**Internal Memo: Jefferson Avenue Firehouse,
Courage Bay**

From: Captain Joe Ripani
To: Squad 1
Re: Warehouse fire reports

All members of Squad 1 are requested to
report for an informal debriefing in my office
tomorrow morning before shift change. Due
to the suspicion of arson in the warehouse fires
at State and 23rd, Courage Bay's finest have
requested we provide them with further details
regarding the first and second call-outs. The
final report will be approved by the chief when
he returns to work. Anyone missing this meeting
had better have a damned good excuse.

On a lighter note, congratulations to our
celebrity truckie Shannon O'Shea. The calls
are still coming in to the station regarding her
televised rescue of the injured Lab from the
warehouse. O'Shea's also being featured in an
article for a women's mag. (Take note, guys:
there'll be no living with her from now on.)

One final notice. I've been informed that the
vacant position in our unit has been filled.
John Forrester is an experienced firefighter from
New York and will make a great contribution to
our team. Squad members are expected to make
him feel welcome.

About the Author

CODE **RED**

BOBBY HUTCHINSON

is a multitalented woman who was born in a small town in the interior of British Columbia. Though she is now the successful author of more than thirty-five novels, her past includes stints as a retailer, a seamstress and a day-care worker. Twice married, she now lives alone and is the devoted mother of three and grandmother of four. She runs, swims, does yoga, meditates and likes this quote by Dolly Parton: "Decide who you are, and then do it on purpose."

code **RED**

BOBBY HUTCHINSON

SPONTANEOUS COMBUSTION

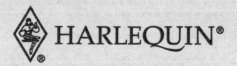

HARLEQUIN®

TORONTO • NEW YORK • LONDON
AMSTERDAM • PARIS • SYDNEY • HAMBURG
STOCKHOLM • ATHENS • TOKYO • MILAN • MADRID
PRAGUE • WARSAW • BUDAPEST • AUCKLAND

HARLEQUIN BOOKS
225 Duncan Mill Road, Don Mills,
Ontario, Canada M3B 3K9

ISBN 0-373-61284-2

Bobby Hutchinson is acknowledged as the author of this work

SPONTANEOUS COMBUSTION

Dear Reader,

Research is always a fascinating part of the writing process. For Code Red I needed to know about firefighting, which meant interviewing my son, Dan, a seasoned firefighter with the Vancouver Fire Department. Having him share tender and funny incidents as well as more tragic moments made my job easier—but as his mother, the stories he told also struck terror in my heart. I understood as never before exactly what his job entailed, the horrific dangers, the profound compassion and the simple, boundless bravery in the hearts of all those who choose to serve humanity during crisis situations.

As always, writing this book was a delight, but as usual I learned from the characters I was creating. As firefighters, they had certain necessary characteristics— bravery, certainly, a sense of comradery and humor. But most of all they shared a single admirable trait: they just never quit. Even in extreme circumstances, when hope seemed extinguished, they went right on trying. I hope I was able to capture that nobility. I hope I'll be able to incorporate it in some measure in my own life.

Thank you, and much love,

Bobby

CHAPTER ONE

THE WAREHOUSE FIRE in Courage Bay occurred on a Tuesday afternoon in late August. It was seventy-eight degrees, and sunny, with no clouds in the blue California sky.

Just before the call came, Shannon O'Shea was sweating up a storm, but not from basking in the sun. She was flat on her back, using the bench press machine in the workout room at the Jefferson Avenue Firehouse. She'd recently upped the weights from 140 to 150, and doing ten reps three times was challenging her to the limit when the alarm, like an insistent doorbell, resounded through the hall.

The dispatcher's voice came on. "Engine One, Rescue One, Ladder One. First alarm to warehouse fire, State Street and Twenty-third." There was a ten-second break, and then the alarm was repeated.

Shannon hurried out to the bay. She pulled her turnout gear over her sweat clothes and climbed on the truck with the rest of her crew, heart pumping and adrenaline soaring. She'd completed her probationary year eighteen months ago, but the feeling she'd had when she'd gone to her very first fire was the same one she had now—a little apprehensive, more than a little pumped, eager to do her job.

Fire was the enemy, speed was of the essence and small mistakes could be deadly. As a firefighter, those facts ruled her working life.

The sounds were familiar as the vehicle pulled out of Bay One and gained speed. There was the wail of the siren, the honk of the air horn at intersections and the low-keyed comments of the men. Louie Chapa, a five-year veteran, was behind the wheel, and as he neared their location, Shannon could see black smoke coming from the roof of a dilapidated warehouse.

While some of the crew began to stretch a line from the pumper, Shannon took a long and careful look at the building, as she'd been taught at the academy. *Size up the building, size up the construction, size up the means of escape.*

This one was big and rambling, two stories, a combination of wood and brick, very few windows. From where the truck was parked, she could see only one set of double doors. There must be a larger loading bay at the side or back.

"O'Shea, you go in with Lucas—place is supposed to be empty, but there could well be vagrants camping in there," Chief Dan Egan said, and Shannon's heart thumped with excitement.

It wasn't that long since she'd been a rookie on the pumper, only assigned to the nozzle after the fire was practically out. When she was brand-new, her crew had taken care of her. Now she was a seasoned veteran looking out for other rookies, like Lucas Ferrintino.

She'd gone from a six-month assignment on the engine to her present, prized assignment as a truckie. Truckies were in charge of forcible entry, using sledgehammers and axes to burst through steel doors. They worked with the ladders, rescuing people trapped in high places. They climbed on roofs and broke windows for ventilation, and most of all, they did search and rescue. Being a truckie was a comment on her superb strength and high level of physical conditioning. She was proud to be considered worthy.

She grabbed her tools, and she and Lucas went inside the building, following the guys stretching the line.

Stay low. Heat and smoke rise. That was one of the first lessons drummed into a firefighter's brain. Shannon didn't have to consciously think about crouching as low as she could.

After a few years on the job, it was as natural as breathing. *Stay low, you go, stay high, you die* was the mantra instilled into a trainee's nervous system. She motioned with her hands to Lucas, reminding him.

Most of the flooring and many of the joists inside the building were made of wood. The support system for the second story was massive wooden beams. The place was cavernous, and at first Shannon couldn't detect much indication of fire. But the farther she advanced, the thicker the smoke became, descending from the upper floor in slow, steady billows until it was like a black cloud surrounding her.

She dropped to the floor and secured her face piece, turning on her self-contained breathing apparatus. She had twenty minutes worth of air, as long as she breathed properly and didn't hyperventilate. She'd done that a couple of times as a rookie, but she'd learned, the way all novices did, to control her breath and conserve her air supply.

It was the noise she was aware of, even more than the heat. Roaring and strange whispering sounds came from all around her, the eerie madness of the archenemy. And beneath those noises she heard another sound, long and drawn out, faraway, like someone wailing, crying out with pain. She listened hard, trying to figure out where it was coming from.

Someone's alive in here.

She signaled Lucas. He heard it, too. It was impossible to localize. She pointed, indicating that she was heading in one direction and he should go in the other, each of them following one of the hose lines the engine crew was operating. Following a hose into a building meant that you could turn and follow it out again.

They parted, sweeping their flashlights in wide arcs, and within moments Lucas was out of Shannon's sight. The cries seemed to be coming from her right, and she crab-walked in that direction, still following the line, using her flashlight to illuminate the space ahead of her.

The men on the hose were pumping water into the flames, and smoke was thick and oily all around her. Off to her left, ceiling beams were catching on fire, crackling and roaring in an increasing cacophony of sound. The place was going up surprisingly fast, but she could still hear the disturbing cries. She veered again, trying to determine where they were coming from.

Using her light to peer around, she realized that she was alone now, without the reassurance of the hose to lead her back out. She turned, about to retreat, but again she heard the sound. It was a whimpering, whining plea for help. She had to find whoever it was, and she had to do it quickly. Those overhead beams were going to start crashing down at any moment.

Shannon struggled through the dense smoke toward where she thought the sound was coming from. Rounding a corner, she'd reached another section of the warehouse. The smoke wasn't quite as thick here, and although there were flames, they were off in the distance. She turned her head from one side to the other, searching the floor. The cries came from nearby.

Ahead of her, a beam had already fallen, cracking in half, and underneath it, her light picked out a black dog, a Lab. He was pinned by one hind leg, and scrabbling frantically at the wooden floor with his front paws, desperately trying to drag himself free. He was alternately yipping, howling and coughing from the smoke. His big, soft eyes were frantic with pain and terror, and when he spotted Shannon, he began to bark and whine, as if to say, *Here I am, please, please, don't leave me.*

"Hey, boy, easy now. Calm down. I'll get you loose…"

Shannon got to her feet, slid her gloved hands under the timber and bent her knees. She grunted and strained, putting her considerable strength into raising the heavy beam and releasing the dog, but the wood was incredibly heavy. She wished with all her heart that she had one of the K-12 saws, but they were back on the truck. No time to go and get one.

She tried again, using the strength in her legs to lever the weight. It wouldn't budge at first, and then slowly, slowly, it moved, but she sank to her knees with the strain, almost losing her grip. With one final desperate shove, using her shoulder, she heaved against the timber, and sent it toppling.

She fell forward—hard—from the momentum, but at least the dog was free. The moment he felt the weight lift from his body, he scrambled toward her, dragging his crushed hind leg, barking and choking from the smoke.

"Poor baby." Shannon's heart was racing and she was puffing hard from the effort. She wondered for an instant how much air she had left. The smoke was growing denser by the minute.

"Gotta get us out of here fast, fella," she muttered. A rapid, horrified glance around told her that the fire had accelerated, and above her head, flames were leaping from one wooden beam to the next in a macabre, gleeful dance.

"Let's go. C'mere, dog." Shannon grunted, lifting the animal in her arms. Still crouched down, she scuttled back in the direction she thought she'd come. Her equipment weighed sixty-eight pounds. The dog was easily another sixty. Skinny as he was, he was big-boned and rangy, but at least he didn't resist.

She did her best not to bump his damaged hind leg—she wondered for an instant if he'd bite—but he only yelped in agony as she hoisted his forepaws farther over one shoulder, trying to support his broken limb and steady him with one hand, while still hanging on to her flashlight with the other.

"Now, where—oh darn, oh Lordy—"

A wall of flames sent her staggering backward. She looked in the other direction, but roiling smoke made it impossible to see. The powerful beam from her flashlight barely penetrated the darkness, and the noise of the fire had grown into a rushing, eerie roar that sounded at times like some demon chortling with glee.

We're in trouble here, pooch. I don't know where the lousy line is anymore. I came around some sort of doorway...

Shannon felt panic begin to nip at her brain, and resolutely shoved it away. *A trapped firefighter who panics is going to die.* There was a way out of this—there had to be. She just had to find it. She turned in a circle, searching, and now she was also silently praying.

Dear God, help us. Get us out of here, please show us the way...

But the flames roared closer.

Please, God, we need a miracle here...

At that moment a nearby beam gave an ominous creaking groan as fire snaked up its length. In another few moments, it would collapse, and unless she got out of the way, it would crush her and the dog beneath it.

She pulled her mask away.

"Hello, anybody there?"

She hollered again, as loud as she could, but there was no answer.

Heat seemed to envelop her on every side, and as she clamped the mask on again, she imagined that her air was running out. The stink of smoke filled her nostrils, and she gagged and choked. The terrible, awesome sound of the flames built into a crescendo.

Of all the fires she'd been on, was she now about to die in a stupid vacant warehouse, rescuing a dog?

Don't panic. She tried to calm herself, to stay in control and figure out what she ought to do next. But instinct and reason both told her she was trapped, that she and the poor animal in her arms were going to die together.

And then from the wall of flames a shape appeared, a huge form in a silver outfit that enveloped the entire body of whoever—whatever—was inside it.

Shannon gaped, certain that the smoke had gotten to her. She knew she was hallucinating, because ordinary firemen just weren't issued the mega-expensive silver suits.

Maybe this was the angel of death?

CHAPTER TWO

WHOEVER HE WAS, Shannon thought he looked far more like an astronaut than a firefighter.

A full-face dark helmet obscured his features. His suit was a silver, and Shannon knew it was issued only to those elite few who worked around chemicals that generated extreme heat, much greater than the temperatures that occurred in an ordinary fire such as this. As far as she knew, the Courage Bay fire department didn't own a silver.

He came toward her, and in a single motion took the dog from her. Gently but firmly he flipped the animal up and over his shoulder in the traditional fireman carry Shannon had been using, and then he reached out and grabbed her gloved hand.

Crouching, moving so fast she had to run to keep up, he headed through the wall of smoke as if he knew exactly which direction to go.

Behind them, Shannon heard the crash as timbers collapsed close to where she'd been. She winced and then stumbled. He released her hand and wrapped one arm around her, pressing her close to his side, half lifting her. She gulped what had to be the last of her air and felt stinging heat on her ears and neck. An instant later they burst through impenetrable smoke into blessed daylight.

They were a safe distance away from the burning building when he let her go. Shannon sank to the ground, ripping the mask from her face and gulping in huge lungfuls of fresh air, which brought on a fit of coughing so intense she couldn't get her breath. Her eyes streamed with tears and she bent double, head on her knees, panting and gasping.

The man in the silver deposited the dog gently on the ground beside her, and the animal licked her hand. She patted him, concentrating on drawing air into her parched lungs.

When at last the coughing stopped, she wiped her stinging eyes and looked around. They'd come out a side exit. She could hear raised voices and the sounds of the trucks and pumps from a corner fifty feet away. The man in the silver must have either headed that way or gone back into the warehouse, because she couldn't see him anywhere.

She needed to thank him. He'd saved their lives. More than a little unsteady, she got to her feet and carefully lifted the dog. In a staggering lope, she made her way around the corner.

Here was controlled chaos. Firemen scurried from trucks to the burning building, and the police had set up a barrier behind which a growing crowd of spectators stood, including several reporters with camcorders. She was aware of flashbulbs going off, of cameras aimed her way, but she was coughing again, and she veered away from the crowd, finding a relatively isolated patch of grass, where she set the dog down.

A reporter came over, but she waved him away and scanned the crowd, searching for the giant in the silver. There was no sign of him. Where the dickens could he be? The size of him, dressed the way he was, meant he couldn't very well blend into the crowd. He must have gone back inside.

After another fruitless look around, Shannon sank down beside the dog, stroking him, touched by the way the animal put his head on her lap. He had to be in pain, but he sure wasn't a complainer. In a minute, she'd get back to work, but right now, she needed to rest.

For a surreal moment, she and the whimpering dog sat there, and then the chief spotted them and hurried over.

Dan crouched down beside Shannon. "You all right,

O'Shea? Lucas said the two of you heard somebody in there. It was this dog, huh? Thank God you got out when you did. I just ordered everybody else out, too. Damn place went rotten all of a sudden."

He frowned and shook his head. "There have to be combustibles involved for it to go up this way. You gave me a scare. I was thinking I'd have to send a crew back in after you when I saw you come around the corner."

"I'm fine, Chief. Just catching my breath. The dog was trapped under a collapsed timber—his back leg's crushed pretty bad."

"Poor old fellow." Dan stroked the dog's head. "Gonna have to call you Salvage, getting rescued out of a blaze like that." He turned back to Shannon. "Anybody else still inside there, you figure? Vagrants? More animals?"

Shannon shook her head. "Not that I could see. Unless the guy that brought us out went back in." She coughed again, and when she got her breath back she said, "Who was he, Chief? That big guy in the silver who brought us out?"

Dan shrugged and shook his head. "No idea. I didn't see anybody like that." He frowned and gave her a speculative look. "You stay here, O'Shea. Take it easy. I'm going for a paramedic, get him to look at you and the dog."

In another moment, the medic was beside Shannon. She assured him she was fine, that she'd inhaled only a small whiff of smoke. She motioned to the dog. "Can you help my friend, here? He's the one in bad shape."

"Sure can. I'll stabilize that leg, but he's going to need to see a vet. Want me to drop him off somewhere for you? We'll be leaving in a few minutes. The driver won't mind a canine patient."

"Could you take him to the Courage Bay Veterinary Clinic?"

"Sure, I know where that is."

This was one of the advantages of living in a relatively

small city. Given Courage Bay's population of only eighty-five thousand, the medical services personnel didn't need directions to most locations.

"One of the vets there is Lisa Malloy—she's a friend of mine," Shannon added. "Tell her to fix this guy up for me. I'll call later and find out how he's doing. Right now I've got to get back to work."

Once the main body of the fire was extinguished, it was the job of the truckies to do demolition with axes and saws, to make absolutely certain the blaze wouldn't reignite.

The work was physically demanding. It involved knocking out walls, tearing down ceilings. It took a while before the fire was under control, and by the time Shannon and the rest of the crew started their job, a lot of the smoke had cleared. The warehouse was fairly open inside, and the job was soon completed.

As she worked, Shannon asked one person after the other, "Where's the guy in the silver? Did you see the big guy in the silver?" It was becoming an obsession. She had to find him, let him know how grateful she was—and also try to convince him she wasn't a total idiot, that she actually had some experience under her belt.

The answer was always the same. "I didn't see any guy in a silver."

Or, "A silver? Where the hell would anybody get one of those babies?"

And the responses were more often than not accompanied by a look that suggested maybe she was having a delusionary episode.

Shannon felt mystified, but she was also losing patience fast. How could anyone miss him? He'd been a good six feet five, and strong as a bull. She could still feel his fingers, like iron clamps inside his glove, hooked around her wrist. His arm had been a rigid length of sheer muscle looped around her waist as he'd pulled her through the smoke and out that side door.

On the way back to the station, Shannon tried again. "C'mon, you guys, where'd the guy in the silver go? Somebody has to have seen him, right?"

All she got were blank looks and a chorus of denials.

"I didn't see anybody wearing a silver."

"Why would anybody have one of those rigs at a warehouse fire, anyhow? There weren't any chemicals around."

"There was nobody like that—you're hallucinating, O'Shea. Smoke's gone to your brain."

"Yes, there was," she insisted. "I lost track of the line, and this huge guy in a silver brought me out, me and the dog."

Louie grinned. "You sure you weren't fantasizing, O'Shea? Was he riding a big white stallion? I've heard of white knights, but never a silver one."

The guys laughed and teased her, and Shannon didn't mention it again.

Back at the station, she showered and gulped down four aspirin to ward off the smoke headache that was thumping in her skull, a result of carbon monoxide fumes she'd taken in.

One of the probies had made a huge pot of stew for dinner, and she was ravenous. The twenty-four-hour shift meant that she wouldn't be off until six the following morning. It was late by the time dinner was over, but it was also quiet. Before she went up to bed, she called Lisa's cell number to check on the dog.

"Hey, Shannon, that black Lab's leg was too damaged to save. I had to amputate, which is how come I'm still at work. I wanted to make certain he came out of the anaesthetic okay. He seems to be doing great, so I'm heading home soon. You okay? The shape the Lab was in, I couldn't help but worry about you."

"I'm okay, just tired. I'm really sorry about his leg. I knew it looked pretty bad."

"Where'd you find him? The medic that dropped him off was in a hurry. I didn't get much out of him except that you were still at the fire and you were sending the dog to me for repairs."

"That old warehouse on State Street burned. Nobody got hurt except the poor old dog. A beam fell on his leg—that's how it got crushed like that."

"Fire and falling beams—gee, I'm glad to hear you weren't in any real danger," Lisa said. "So tell me exactly what happened. You went in to rescue the dog?"

Shannon filled Lisa in on the details of the fire. "The Lab was trapped, and the beam weighed a ton," she explained. "I managed to heave it off him, but by then the fire had us pretty much surrounded." Just thinking about it sent a cold shudder up and down her spine. "I can tell you, I was praying really hard. And then the weirdest thing happened, Lise. This guy came along and hauled us both out—some huge guy in a silver suit, with arms like a couple of anvils."

"A giant in a silver suit saved you? Who was he?"

"That's the spooky part. Nobody seems to know."

"What kind of silver suit was he wearing?"

Shannon explained about the suits being unusual and rare. "I asked around, but nobody seems to have noticed him except me. What I can't figure out is how anybody could miss a giant wrapped in aluminum foil, hauling a six-foot woman and a black Lab out of a burning building. There were photographers there, for gosh sakes. Surely someone must have gotten a picture of him. He wasn't exactly inconspicuous."

Lisa was quiet for a minute. "Obviously the guy was an angel, Shannon."

"Yeah, right."

"Well, you said you were praying. And along comes somebody larger than life, wearing silver clothing, who saves you from disaster. Sounds to me like he must have been a visitor from the Other Side."

"So why would an angel need protective clothing, Lise? Tell me that."

Lisa giggled. "Beats me. You got a better explanation?"

"Actually, no. But I'm sure not gonna pass yours on to the guys. They've already given me a bad enough time about this. If I produce the angel theory, they'll declare me officially loopy."

"Loopy or not, be glad the angel came along. And while we're on the subject of angels," Lisa said, "how's Linda feeling? Is she still upchucking 24/7?"

Shannon's oldest brother, Sean, and his wife, Linda, had recently learned they were pregnant, which accounted for the persistent stomach flu Linda had endured before, during and every day since their wedding six weeks ago. It was impossible to keep a secret in the O'Shea family, and everyone was overjoyed at the news, but no one was more thrilled and proud than Sean. He grinned his way through all the good-natured teasing from his family and the crew at the firehouse, and Shannon thought she'd never seen him this happy.

"Is she showing yet?"

"Hardly. She figures she's barely two months along."

"I'll bet you'll hardly be able to tell, even when she's full term," Lisa said. "Me, I'll sprout a gut the size of the Goodyear blimp. You long, lean women have way more room for expansion than us vertically challenged ones."

"Yeah, well, I'm not about to test your theory quite yet. Before I get pregnant, it would be nice to find a partner. Sometimes I think I missed the bus that's heading for happily ever after. I can only hope it comes by again before I'm forty."

"So you've got twelve good years left, don't sweat it."

"I'm not, but my mom's getting a little antsy."

"I'll bet she's excited about being a grandma again."

"Excited doesn't half cover it. She adores my brother Patrick's two kids, but she's over the moon at the prospect of a new baby to cuddle. She's been so consumed since she found out about Linda's pregnancy, I haven't had a single lecture about the advantages in finding another line of work."

"She still hasn't accepted that being a firefighter is what you want to be when you grow up?"

"I doubt she ever will. She's a worrier, my mother."

The fights she'd had with Mary O'Shea when she'd first mentioned becoming a firefighter still bothered Shannon. She had two brothers, both older, and as the only girl in the family, Shannon had found her mother to be her staunchest ally, her best friend, her confidante. It hurt to have her withdraw that support, to know her mother had never accepted her choice of career.

"Worrying is a mother's job," Lisa said.

"Yeah. I guess. There should be an expiration date, though, I've been a firefighter for a while now—you'd think she'd get over it. Anyhow, the prospect of this baby coming has taken a lot of the heat off me. Mom's already buying baby clothes. Linda says by the time it finally arrives, she's gonna have to get Sean to build on a separate wing just to hold the baby's wardrobe."

Lisa laughed. "Well, if it's a girl, she can never have too many clothes."

"Goes right along with being too rich or too thin. Guess I strike out on all three counts."

"Can't comment on the money part, but have you looked in a mirror lately? You've got gorgeous going for you, O'Shea. You don't need clothes or money or diets. I'd kill for your cheekbones. And then there's that winning combo of black hair and blue eyes."

"Yeah, right." Shannon blew a raspberry. "You're just buttering me up because you've got another impossible stray over there you need a home for, right?"

"You are *so* suspicious. You're supposed to just say thank you when someone pays you a compliment. Especially when it's true."

"Thank you, Lise. I'll come by on my way home from work in the morning and buy you breakfast for saying such sweet things."

"Sounds good to me."

"Okay, tell old Salvage I'll see him in the morning."

"That's his name? Salvage?"

"I have no idea what his name is. He wasn't wearing a collar or anything. The chief named him Salvage because he got saved from the fire. I don't know what he was doing in that warehouse in the first place. Far as we could tell it was deserted."

"Probably hiding out. I'd guess he's a stray, by the looks of him. Skinny. Rough coat. It's too bad about his leg, but dogs do just fine on three. I've given him antibiotics, and a vitamin shot, as well. You gonna turn him over to the SPCA?"

"I'll advertise, see if anybody claims him," Shannon told her.

"And if they don't?" Shannon knew from the sound of her voice that Lisa was smiling. "You'll take him home to make friends with the odd couple, right?" Lisa guessed.

"I suppose he can hang out at my sheltered workshop for a while, but I'll have to find a permanent home for him pretty quick," Shannon said. "He's number three, which is two dogs more than the one small one I wanted in the first place. You do remember I said one *small* dog?"

Lisa giggled. "You've got one."

"I've got two—one small, one enormous—and they're both candidates for the funny farm. Plus, I spend more money on dog food than large families do on groceries."

When she'd bought her first house the year before, Shannon had told Lisa she wanted a small stray as a pet. The very next day, Lisa had brought her Cleopatra, a lovable teddy bear of a dog whose only trick was to lie on her back and wave her paws in the air. It was readily apparent that Cleo would never qualify for the doggy version of Mensa. She was a mentally challenged Saint Bernard with a psychological glitch that made her think she was a lapdog.

"You've got to admit that Pepsi doesn't eat much," Lisa argued.

"And that's the only thing that wretched animal has going

for him," Shannon said. "If Pepsi was a person, he'd be tell-ing dirty jokes, smoking a cigar and packing a pistol."

Lisa giggled. "You're right, you know."

Pepsi, a tiny, long-haired, peculiar-looking mongrel with a bad attitude, had been abandoned on the porch of the clinic, and Lisa had convinced Shannon that Cleo needed a friend. Amazingly enough, the two dogs had bonded. Unfortunately, Cleo was the single exception to Pepsi's universal hatred of both humans and animals. Biting and urinating were his cho-sen methods of communication.

Shannon yawned. "Gotta go to bed, Lise. I can barely keep my eyes open here. I'll see you in the morning."

They said good-night, and Shannon headed off to the bunk room.

Her last thought before she dropped like a stone into sleep was of the mysterious man in the silver suit. Even she was be-ginning to wonder if she'd only dreamed him.

CHAPTER THREE

THAT NIGHT WAS QUIET, which was a blessing. There were no call-outs until four in the morning, when Shannon's crew was sent to treat a man having a seizure on a downtown street. He was a wino, and her team did what they could until the ambulance arrived and took him to hospital.

Just before she was due to go off shift at six, Dan called her into the office.

Great, she thought. *Finally, he's located the guy in the silver.*

But it wasn't that at all.

"The warehouse fire got some coverage on the TV late news last night," Dan began. "They had a shot of you carrying that dog. They made a big thing over how you'd risked your life to save him. How's he doing?"

"He lost his back leg. It was too damaged to save, but he's recovering." Shannon couldn't mask her irritation. "I really wish they hadn't zeroed in on me and the dog. Why couldn't they include the entire team? I was only—"

Dan held out a hand, stopping her in midsentence.

"I know, I know, you were just doing your job, O'Shea. But the fact is, a little PR never hurts. The bosses like it. And if we're lucky, we might end up getting some public funding that would pay for another shower, one with your name on it. See, I got this call just now from a journalist. Some woman's magazine wants to do a feature article on you." He rummaged among scraps of paper and held one up. "*California Woman,* the magazine's called."

Shannon's immediate reaction was to refuse point-blank. She was basically shy, and the thought of being interviewed made her cringe.

"Why not let them talk to Dana?"

Dana Ivie was the other woman firefighter at the station. The schedule for the two squads at Jefferson Avenue was twenty-four hours on, thirty-six off, then twenty-four on, followed by five days off. Dana worked opposite shifts from Shannon, and was already on days off.

"They specifically asked for you, because of the news coverage. Besides, Dana's on her long break and they want to do this right away. It's some kind of rush for the next issue."

Shannon didn't enjoy being the center of attention, and she certainly would never seek out the limelight. There'd already been several articles in local papers about her and Dana, just because they were the only female firefighers on the Courage Bay crew.

She made a face and shook her head. "I dunno, Chief. I hate having a big fuss made just because I'm a woman. If it had been one of the guys with the dog, would they still want an interview?"

Dan smiled and shook his head. "I doubt it. You gotta take into account that there aren't that many women who make it through the application process, never mind the academy. You and Dana are exceptions. If you did this, it'd be good publicity for the department. Look what that documentary on your brother accomplished. We got new uniforms out of that."

"Yeah, but Sean's also a smoke jumper. That's different than being singled out just because of my gender."

Dan was sticking to his guns. "I think it's a real opportunity, O'Shea. Like I said, never hurts to have some good PR, especially since we always need funding. But don't let me influence you one way or the other. It's entirely up to you...your decision."

Of course it was—*not*. As if she was going to refuse when

her chief was practically saying it was her civic duty, not to mention holding out the carrot of a private shower, which she had lascivious fantasies about. One of the biggest hardships she and Dana had here at the station was having to juggle the use of the common showers with the guys. Shannon usually got up an entire hour early just to get in there before anyone else.

Shannon heaved a resigned sigh. "Okay, tell the interviewer to give me a call."

"Good. Can I give her your home number?"

"Sure, go ahead."

Dan grinned and thumped her shoulder. "You're a good man, O'Shea."

"Thanks, Chief." He was a great guy. The department was lucky to have him.

And he was a manipulator.

Shouldering her backpack, Shannon set off at a jog for the veterinary clinic, looking forward to a good long run. Lisa's clinic was some distance away, and Shannon had left her car at home. Jogging to work and back was one more way to stay in shape. When her lease came up on her apartment a year ago, Shannon had decided the time had come to buy something of her own. She'd searched for and found a small house only a mile from the fire station. It was in a neighborhood that was going through change, which meant that some houses were dilapidated while others were being yuppified. Her house was unquestionably in the run-down category, but being in her minimal price range and also close to work meant it was made for her. So it needed repairs. She'd get to them one by one.

As she ran, she was thinking about all the things that needed fixing, but she was also enjoying the scenery. Below she could see the Pacific Ocean and glimpse stretches of the ten-mile, clean, white sand beach. Years before, the little town of Courage Bay had clustered along the half-moon strip of verdant tableland below, but with time had come expansion. Now the streets wound up and down the steep side of the forested mountain that formed a backdrop to the old portion of the city.

The route Shannon followed was particularly hilly, and she pushed herself extra hard on the inclines. She'd been blessed with long, strong legs, and she needed them. Lifting ladders over her head and carrying people out of burning buildings required muscles.

She thought again of the mysterious stranger in the silver. He was well up there on the strength meter, all right. One way or another, she was determined to track him down, if only to prove to her crew that she wasn't losing her marbles.

She sprinted the last half mile and burst through the door of the clinic, dripping sweat and puffing. Two elderly women, obviously sisters, looked up and smiled at her. Each held a small pug dog on her lap. They were staying as far as they could from the teenager with the Iroquois hairdo and multiple piercings, who was stroking a ferret on a leash.

Beside him sat a skinny woman covered with tattoos who looked to be high on drugs. Her eyes were closed, and her body was weaving back and forth to some unheard rhythm, while a monstrous cat on the chair beside her growled low in its throat and viciously ripped the stuffing out of the cushion on the chair. The animal was the size of a small cougar, and Shannon gave it a wide berth as she made her way to the reception desk.

The receptionist, a twenty-something ringer for a Barbie doll, was on another planet. She barely glanced up when Shannon appeared. She was painting her inch-long fingernails deep blue. The phone was ringing, but she ignored it, blowing on her nail polish. Shannon did a mental eye roll. For this, Lisa was paying well above minimum wage?

"Hi, Agnes. Lisa in the back?"

"Oh, yeah. Hi, umm…yeah. She said to tell you to just go right back." Agnes had met Shannon maybe fifty times, and the hapless girl still didn't remember her name.

Shannon headed along the narrow corridor to the examining rooms. The door to the first one was open. Lisa's partner, Greg Seaborn, was in there, bent over a small ginger kitten. An elderly woman was hovering anxiously near his right shoulder, so Shannon just waved a hand at him and hurried on down the hall.

Lisa was in the second treatment room, applying an adhesive patch to the shaved belly of an unconscious black-and-white spaniel. The intense expression on her pretty face softened into a wide smile when she saw Shannon. "Hey, girlfriend, I'm almost done here." She stripped off her surgical gloves and ran a hand over her mop of chestnut curls. "Greg says he'll handle the waiting room for an hour while we eat. I missed breakfast and I'm starving."

"He's got his work cut out for him. There's a monster of an evil cat out there I wouldn't go near. He's ripping up one of those cushions you got for the chairs, and his mother looks as if she's tripping."

Lisa rolled her eyes and groaned. "Don't tell me Candy's here with Tinkerbell again."

"That monster's called Tinkerbell? It's bigger than Pepsi and twice as mean looking, which is saying something."

"Tinker's one of the largest cat breeds. He's a Blue Colourpoint Ragdoll, and he's not a happy camper. Those and Norwegians are the giants in the cat world. They're usually good-natured, but Tinker's a notable exception."

"Well, if Candy deserts that animal here, don't factor me into the equation when you try and find a home for him."

"I wouldn't do that. I know you're a dog person." Lisa stroked the sleeping spaniel. "Now, Franklin here is a sweetheart, but he was a really *randy* sweetheart. So I did the inevitable—he'll wake up and wonder what the heck happened to his libido while he was napping."

"Salvage must be wondering the same thing about his back leg. How's he doing?"

"Come and see for yourself." Lisa picked up the limp spaniel and headed into the large room where the cages were. She gently placed him in one and pointed at another, where Salvage was lying.

The moment he saw them, the black Lab struggled to his feet and started to bark with excitement. Shannon went over to him. "Hey, old buddy, look at you, already getting used to three legs." She opened the cage door and the dog practically leaped into her arms.

"Whoa." Shannon staggered back a little, laughing, as Salvage lathered her face and whimpered a joyful greeting. "I guess this means we're buddies, huh?" She set him down and crouched beside him, taking his head between her hands. "You're not a bad-looking guy, considering how skinny you are and what you've been through."

"He inhaled his breakfast, and we gave him a bath. He was pretty dirty."

Shannon petted the dog. "He cleans up good, huh? I wish he could talk. He'd be able to tell us his story."

And back her up about the mysterious guy who'd rescued them.

Together, Shannon and Lisa put the Lab back in the cage. He whined pitifully when they left the room.

"When I get back, Greg will take you out for some exercise," Lisa called to him. "I'll keep him here for four or five days," she told Shannon, "until the incision is healed. Dogs adapt really fast to amputation. In a short time he'll be running around as if he was born with three legs."

They washed up in the bathroom, and then Lisa said, "Let's sneak out the back. If Candy sees me, I'll never get away. She has the mistaken idea that Tinkerbell likes me."

Lisa went to have a word with Greg, and then they escaped through the back door, down a short alley and along the street to a comfortable little café they both knew and liked. They sat at the counter and ordered eggs, hash browns and pancakes with their coffee.

"I had a bowl of oatmeal earlier, but I'm hungry again," Shannon said. "Although if I eat all this, I won't be able to run home."

"I'll give you a lift—anything to avoid dealing with that cat."

While they waited for their order, Lisa said, "How's your new tenant working out?"

Shannon had just rented one of her two upstairs bedrooms to an older woman, Willow Redmond.

"I haven't seen much of her. I've been working and she just moved in the other day, but I like her. She's an advertisement for mature women. Even at sixty something, she looks hot in jeans."

"You said she's an old friend of your mom's?"

"Yeah. They were friends years ago. She used to play guitar for the group Mom sang with. But they lost touch. Willow got married and moved to New Jersey, and Mom met Dad and settled here." The waitress came with their orders, and they were quiet for a few moments as they both attacked their food.

Lisa swallowed and took a sip of coffee. "So how'd she end up in your upstairs bedroom?"

"According to Mom, she's left her marriage. Willow and her husband had been together something like forty years, and I guess he's always been a pain in the butt, controlling and really jealous. Apparently he accused her of having an affair with one of her night school instructors, and she just up and walked out with two suitcases, a guitar and something that looks like a toolbox." Shannon cut up her pancakes and added more syrup.

"A toolbox, huh?" Lisa laughed. "I like her style."

"Me, too. She's one feisty lady. Mom says Willow flew to L.A. for no other reason than because it was a long way from New Jersey, and one night after she got here she saw a rerun of that documentary Linda did about Sean."

A renowned television news photographer, Linda had been sent to Courage Bay to make a film on smoke jumpers. That's how she'd met Sean.

"Willow recognized the name O'Shea," Shannon added, "and she called Mom. Of course Mom invited her here for a visit. She stayed with my parents for a week and decided she wanted to live in Courage Bay, but she didn't want to impose on my folks any longer. So Mom asked me about renting her my upstairs bedroom."

"Good thinking. It probably helps with the mortgage."

"Yeah, and she also likes the dogs. She's offered to take them for walks and feed them while I'm working, which lets Dad off the hook."

"Willow's an unusual name."

"It suits her. She's a pretty woman."

"She got a job? Or isn't money an issue?"

"It has to be, or she wouldn't be living in my attic. It's not exactly the Ritz up there."

"Think she might want to work at the clinic? If she has any computer skills, that is. That dipstick Greg hired is leaving, thank goodness. Get this, Agnes says the job isn't fulfilling her spiritually."

Shannon laughed. "I don't suppose it's doing much for you and Greg, either."

Lisa rolled her blue eyes. "You got that right. They say everybody has the capacity for murder, and Agnes brings mine to the surface."

"No wonder, she's a total ditz. I bet Willow would jump at the chance to work for you. I heard her telling Uncle Donald she knows about computers. You want to meet her first, size her up for yourself? I don't know her all that well. You might have a different take."

"If she's home this morning, you can introduce us when I drop you off. Otherwise, you talk to her. If she's your mom's friend, and you like her, that's good enough for me. If she wants the job, send her over to fill in the forms. Agnes, of course, didn't give us any notice. She's history the end of the week."

"Shouldn't you check with Greg?"

"Nope. He hired Agnes. Anything I do has to be an improvement."

The waitress refilled their coffee cups, and then Lisa said, "Of course, I was fantasizing about some incredible hunk with a gentle soul sitting out there, but what the heck. Maybe Willow has hunky sons who'll come to visit."

"I think Mom said she has one. Didn't that good-looking guy with the parrot ever call you, Lise?"

"Yeah, I went out with him twice. He's weird in an intriguing way, really sexy, but I have a hunch he's married. I heard him on his cell, having this intense conversation. He said it was his sister."

Shannon blew another raspberry. "Yeah, right. Men. Wouldn't you think they'd be able to come up with something more believable than that?"

"Somebody ought to write an instruction book for them," Lisa declared. "How about you. How's it going with that new resident from the hospital? What's his name again?"

"Diego Larue. Great name, great guy, really great hair, rides a honking big Harley, which intrigues me. I've always lusted after one of those babies." Shannon sipped her coffee and gave a wry grin. "Now, that would drive my mother right over the edge on the worry meter, if I bought a Harley. Anyhow, he took me for a spin a couple Sundays ago. I loved it. But I've decided not to go out with him again."

"Why ever not? He sounds hot, and nice to boot."

"Nice, yeah, but no sparks. And it would never work timewise. I'd be at the firehouse, he'd be at the hospital. I've tried that before. I dated that obstetrician for a while, remember? It was crazy-making. We hardly saw one another."

"Wasn't he the one who bought you all that gorgeous underwear?"

"Yeah, just before I dumped him. That was part of it—it was all size six. It made me think his fantasies weren't really about a six-foot lady who wears size ten." Shannon shook her head. "Sometimes I think my only option is to hook up with a firefighter. Who else would understand the hours? And they're usually bigger than I am, which is not an insignificant advantage. But then we'd be on different shifts, so we'd barely see one another."

"A match made in heaven—no time for conflict. So did Diego give up that easily?"

"He's called a couple times, but there's not enough chemistry there for me. You wanna meet him, Lise?"

"Nope. Leftovers never work."

"You ever thought of giving Greg a little encouragement? I've seen the way he looks at you."

Lisa shook her head. "Greg's a super guy, but there's no sparks there, either. He's like a brother. By the way, he said he saw you on the late news last night. There was a shot of you carrying Salvage outside that burning warehouse."

Shannon groaned. "Everybody's seen that but me. Because of it, I got roped into doing an interview for *California Woman* magazine." She told Lisa how Dan had pressured her into it.

"I think your chief's right—that'll make a great story," Lisa declared. "Other women get inspired when they find out you're a firefighter. Greg said the clip was really moving. You were holding Salvage up over your shoulder."

"It must have been right after your so-called angel dragged us out of the inferno. I can't figure out why nobody got a shot of *him*."

"You find out any more about him?"

"Nothing. It's as if he disappeared into thin air. And the guys are giving me a real hard time, saying I imagined him."

"I told you he was an angel."

"Yeah, well, if he was, I wish he'd reappear at the firehouse so I don't get permanently labeled as a loony. I'm beginning to be sorry I ever mentioned him."

BY LUNCHTIME THAT DAY, Shannon had even more reason to regret ever referring to the man in the silver suit. The phone had rung nonstop from the moment Lisa dropped her at home. Willow wasn't in, so Lisa hadn't had a chance to meet her.

The first call was from her mother, and Shannon braced herself. When it came to her job, her mother always made her feel defensive, and this time was no exception.

"I saw you on the news," Mary said, sounding hurt. "Why didn't you phone and warn me? Seeing you on TV with that warehouse blazing behind you and your face all black with soot scared me half to death. You looked as if you were dazed, Shannon, standing there holding that dog. And you were coughing. Did you get smoke in your lungs? You know what that does to you long term. Goodness knows you should. Your father gets pneumonia every single time he gets a cold, and it's from his years as a fireman."

Shannon sighed and tried to stay calm. "I'm not going to get pneumonia, Mom. I did get a little whiff of smoke, but not enough to do anything but make my nose run."

"And cough. I'll bet you coughed half the night." Mary figured she knew everything there was to know about firefighters and the injuries they could suffer on the job—and she probably did. Shannon's father, Caleb, had been a firefighter all his life, and her brother Patrick had been fire chief before becoming mayor. With both Shannon and her brother Sean still working in the profession, Mary had become paranoid. With good reason, Shannon had to admit. They'd all had close calls at one time or another. But knowing that her mother had some legitimate concerns didn't make it any easier to deal with accusatory calls like this one.

"Honest, Mom, I'm absolutely fine," Shannon insisted. "And I didn't save the dog on my own. There was a guy in there helping me." She gave an expurgated and revised version of what had occurred. Shannon and Sean, like their father before them, had an unspoken agreement that the less Mary knew, the better she'd sleep at night.

"That man was an angel," she declared when Shannon finished. "He was sent to rescue you. It wasn't your time to go, thank God."

When her mother, a deeply religious woman, said things like that, Shannon usually bit her tongue to hold back some smart remark. But this time, she remembered being surrounded by fire and truly thinking that she was about to die. After all, who was she to argue against angels? Whoever he was, the dude had certainly gotten her out of a tight spot.

"So how's Linda feeling?" Shannon had learned that her sister-in-law's pregnancy was a good way to divert her mother. For the next ten minutes, she listened to details about Linda in particular and pregnancy in general, and finally her mother ended the call.

The next caller was Linda herself. She, too, had seen the news, and Shannon related the story again, this time sticking a lot closer to the truth.

"So some huge hunk in a silver suit dragged you and the dog out of a burning warehouse? Wow, that's so romantic. Also good drama. Care to tell it on camera for the human interest portion of the news?"

Linda had just started working at the local television station, interviewing and photographing newsworthy people and events in Courage Bay.

"Sorry, I'm already booked." Shannon told her about the upcoming interview with *California Woman*.

"You gonna talk to them about your hero in aluminum foil?"

"Not in this lifetime," Shannon said vehemently. "Everybody thinks he's either an angel sent from heaven, or a definite sign that my mental health is deteriorating, and I've had it with the whole subject. Let's discuss your morning sickness instead."

Linda, like Mary, was easily diverted. "It's my bladder, actually. I've started considering just sleeping on the toilet. It would save getting out of bed fourteen times a night."

They chatted a few more minutes, and Shannon had no sooner hung up than the phone rang again. Groaning, she picked up.

"Morning, Ms. O'Shea," a professionally cheerful voice said. "My name is Melissa Child. I'm a staff writer with *California Woman.*"

Shannon's heart sank. Melissa Child hadn't wasted any time.

"I spoke with Dan Egan earlier this morning, and he tells me you wouldn't mind talking to me about your job as a firefighter?"

Shannon felt like saying that at this moment, talking about her job was right up there with sticking pins in her eyeballs. Instead, she did her best to be polite, and ended up agreeing to an interview the following day. Might as well get it over with.

"We'll want photographs of you at the station," Melissa said. "I know your chief said you're starting days off, but maybe you wouldn't mind going over there—"

"Nope, that would be fine for photos. But I'd prefer doing the interview at my place." She knew the guys. They'd find endless excuses to listen in. She gave the woman her address, thinking that she'd have agreed to almost anything just to get off the phone. She needed to use the bathroom.

When Melissa finally hung up, the damn thing rang again almost at once, and this time Shannon let the machine pick up as she headed down the hall.

Behind her, she heard her brother Sean say, "Shannon, are you there? I don't know if you heard, but that damn warehouse reignited. The word's out that it was—"

Shannon snatched up the phone just in time to hear Sean say, "Arson."

CHAPTER FOUR

"SEAN? I'm here, talk to me. What happened?" Shannon could feel adrenaline pumping. Her stomach hurt all of a sudden.

Having a fire reignite was a black eye for the entire fire department, but particularly for her and the other truckies, whose job was to see that such a thing never occurred. In her head, she started frantically reviewing what they'd done.

Sean's voice was somber. "There was an explosion just after ten this morning. It set off a new blaze. We just got back to the station."

Shannon felt herself tense. She knew in her gut there was bad news coming.

"Dan and Sam Prophet were there when the thing went off." Sam Prophet was the arson squad investigator.

"Oh, no. Oh, Lordy, Sean." Shannon placed a hand over her pounding heart. "Are they—"

"They're in hospital. Dan's got a concussion, contact burn to his side—not good but not too bad. Sam's in worse shape. He has a compound fracture of his leg, dislocated arm, six-inch gash on his shoulder. They're both lucky to be alive at all. They were close to the blast when it went off. Fortunately, we got them out in time, because within minutes it turned into an inferno."

Shannon swallowed hard. "I just don't get it. What caused an explosion?"

"Not what...who? Sam figures an arsonist. Apparently he now thinks the blaze yesterday was arson, as well. There'll probably be no way of telling because this one today burned pretty hard before we got it out. They're sending in a bomb squad specialist anyway, to investigate."

"Anybody we know?"

"Nora Keyes. She's a detective with the police department."

"I've never met her. I hope she finds out who's doing this."

"Me, too. Gotta go, sis. I haven't even cleaned up yet."

"Thanks for calling me, Sean. I'm going over to the hospital right now to see how they are."

"Call me back and let me know how they're doing. We're all pretty concerned about them down here."

Shannon promised.

Controlled chaos pretty much described the scene at the hospital. Whenever a firefighter was injured, fellow members who were off duty gathered immediately to see what they could do to help. The waiting room was packed with firemen.

Sam was still in surgery, but after Shannon had been there a few minutes, an orderly pushed Dan, on a gurney, out of a treatment room. His dark brown hair was singed along one side. His ears were fiery red, and there were raw, red burns on his cheeks as well as his arms and hands.

Shannon felt her gut contract. The firemen were like family, and it hurt to see one of them injured. It always brought home hard that their job was risky.

In a moment, Dan's stretcher was surrounded. Shannon hung back a little.

"Chief, hey, man, how you doing? Anything we can do? Anything you need? Something you want done at home?" Voices crisscrossed one another. Everyone wanted to help, needed to show their support and their affection.

"Hello, guys." Dan's voice was rough from the smoke he'd inhaled. "Thanks for coming down. I'm fine. I want to get out of here, but they're making me stay a couple more hours. You wanna do something, send Sam good thoughts. He needs them more than me."

Shannon found a moment to silently put a hand on the fire chief's arm before the orderlies took him off to his room. Then, along with the others, she waited for word about Sam. It took the best part of an hour before a doctor finally came and told everyone that Sam was out of the operating room. His fractured leg had been repaired successfully, and he was in recovery.

There was nothing more to be done, so Shannon drove home, thinking about the fires, sickened by the fact that two men she respected and worked with had come close to dying because of arson.

Why? Who would do such a thing? Was the second explosion a deliberate attempt at covering up whatever had caused the first fire? What had been in the warehouse? What could be important enough to warrant a near homicide?

Drugs, probably, but there was no way of knowing for sure. She thought again of the man in the silver. This arson thing put a whole new spin on both his presence and his disappearance. What was he doing there, and why had he been so elusive?

More important, where the heck was he now?

At home, Shannon fed the dogs and took them for a little walk. As she headed down the sidewalk, she knew the three of them looked ridiculous, and somehow that lightened her mood. Gigantic Cleopatra minced along like the petite, svelte little dog she believed herself to be, while tiny Pepsi swaggered and growled and postured as if he were the Saint Bernard.

They made her laugh, and temporarily, she forgot about arson and injuries and men in silver suits, giving herself over to the perfection of the California day and the ridiculous antics of her animals.

It wasn't until bedtime that she remembered the interview she'd promised to do the following morning. She lay awake then, wondering if the interviewer would question her about the warehouse fires, and worrying over what she ought to reveal. Should she mention the man in the silver? She wouldn't say anything about arson. But what if the interviewer asked her why the second fire had ignited? She couldn't make up her mind how to answer that one, and it took hours before she finally slept.

SHE SHOULD HAVE GUESSED from her perky voice that Melissa Child would be a tiny, fashionable woman with meticulous makeup. That brand of fellow female always made Shannon tense, because she and they were at opposite ends of the feminine spectrum.

In contrast to Shannon's thick black braid, Melissa had a short and carefully careless streaky blond hairdo. In a fit of fashion nerves, Shannon had pulled on her newest jeans. Melissa wore a pair of cream silk cargo pants that Shannon couldn't help but covet. The woman also had eyes the exact color of violets. Was she wearing colored contacts? Shannon couldn't tell.

Melissa had arrived at Shannon's house exactly on time, and she even managed to smile when Cleopatra put her massive head on the cream silk pants and drooled.

The interviewer was a little less forgiving when Pepsi lifted a leg beside her fashionable high-heeled sandals.

Fortunately, Shannon intervened before more than a few drops had hit their mark. While she exiled the dogs to the backyard, Melissa set up her tape recorder at the kitchen table. As she started the recorder, Shannon served coffee and the cinnamon buns she'd bought.

Shannon's stomach did flip-flops as Melissa clipped a mike to her shirt. Lordy, she hated this. What should she say when the warehouse fires came up?

But the first question was easy. Melissa simply asked how long she'd lived in Courage Bay.

Shannon took a deep breath and realized her voice was actually working.

"I was born here," she explained. "My family's been here for generations. In fact, there's a family legend that says one of my great-great-grandmothers on my father's side was a high-born member of the Chumash native people."

Melissa's eyebrows rose and she said enthusiastically, "So you have native heritage. I should have guessed from those wonderful cheekbones and your lovely black hair. Where do the amazing blue eyes come from?"

"My great-great-grandfather was Irish."

"Ahh. The eyes and the creamy skin." Melissa sighed. "Lucky you."

Shannon wanted to squirm, but she remembered what Lisa had said about compliments. Just say thank you, her friend had advised.

"Thanks."

"You're a beautiful woman, but I expect you know that already," Melissa purred. "Now, what made you decide to become a firefighter?"

"It's genetic," Shannon told her, relieved beyond measure to talk about something besides her hair and skin. "I'm a fire department brat. Firefighting is the family business. My father was a fireman all his life. He retired six years ago. My brother Patrick was a fire chief, and my brother Sean's on the opposite shift to mine. He's actually a smoke jumper, but he also works at the firehouse."

"So you knew as a teenager what you wanted to do?"

"Nope." Shannon shook her head. "I went to college and sort of thought I wanted to go into medicine." That had made her mother ecstatic. More than anything, Mary had wanted her daughter to be a doctor. "So I took maths and sciences, and when it came time to really make up my mind, I realized I didn't want to spend seven years training. I did want to help people, though, so I became an EMT, an emergency medical technician. I did that a couple years and realized I really wanted to be a fireman. The EMT training was good on my résumé."

"Was it tough to qualify?"

Shannon was feeling a little more relaxed. This was familiar ground. "Yeah, it sure was. There were five thousand applicants for thirty positions." She still felt incredible gratitude that she'd made the cut—and remembered that her mother had burst into tears when she'd given her the news. Not joyful tears, either.

"The written exam isn't too bad. It's a general intelligence thing, but the physical is another story. I'm lucky, because I'm really strong. I had to train hard to complete the physical requirements, but most guys do, too. The physical part of the exam is tough for everybody."

Melissa nodded. She tipped her head to one side like a curious parakeet. "So what did your training consist of?"

"Running upstairs with a hundred pound dummy over my shoulder, dragging weighted duffels across a gymnasium. Scaling walls. Lifting weights. Shinnying up ropes. Doing push-ups and pull-ups. Running, short and long distances." Shannon grinned and added, "And lots of vomiting, just from sheer physical exertion."

Melissa pursed her mouth and whistled. "Impressive. I can't even do one push-up myself. And once you got through the preliminary testing, what then?"

"Three months at the training academy."

"What do you wear to work?" Melissa asked, her violet eyes traveling up and down Shannon's jeans and simple blue T-shirt.

"My uniform, with my turnout gear over the top when we go on a call. Sweat clothes for working out. And the first thing I do at the beginning of my shift is put my turnout clothes and all my gear near the truck, so I can grab them fast when there's an alarm."

"What's turnout gear?"

"Protective boots, pants, jacket and helmet. And a breathing mask for heavy smoke."

"And you work twenty-four hour shifts. Where do you sleep?"

"In the bunk room with everyone else. There's dividers between the beds, but no private rooms."

"And do you have your own bathroom?"

"Nope, it's not practical with two women and nineteen men. Well, usually nineteen. We're one man short at the moment." The position had been posted and the crew was waiting to see who'd fill it.

"That must be a stretch for you gals, sharing a toilet with all those guys."

Why were people always so interested in these basic things? Sooner or later, almost every woman Shannon talked to got around to the sleeping arrangements and the bathroom facilities at the firehouse. "There're two bathrooms, but only one common shower room. All of them have a two-sided sign on the door, the male and female symbols. Dana and I just turn the sign over if we're in there."

"Do you have to do more household chores than the men? More cooking, for instance?"

Shannon laughed and shook her head. "Everyone takes a turn. The only time you do more cooking is when you're a probie, and that's a year of challenge all around, but everyone's treated the same when they first come on. You're always learning or drilling or cleaning, and you're not called by your name. It's 'boot' or 'probie,' or 'hey, you.' It's pretty cruddy. But it's not gender selective."

The questions so far had been a little frivolous, Shannon mused, but they were probably valid. Maybe readers would be interested in what she wore and where she peed. So far, she hadn't had to say anything about the warehouse or the man in the silver.

"How does it feel to be in the minority, one of two women among so many men?" Melissa asked next.

It was another question women asked her all the time. Shannon smiled and shrugged. "We're a team," she explained. "Male and female doesn't really enter into it. We have work to do, and we do it. We're a tight knit group. We have to be, because often our very lives are dependent on our buddies."

"Have you ever experienced sexual harassment on the job?"

"Nope," she lied. "A few of the older guys aren't used to having a woman around, and they gave Dana and me a bad time until they saw that we could do our job, but they give all the probies a bad time, so that wasn't sexual. It was ordinary. Now I'm just one of the crew. I'm sure Dana would say the same." She'd guessed Melissa would ask that question, and she knew she couldn't be honest about it.

For the most part, it was true that the guys didn't harass her. But there'd been one man who'd run his hand over her butt in a suggestive way. More than once, he'd made a point of brushing up against her boobs. And he'd deliberately come into the shower room when she'd had the sign prominently displayed. It put her in a really tough position, because he was the battalion chief, Victor Odom.

Odom was way out of line, but what was she supposed to do or say to the guy? He had the power to make her life hell, so she gritted her teeth and ignored it. He wasn't around the station all that much, so she could stay pretty much out of his way, which was good. The slimeball gave her the creeps.

"And what about your social life?"

Shannon shrugged. "What about it?"

"C'mon now," Melissa said with a suggestive wink. "A beautiful single woman like you, and all that beefcake around for so many hours every day. Aren't you tempted once in a while? Don't the guys hit on you?"

"I've been asked out on dates, sure. Once in a while I've dated firemen, but not often." Truth to tell, she'd scared a lot of guys off. When she'd first come to the firehouse, one of the other probies had asked her out and kept asking, even when she politely and then not so politely turned him down. She'd finally lost patience and said she'd go out with him if he beat her in an arm wrestling competition. He lost, which resulted in his nickname—Nubs, which stood for no upper body strength. And of course she'd been labeled Biceps.

The moniker had stuck, and the story was still told over and over again among the firemen. She wasn't about to tell it to Melissa, however. And she could only hope that no one else would.

"It's not a good idea to date the guys you work with," she said. "If it ends badly it can cause repercussions, because we live in close quarters and have to see one another all the time."

"Are there hard and fast rules in the fire department about—what do they call it in the military—fraternizing?"

"I don't know of any rules of that sort. I've heard of female firefighters marrying male firefighters. I'm just not personally involved with any of the guys."

Melissa gave her a look, switched off the recorder and then leaned in close. "This is off the record."

Oh, lordy. She was going to ask about the warehouse fires and the guy in the silver. Shannon tried to stay calm.

"You're one gorgeous, sexy lady, Shannon O'Shea." Melissa opened her mouth a little and ran her pink tongue around her glistening lips. "How about having a drink with me when this is done?"

Omigod. It finally dawned on Shannon that Melissa was hitting on her.

CHAPTER FIVE

"SORRY, NO, I CAN'T. I'm, umm…" Shannon knew she was stammering like an idiot, but how did a person phrase this tactfully? She couldn't just challenge the woman to an arm wrestle. She felt hysterical giggles threatening and did her best to control them, finally managing to blurt out the bald truth.

"I'm heterosexual, Melissa. Totally."

"Bummer." Melissa wrinkled her nose. "Well, if you ever want to try the sunny side of the street…" She pulled out a card and scribbled on the back. "My private number. And a guaranteed good time."

Shannon took it and shoved it in the pocket of her jeans. She'd tear it up at the first opportunity, but right now, she had to get through the rest of this debacle with some show of grace.

There were a few more questions, and then Shannon felt gratitude and relief when Melissa said, "I think that's about it." But then she added, "Could we take some photographs of you down at the station, Shannon? We should have some of you in your uniform and also in your—what did you call it again?—your turnout gear. I'll have Becky, our staff photographer, meet us there."

Feeling like a prisoner being led to the gallows, Shannon reluctantly agreed.

When they got to the hall, of course, the guys all found excuses to hang around the area where the photography was taking place, especially when Becky turned out to be a willowy green-eyed blonde in a pair of short shorts. And of course they had no way of knowing that the lovely Melissa wasn't impressed by either their pecs or their patter.

Shannon felt like a total dork as she posed in the workout room doing sit-ups on the incline board. Then the photographer posed her in front of the truck, in her blue uniform, balancing on one knee with her hat perched on the other like a total and complete doofus.

By the time Becky had her sit behind the wheel of Engine One as if she was driving the damn thing, Shannon's skin was hot and her nerves frayed. By the time the two women got around to having her hold the hose, and then slide down the pole, she figured she'd pretty much bottomed out as far as mortification went.

Except she hadn't.

"You oughta get one of Biceps arm wrestling," one of the guys suggested with a wink in her direction. "She's real good at that."

Shannon glared at him and decided that murder was actually an option in this case.

Of course, Melissa wanted to know what the Biceps thing was all about.

Maybe they saw the look in her eyes, because none of the guys ratted her out, but Shannon was sweating and shaking by the time the session was finally over.

As she said goodbye to Melissa and the photographer, Shannon gritted her teeth and vowed that never in her entire life would she agree to another interview, private shower or no private shower.

AT HOME AGAIN with Cleo and Pepsi underfoot, she called the hospital to check on Sam. He was resting comfortably, the desk clerk said. Shannon doubted that—she'd only been in hospital once, to have her appendix removed, but she remembered all too clearly the rigid routine and the fact that getting any real rest had been almost impossible.

Next she placed an ad in the local paper, saying that a black Lab had been found, and the owner could call her number to claim him. Judging by the neglected state Salvage was in, she doubted anyone would answer it.

When she was done with that, she felt herself relax for the first time all day. She was on days off now. What needed doing the most? The list of repairs to the house seemed endless. Much of the work was structural, which meant she had to have help. She was no carpenter. The tiny deck off the kitchen was rotting through in places, as were the stairs. The front steps were also rickety. The windows in the two upstairs bedrooms had no screens. Her father and Sean had rewired the house for her before they'd let her move in, and the places where they'd had to poke holes to run wire awaited patching and plastering. The kitchen could use new countertops—the old white Arborite was stained and curling up at the edges. The kitchen sink and both bathrooms needed some plumbing; all the taps leaked.

Well, she wasn't about to tackle any of that today. She had laundry and grocery shopping to do, and she was almost out of dog food. Where were the heirs to dog food empires when she needed them?

She opened the fridge, expecting mold to reach out and grab her by the throat, but it was gleaming. Either Willow had cleaned it or Shannon had acquired a kitchen angel along with the one from the fire. Her money was on Willow, and now that Shannon was paying attention, it looked as if she'd also washed the kitchen floor. There was even fresh newspaper under the dogs' food and water bowls. Having a boarder must be something like having a wife. No wonder guys wanted one.

The living room still had dog hair everywhere, so a good vacuuming was in order. With some difficulty and much resistance, Shannon dragged the dogs outside and put them in the screened run. They whimpered and looked betrayed. "So learn to vacuum your own mess up, you deadbeats," she told them. Inside, she dragged out the machine and got to it.

Willow came in just as she finished.

"I was going to do that," the woman said, "but I decided on a long walk instead. With the pittance I'm paying you for rent, Shannon, you should make me a job list. I'll happily do whatever."

"You already did the fridge and the floor, thanks so much. I don't expect you to clean for me, Willow. It's enough you help take care of the dogs."

"I've never been one to sit. I need jobs to do." Willow's smile encompassed her entire face, and Shannon couldn't help smiling back, thinking how incredibly young-looking her boarder was for sixty-something. Tiny and slender, Willow had a short cap of snow-white hair that she moussed until it stood wildly on end. Her clothes were dramatic and colorful and youthful, and she oozed energy. Today she was wearing a slim denim skirt that bared excellent legs, a pink tee and an assortment of bracelets that jangled on her arm. She actually made growing older look appealing, Shannon mused.

"Speaking of jobs, there's one you might want to look into." She told Willow about Lisa and the vet clinic.

Willow's hazel eyes sparkled, and she clasped her hands under her chin. "Oh, that sounds like such *fun*. I love animals, as you know." Her face registered uncertainty. "But I haven't had a real job in years. Steve had a thing about me working."

Steve sounded like a real winner, Shannon thought. Good for Willow for doing a bunk. "So how did you spend your time if he didn't want you to work?"

"Oh, I took a zillion classes on everything under the sun, including carpentry. I don't really have any sort of work résumé, though."

"I don't think Lisa gives a hoot about a résumé. She just wants somebody who knows something about computers and doesn't paint their nails or ignore the telephone while a vicious cat tears up the waiting-room cushions."

"Is that all?" Willow had a wide, quirky grin. "I'd promise to do my nails on my own time. And as for the cat—surely there's catnip growing somewhere around here that we could bribe the animal with?"

Shannon laughed. "There you go. Just tell Lisa that and she'll hire you in a heartbeat."

"Thank you so much, Shannon. I didn't expect you to come up with a paying job as well as a place to live. Now, there's something else I was wondering about." Willow hesitated as if she was nervous about asking a favor. "Do you think I could maybe help with the things around the house that need fixing? I noticed you have drywall that should be patched, and the banister on the stairs is loose. And both sets of steps are a little dangerous." She clapped a hand over her mouth. "Oh, fudge. It sounds like I'm criticizing your house. Please don't take it that way. It's just that lots of my night-school classes were in carpentry and I'm pretty good at it. The back deck could use some new flooring. I know how to do that. We'd use treated cedar, I'd nail it on an angle—whoops, there I go again. Tell me just to mind my own business."

Shannon was flabbergasted. Dainty Willow, fixing her deck? Although she shouldn't be surprised; there *was* that toolbox.

"Me mind? Are you nuts? A carpenter, living right here—it feels like I've won the lottery. I'd think I'd died and gone to heaven if even two of those things got done. Just make a list of all the supplies you need, and I'll get them." Shannon's imagination was taking off. "My uncle Donald has power tools he never uses. He was going to build a boat when he retired from the insurance business, but that hasn't happened. I'm sure he'd loan them to us if we need them, so we're solid there." She reined in her enthusiasm. "But, Willow, please don't feel you have to."

"Have to? No 'have to' about it, it's my hobby. Besides, I get restless without enough to do."

"Just don't kill yourself. You might find you won't have the energy if you take the job at the clinic. It can get pretty hairy over there." She grinned. "No pun intended."

"Honey, I've lived for forty-three years with a man who criticized almost everything I did. He wasn't what you'd call supportive. It feels as if I just got let out of prison, and besides, I've got that post-menopausal zest thing going for me, as well. I have energy to burn."

"Then let's drink to freedom." Shannon got cola from the fridge and two glasses, and they sat at the kitchen table.

Willow took a sip and then said, "Is that black Lab you saved from the fire doing okay? I saw you with him on TV. And apparently that fire started up again, and two firemen were hurt. That's horrible. Are they okay?"

"Yeah, they're doing fine, but that warehouse is turning into a nightmare for all of us. And the dog lost his back leg. Lisa couldn't save it. He's still at the clinic, and he'll be there another couple days. I'm calling him Salvage. I advertised for his owner, but I think he's a stray, so I'm gonna have to find a home for him, because I just can't afford another dog—emotionally or financially. Cleo eats twice her body weight in dog food every day, and it's a wonder I haven't ended up getting sued over Pepsi's behavior."

"He *is* a little peculiar. He seems to have a problem with his bladder."

"That's a tactful way of putting it. The truth is he's a miserable little cuss whose favorite expression is 'Piss on the world.'"

Willow laughed and then said, "It's too bad Salvage had to lose his leg, but it's sure better than dying in that fire. I really like his name. What about the firehouse? Don't firehouses usually have a mascot?"

That hadn't occurred to Shannon. "You know, that's not a bad idea. I'll talk to the guys, see if anybody has any objections."

"My son always wanted to be a firefighter, but he'd never be able to pass the physical," Willow confided.

"Why would he have trouble?"

"Didn't your mother tell you? Aaron was born with one leg twisted and much shorter than the other."

Shannon was shocked. "That's really rough. Do the doctors have any idea what caused it?"

Willow shook her head. "My mother was psychic. She's dead now, but she always said it was from past life stuff, and I'm sure she's right."

"You believe in all that, reincarnation and multiple lives?" Shannon had read about it, but she was undecided.

"Oh, absolutely. Astrology, reincarnation…it makes perfect sense to me. We bring challenges with us from other lives and do our best to work them out. Everyone we meet here is both our teacher and our student, and we've all agreed beforehand to play our part in one another's lives. There are no accidents."

Shannon drank the last of her cola and smiled at Willow. "That would sure make you view things differently." She was thinking of her mother. Maybe if Mary believed everything was already decided, she'd lay off Shannon about her choice of career.

"It's comforting," Willow said. "It takes away the whole issue of why somebody might treat us badly. Leaves no room for self-pity. Maybe last time around, we did something similar to them."

"What about relationships? You think we're fated to meet a certain person at a certain point in our lives?" It was something Shannon had always wondered about.

"Oh, absolutely. An astrological chart can predict exactly when it'll happen. The interesting part is that we're simply drawn to them. We have no idea whether it's going to be heaven or hell to actually *live* with them." She looked pensive, and Shannon figured Willow was thinking about her husband. "They're the right person to make us grow, that's all," she added after a minute. "The universe has no respect for our comfort zones. See, I could bemoan the fact that I ever met Steve…berate myself for marrying him."

Shannon nodded. "That would be the usual response, all right."

"And it would make me miserable. Life's way too short for that. Looking back, I can see that I would never have gained what little determination or self-esteem I have without Steve always being negative and questioning me at every turn."

Shannon nodded again, even though she figured she would have walked out on Stevie baby way sooner than Willow had. Like ten minutes into the honeymoon.

"In the end, I knew it was either lose myself completely and turn into a blob, or get strong and walk away." Willow's voice quavered a little. So she wasn't quite as tough as she seemed. "I got strong. He's been my greatest teacher. I'm grateful to him for that."

"Wow. You must drive your divorce lawyer nuts. How's he gonna make any money if you don't get mad and mean and want to fleece the guy for everything he's got?"

Willow laughed. "Oh, I haven't thought about divorce yet. And according to the laws in New Jersey, I'm entitled to half of what we have. When the time comes, that'll be more than enough for me."

"Enough people like you, and divorce lawyers would have to go out of business." Shannon hesitated, but curiosity got the best of her. "So what's your son doing now?"

"Aaron works for a contractor. He was the one who inspired me to do the carpentry thing. Here, I have a photo of him." She dug in her handbag and then flipped open her wallet.

"Wow. He's really good-looking." Aaron was a hunk, whatever length his legs were. He had a big smile, even features, a shock of thick hair. Nice smile lines around his eyes. He had a gentle look about him.

"Thank you. I think he's wonderful, but then, I'm his mother. I do know he has amazing talent as an artist, but Steve insisted he get training in something practical instead of getting a degree in art." Willow sighed. "Aaron always tried hard to please his father."

"Maybe he'll decide to be an artist when he's older."

"Maybe. He's thirty-six, so there's lots of time."

That made Shannon blink. This guy they were talking about was eight years older than she was, and still conflicted about what he wanted to be when he grew up? At least her mother hadn't had that problem to contend with.

"I'm hoping he'll come out here for a visit," Willow said. "I'd like him to meet you. And your brothers, of course. All of you are so confident, so sure of yourselves. But you get that from your mother. When we were performing together, I used to have terrible stage fright, but Mary just loved every moment of it." Willow shook her head, a faraway look in her eyes. "I was sure she'd be famous someday. She had that marvelous voice, and she wasn't afraid of anything."

She wasn't afraid of anything? Could this be the same Mary O'Shea who made herself sick worrying over her kids, and was giving Shannon a bad time about her job because it was dangerous?

"She led your father a merry chase, you know. He was so in love with her, but for the longest time, she wouldn't agree to marry him. She was determined to have a singing career."

This was news to Shannon. "What do you think changed her mind?"

"Oh, I have no idea." But the way Willow averted her eyes told Shannon she knew very well. "You'd have to talk to her about that."

Maybe she would, Shannon decided. Her mother, like Willow, had never really worked outside her home. Sure, Mary was talented at acting, and everyone knew she could sing. She'd always belonged to the local little theater group, and she performed at church concerts, but Shannon had never thought much about what Mary's dreams might have been as a young woman. She'd just assumed that her mother had exactly the life she wanted.

Willow changed the subject. "Let's make a list of things that need fixing around here, and then I'll figure out what supplies we need, okay? And then I'm going over to your friend's clinic to apply for that job."

For the next hour, they walked through the house and Willow jotted down in a notebook all the things that could stand improvement. The longer the list grew, the more excited she became.

Shannon got into the spirit of the thing. She called her uncle Donald and asked to borrow his pickup, and when he dropped it off, she and Willow set off for the hardware store.

On the way, Shannon stopped and introduced Willow to Lisa and Greg and Salvage, and within fifteen minutes, Willow had the receptionist's job.

"I'm so grateful to you, Shannon," Willow said when they were once again in the truck. "I can't believe I'll be getting paid to work there. I'd happily do it for free."

Shannon laughed. "That's exactly how I felt at first about being a fireman."

"I feel as though I've gotten a chance at a whole new life," Willow declared, "just like Salvage. He's going to make the best firehouse mascot ever."

"I think so, too. Now all I have to do is convince the guys at the station that you're right."

A WEEK LATER when Shannon arrived at the station for her morning rotation before another five days off, she was mentally planning her campaign to have Salvage adopted. She could hear voices in the kitchen, and after she stowed her gear, she headed that way, going over in her head the list of reasons why the firehouse needed a mascot.

The kitchen was the place where the incoming and outgoing shifts chose to brief one another. The outgoing crew was gathered around the table, and most of the guys on Shannon's shift were there, as well. So was a man she hadn't met before, and her carefully prepared speech on Salvage's behalf went right out of her head when she looked at him.

There was something about him...

"Shannon O'Shea, meet John Forester, our newest squad member," said Rolando Martinez, the acting chief. "John's posted here from New York. Shannon's one of our two female firefighters, John."

"Hey, Shannon." John got to his feet and held out a massive hand. "Pleasure to meet you," he said.

"And you, John." Shannon took his hand and looked up at him—*way* up. He had to be six and a half feet tall, and with the height went a spectacular build. She'd seldom met anyone as tall and fit as her brother Sean, but this guy was a strong contender.

What was it about him...?

A quick assessment told her he was probably close to three hundred pounds of sheer muscle. His eyes were a soft, dark brown. They looked kind, and the laugh lines around them suggested a sense of humor. His hair was a match for his eyes in color, thick and soft, waving a little over his forehead. He had a quirky, lopsided grin, great teeth and that indentation in his chin that women adored. He also had dimples when he smiled.

As far as looks went, Forester would qualify as a hunk by even the most exacting woman's standards. And if he turned out to be passive aggressive and chauvinistic as hell, at least he'd be fun to have around. Eye candy, Shannon told herself.

But why would the department parachute an applicant in from New York when Shannon knew of at least three great guys who'd finished their training right here in Courage Bay, and were perfect for the job?

There was going to be some controversy about this posting, that was certain. But then, who knew what the higher ups were thinking? Maybe this guy had more experience. Or maybe he just had pull with the powers that be.

"O'Shea will give you a guided tour of the firehouse, John," Rolando added. "And if you're available tomorrow evening, we'll all introduce you to our favorite hangout, the Courage Bay Bar and Grill, just down the street."

"I'll look forward to that." He turned to Shannon and raised an eyebrow. "Good to go, tour guide?"

"Absolutely, just follow me," she managed to say in a cheerful, helpful tone. She smiled up at him, acting cool even though inside she was trying to figure out why this huge man should be having such a weird effect on her.

She'd felt sexual attraction before—what red-blooded woman hadn't? But this immediate and powerful reaction was different. She felt she'd actually *known* this man before, and yet she could swear she'd never met him.

CHAPTER SIX

JOHN FORESTER WASN'T exactly somebody who'd slip a normal woman's mind—not unless she had Alzheimer's, Shannon told herself.

Maybe there was something to this reincarnation thing that Willow had talked about. Maybe Shannon had known Forester in another lifetime. Because he made her nervous as hell in this one, and the result was she talked too much.

"You probably noticed that the police headquarters are right across the compound from us—we share the outside exercise area. So far we're beating them at basketball. With your height, you'll be a welcome addition to our team. Losers have to supply the barbecue on the outdoor grill. Now, the grand tour. Here we have the workout room, and this is the TV room. *Ta da*—these are the offices, here's our kitchen, and of course you'd never guess these are the three bays where our trucks live, one engine, one ladder, one rescue. The fourth bay is maintenance. Two entrances, one on Jefferson, one on Fifth. Two bunk rooms, two bathrooms, common shower. If the sign's turned over, it means I'm in there."

Cute. Not. Stop it, O'Shea. You sound like a wound-up Energizer bunny. Ask questions. Get him talking. Let yourself off the hook.

"So you're from New York, John?" *Brilliant, just brilliant.*
"Born and bred. How about you, Shannon?"
Neat, fast turnaround. "Courage Bay, born and bred." Two

more members were just coming in, and Shannon introduced them. Then she led the way to the garage area.

"Bud Patchett, John Forester," she said next. "Bud does all the maintenance and repairs on our trucks, and he also gives free advice when my poor old car breaks down." She liked the friendly mechanic. Everyone did. "John's our newest member, Bud, just in from New York."

"Good to meet you." Bud wiped off his fingers with a cloth before he shook John's hand. "Hope you like our little city. Must seem small compared to New York."

"I haven't been here long enough to really look around, but I think I'm gonna love it," John assured him.

Before they could say any more, the bells sounded and the dispatcher's voice came over the loudspeaker. "Engine One, Rescue One, Ladder One. First alarm to Forty-fifth and Smythe. Report of apartment fire."

Shannon joined the general rush for turnout uniforms and jumped on the truck.

The call-out was a false alarm. Some kids had put a flashing red light in an empty apartment, and it looked like flames from the street. But the crew had no sooner arrived back at the hall than the alarm sounded again.

This time it was a thirty-seven-year-old man in a luxury apartment building, who'd had a heart attack. Shannon and the others resuscitated him, and he was breathing when the ambulance arrived, but when they got back to the firehouse, they heard he'd been DOA when he reached the hospital.

No one said much over dinner. Shannon didn't know what the others were thinking, but she kept seeing the young man's face in her mind. He hadn't been much older than her, and now he was dead.

She glanced up from the ice cream they were having for dessert and caught Forester studying her. He gave a tiny nod and a wink, and for some reason she figured he knew exactly what she'd been thinking.

There was a motor vehicle accident just after midnight with three serious injuries, and at three in the morning a woman in labor who didn't have cab fare called the fire department instead. They got her to the hospital in the very nick of time. The baby was a healthy boy, and the atmosphere in the truck on the way back to the station was almost hysterically lighthearted. In some crazy fashion, the baby's birth seemed to balance out the young man's death.

Through it all, Shannon was intensely aware of the newest member of the team, and the feeling grew even stronger as the twenty-four-hour shift progressed. When she did get a few stolen hours of sleep toward morning, she was grateful that Forester was assigned sleeping space in the other bunk room. The energy between them was disconcerting.

By six the next morning, when her shift was over, Shannon felt the usual buzz, a combination of leftover adrenaline and weariness. She was pulling on her runners when John came up to her.

"I wondered if you were going to this Bar and Grill place this afternoon, Shannon?"

"Yeah, of course. Having a beer together is a tradition when a new guy arrives at the hall."

"Where is it, exactly?"

"Right along Jefferson Avenue, a couple of blocks from here. I'll walk over with you now and show you the place, if you like."

"You wouldn't mind?"

"Not at all." But as they started out, she wasn't exactly sure that was true. Being close to him made her hyperaware of being female, a situation that usually didn't come up with the guys at work. They were a team, and gender wasn't an issue.

During the short walk to the bar, the strange and powerful attraction she'd felt earlier was back in full force. He wasn't touching her, but every nerve ending in her body telegraphed awareness. Tension grew, and Shannon again found herself taking nervous refuge in words.

"The Bar and Grill's smack-dab in the middle of the emergency services district," she said. "So it's become an off-duty hangout for the police, the firemen and the medical emergency teams." *And you've become a chatty tour guide.*

"There's a couple places in New York like that, too," he said. "Family places, in a way."

Shannon nodded. "It's got an interesting and tragic history, actually. The owners, Larry and Louise Goodman, geared the place to the emergency teams after their only son, Peter, died ten years ago. He was a paramedic, and he died as a result of treating victims of a chemical spill at a paint factory. They've devoted an entire wall to photos of emergency personnel who've lost their lives in the line of duty." She pointed ahead, relieved that they'd reached their destination. "That's the building there."

"Brick, huh? You'd almost think it was built by firefighters."

Shannon smiled at him and shook her head. "It was an old movie theater, built back in 1914 when movies first caught on. Larry's father bought it in the seventies and converted it to the Bar and Grill. Larry inherited it. He's added a rooftop patio—it's nice up there on summer evenings."

"You can probably use it all year round in this climate." John nodded up at the sky. "Just look at that color."

Above the hills, the eastern sky was still streaked with gold and yellow, remnants of the sunrise.

"We don't have this much sky in New York," John said. "Too many tall buildings."

"Do you miss it?"

"New York?" They'd reached the bar, and he stopped and turned toward her. The guy had a killer smile. "I haven't been away long enough to get homesick."

"So when did you arrive in Courage Bay?"

He named a date.

"That was the day after the first warehouse fire," Shannon said.

"Yeah. I heard all about that. The place went up again, right?"

"It sure did. That would have happened the day you arrived here. Our chief, Dan Egan, and the arson investigator, Sam Prophet, were hurt in that second fire. There's some indication it was arson. I heard they've sent in a bomb specialist. Maybe the first one was arson, too. I was there, and things went bad really fast, much faster than an ordinary blaze should have."

"I've been in some like that. We had one in the Bronx, in a carpet warehouse. Place went up like tinder."

"Was that one arson?"

"Nope." John shook his head. He didn't seem inclined to say any more about it. Usually when guys were loath to talk, it meant something bad had happened, somebody hurt or dead, so Shannon let the subject drop.

"Well, I should be heading home." She adjusted her backpack. "See you here at about five this afternoon."

He nodded and held her gaze longer than necessary. "I'll be waiting, Shannon."

Now what exactly did he mean by that? She had the distinct impression he was watching her as she jogged down the street. But when she turned the corner at the end of the block, she glanced back and he was gone.

So much for an overactive imagination.

WHEN SHANNON GOT HOME ten minutes later, it didn't take any imagination at all to see that her front steps were missing. Nothing but a pile of rubble remained, and Willow was already busy loading the old lumber into a wheelbarrow Shannon hadn't seen before.

Willow set it down and waved a cheerful greeting as Shannon jogged up.

The dogs came racing over to greet her, and Willow said, "Hi, boss. I thought I'd get started early on those steps. They could give out at any time, and I've heard how Californians will sue at the drop of a hat."

Shannon was a little surprised and not a little dismayed. She'd been thinking more along the lines of repairs rather than total annihilation. But what did she know? Maybe the stairs were too rotten to save. And she hadn't been specific.

Cleo was lying on her back on the grass, waving her legs in the air, and Shannon knelt to give her belly a scratch. It gave her a chance to recover. "Did we buy enough wood to rebuild these?" She knew they hadn't. And her charge card was already dangerously close to maxing out.

"Pepsi, don't you dare." Shannon took a swipe at him just as he raised a leg above her right running shoe.

"Don't worry about lumber," Willow chirped. "Donald's going for some when the stores open. He brought over his wheelbarrow, too. We're piling all this junk in the backyard. I thought we could light it and have a wiener roast a little later."

"Good idea." Did she have any wieners? Shannon didn't think so. She was making a mental shopping list as she made her way around the house to the back, dogs trailing behind her.

She stopped short when she rounded the corner of the house, and her jaw dropped. The back deck was also demolished. A ladder had been propped on an angle against the back door, obviously to gain access to the house.

A not so little niggle of concern was beginning to take the place of surprise. It was one thing to knock things down, but it dawned on Shannon that she had no real proof Willow was capable of building them back up again.

"I figured we might as well get the lumber for both," Willow said cheerfully as she wheeled a load past Shannon and dumped it on the already enormous pile of rubble.

"Absolutely," Shannon agreed in a weak voice, noting that the pile was almost as high as the back fence. When they lit that scrap heap on fire for their weiner roast, she'd better have an engine standing by, or the whole neighborhood could go up.

"Don't worry," Willow called after her as Shannon climbed

the ladder into the kitchen. "I'm going to fix up a ramp so the dogs can go in."

Shannon was getting to her feet when she noticed the countertops. The Arborite was gone, leaving a mess of worn wood and old, ugly glue.

"Omigod." She stared at the mess. Exactly how far had Willow gone with this demolition kick? Almost afraid to find out, she made her way through the rest of her house. The walls in the hall had been generously spackled but not yet sanded. Well, that wasn't too bad. They'd needed spackle, although it looked as if Willow had been more than a little generous with the stuff. The banister was now missing from the stairs.

The downstairs bathroom had no glass doors on the tub, which was what Shannon had planned would eventually happen, but neither did it have a rod and shower curtain. That was going to make showering a little tricky, but it wasn't really an issue, Shannon realized an instant later, because there was no longer a shower. Instead, there was a gaping hole in the wall, which exposed the pipes.

"There was a leak in the line, and the shower was rusted, so I just took the whole thing out," Willow said from behind her. "I haven't done much plumbing, but I don't think it's too complicated. After all, men do it all the time."

Take two deep breaths, Shannon cautioned herself. *And then turn around and try to smile. Keep your hands at your sides. Remember, sometimes you don't know your own strength.*

"You don't think maybe you've taken on too much, Willow? I mean, with the job at the vet clinic and all?" Gad, she was proud of herself. She didn't sound furious.

"Heavens no." Willow shook her head. "You know what they say—if you want something done, find a busy person."

"Right." *Get out of here before you explode, O'Shea.* "Well, I think I'll head off to the grocery store for some mustard and wieners."

"That would be nice. I think that's Donald's truck I hear. Good. He's back with the materials we need."

Shannon was exiting via the ladder when her uncle rounded the corner carrying a stack of lumber on his shoulder.

"Hey, how's my girl?" He put the lumber on the grass and came over to kiss Shannon's cheek. He was puffing hard and sweating heavily. Shannon studied him, wondering if he ought to be carting around heavy loads of lumber.

Uncle Donald was a good forty pounds overweight, and from the color of his face, Shannon guessed he might also have high blood pressure. He'd had a desk job all his working life, and he hadn't taken up any exercise more strenuous than table tennis since his retirement four years before.

"I think Willow wants to talk to you," Shannon lied. "Go see what she needs and I'll finish unloading the lumber."

"Okay." Donald's face registered relief. "Oh, Shannon, here's the bill for the supplies. I put it all on my credit card."

Shannon took the slip of paper. One glance, and she could feel her own blood pressure rising rapidly. "I'll write you a check." *And then I'll go see about a loan at the bank.*

"No rush, honey." He headed up the ladder, but Donald wasn't that agile. He slipped halfway up. He caught himself before he fell, but Shannon started wondering about her liability insurance. What, exactly, did it cover?

She carried lumber until she'd cooled down somewhat. Then she went up the ladder herself, determined to lay down the law.

Willow was making coffee in the kitchen. Uncle Donald was sitting on a stool at the counter, looking at her as if she was a multibillion-dollar policy he was writing up.

Shannon took a deep, calming breath. "Willow, I want you to replace at least one set of stairs as soon as possible. I'm concerned about safety." There, that should do it.

"Oh, absolutely." Her eyes went big and round. Donald turned and gave Shannon a wounded look.

"We're planning to do that right away, aren't we, Willow? You don't mind if we just have a cup of coffee first? And a sandwich?"

Shannon felt like crap. They were both pensioners, for God's sake. What was she thinking? "Take all the time you need," she muttered. "There's ham and cheese in the fridge." Shoulders hunched, she turned and made her way out the door and back down the ladder.

She opened the dog pen. Pepsi and Cleo burst out as though they'd been incarcerated for years. "C'mon, you two. I need a walk. And we'd better all hope the geriatric wrecking crew don't decide on some upgrades to your doghouse while we're gone."

By the time she left for the Bar and Grill that afternoon, there was a ramp the dogs could manage that led up to the back door, but that was all. Willow and Donald had made two attempts before they got it right, and it had taken most of the afternoon to construct, which Shannon figured didn't bode well for the rest of the renovations. On the positive side, Willow had decided against lighting the pile of rubble.

"Donald's invited me out for a nice dinner instead of hot dogs," she told Shannon. "We'll have the wiener roast another day."

And she'd make certain she had a hose and maybe an engine standing by, Shannon thought as she headed out the door. She wondered if Willow's husband drank. The woman had been living with her for only a little over a week, and already Shannon felt the need for liquor.

When she walked into the Bar and Grill, the guys from the firehouse hailed her. Some had their wives and girlfriends with them. All of them were grouped around the long, U-shaped bar. John was sitting beside Spike Hilborn.

"Hey, Biceps, c'mon over," Spike said, scooting aside to make room. "We saved a seat for ya." She sat down between the two of them, conscious all over again of the magnetism

John exuded. Was it only her, or did every woman in the room feel it?

"John just got here," Spike said to her. "So I'm introducing him to the guys he didn't meet this morning. This is Monte, better known as the Bull," he related. "And Brian, also known as Sleepy. Gary, and his lady, Maria. That's Chug, and his wife, Belinda. And the beautiful blond bartender is Carolee Pollack. Meet John Forester, everybody. He's our newest member, which means he's buying."

Laughter greeted that announcement. Everybody clapped and raised their glasses to John. Carolee put a brimming mug of lager in front of Shannon so she could join in the toast.

"Welcome to Courage Bay, Forester," everyone chorused.

Just as Shannon had known he would, Spike began the inquisition before their mugs of draft were half emptied. Spike was called the Inquisitor, and he'd earned his nickname fair and square. He leaned forward, squinting around Shannon, and said, "So, John, what brings you here to Courage Bay?"

"I saw the posting in the *Bulletin* and applied."

The *Bulletin* was a national newsletter for firefighters.

"I always wanted to live in California," John declared. "And I saw this documentary a while ago on Courage Bay—looked to be a really nice city."

"You're right about that," Spike confirmed. "Our town's the best kept secret on the coast. Great weather, beautiful gals, nice beaches."

"Not much of a secret after that documentary aired," someone commented.

Shannon had to agree. Her sister-in-law's film had gotten national distribution and won several awards, and obviously it had attracted people to Courage Bay. Willow had seen it and moved here, and now John was saying it was the reason for his arrival, as well.

"Yeah, you're right, I guess that documentary sort of put us on the map," Spike agreed. "That was mostly about Bicep's big brother, Sean, and his group of smoke jumpers. Those guys are real heroes."

Carolee was serving more beer. "Your sister-in-law was the photographer on that film, right, Shannon?"

"Yeah, that's how Sean and Linda met," Shannon confirmed.

"That was so romantic," the waitress sighed. "They got caught in that bushfire up the mountain, didn't they? And the news helicopter rescued them."

Shannon nodded. Carolee might not fully understand the danger Sean and Linda had been in, but she did. It still gave her cold shudders to think of it. It was a miracle they'd ever gotten out. They'd been surrounded by wildfire, just as she had been at the warehouse fire, when her silver angel came along.

Maybe the O'Sheas had a monopoly on miracles.

As if she'd read Shannon's mind, Carolee said, "How's that dog you saved from the warehouse, Shannon? I saw you on the news with him." Carolee loved animals, and had a cat that she brought to work.

"He had to have his back leg amputated, but I think he's gonna be fine." She hadn't brought up Salvage's future yet, but now was as good a time as any. Raising her voice so the others around the bar could hear, she said, "If nobody claims him, what do you guys think of having a dog at the firehouse? He's a black Lab, real nice disposition. Name of Salvage, and a trifle challenged, so he fits right in."

"Sure."

"That's a great idea."

"Sounds good. He could clean up on the dinner scraps—keep Chug from gaining any more weight."

"Bring him around, we'll take a vote."

It sounded as if Salvage might have a new home, and Shannon felt pleased with herself—and grateful to Willow for having the idea in the first place. She sipped her lager. At least one thing had gone right today.

Spike was grilling John again. "So how long you been a fireman, Forester?"

"This is my fifth year. My dad was a fireman. We lived in Queens but he worked at Hall Seventeen in Brooklyn. He died a year ago, and I haven't any other close family."

"Hey, my second cousin worked at Seventeen," Monte said. "Jimmy Reilly. You ever hear your dad mention him?"

There was the tiniest of pauses before John answered, Shannon noted.

"Not that I can recall, but maybe he was there after my father left. Dad was retired for a long time before he died—he had bad lungs. Used to go in with no breathing apparatus."

"Yeah, lots of the old-timers had rotten lungs from that," Monte agreed. "They used to think they were tough—made fun of anybody who used masks."

"I'm glad things have changed in that regard," John commented.

"So, you married, Forester?" Spike asked. "Got any kids?"

Shannon had to hide her grin by taking a sip of her beer. Spike wouldn't rest until he extracted every last ounce of personal information John was willing to share. And about this particular subject, she was all ears.

"Nope. Never been married. And no kids."

"That you know about, right?" Spike joked. "Hell, at our age, there could be a lot of slips we never found out about. Remember that report on *20/20* about guys who sold sperm to those banks, and now the kids are tracing down their biological fathers? One guy could have thirty kids turn up on his doorstep one day, all asking for money for college. Now there's a sobering thought. Any of you guys ever go that route in your younger days, selling your essence to pay the rent?"

There was laughter and denial all round. "How come you know so much about it, Spike?" Chug asked.

"Hey, don't look at me. My sperm are all present and accounted for."

"So do you practice abstinence, or just safe sex?" The wise mouth was one of the two rookies who'd just walked in.

"Porn movies, that's the answer," the other one said. "It's cheaper than dating."

The group erupted with hoots of derision and shouts of agreement.

Taking advantage of the noise level, John turned to Shannon and asked, "How about you, Shannon? Married, divorced, significant other?"

"Never married, so never divorced. Nothing significant or otherwise. And no kids, although I'm about to become an aunt again, which thrills me no end. I already have a niece and a nephew."

He nodded, once again holding her gaze just longer than was comfortable. Damn, this guy raised the hair on the back of her neck just by looking at her. She used her mug as a diversion, taking another sip of beer.

"But kids of your own are in your future?"

She gave a noncommittal shrug. "I'd like to think so. But who knows what the future holds?"

According to Willow everybody did, on some level. But Shannon didn't want to think about Willow and her theories—or her wrecking ball—just now.

"The guys call you Biceps," John continued. "Care to tell me how you got your nickname?"

She smiled and shook her head. "Nope."

But Spike was eavesdropping, as usual. He winked at Shannon. "That started when she was a rookie, and Martin, the guy we call Nubs—you'll meet him—was totally smitten with her, but Biceps didn't feel the same way, see. Anyhow, Nubs hit on her until she got fed up and challenged him to an arm wrestling contest. He's an annoying guy, Nubs. She made the rules. He won, she'd go out with him. He lost, he'd leave her alone. Now, you gotta understand that having a woman as part of the team was brand-new to all of us, so we were really interested in this whole scenario. In fact, the whole damn firehouse laid bets that day."

"Yeah," Chug said with a doleful sigh. "I lost a hundred bucks on that one."

"Not me," Spike declared. "I made a bundle. I figured she was way too smart to get into something she couldn't win."

Shannon was embarrassed by the attention, but she was also laughing along with everybody else. The story had become a legend of sorts at the hall, and she'd heard these guys telling it to every rookie, so it wasn't anything new.

"Anyhow, she took him easy. Which is how he got the label Nubs. No upper body strength. Which made her Biceps."

John pursed his lips and whistled. "Remind me never to challenge you to a duel, Shannon." He was obviously enjoying himself at her expense.

"A duel? I'm hopeless with guns. You'd win easy." *Unless we were using another kind of weapon, up close and personal. That might be a draw.*

John was looking straight into her eyes, and she felt color come to her cheeks.

"No really smart guy would take that route to win the heart of a lady, anyhow," he said.

"No?" Chug leaned forward. "So give us your tried and true big-city formula for romance, there, Big Bad John."

Big Bad John.

Shannon knew at that moment that John had passed the test. New members only got a label when the other guys took to them—or when they made a serious error. Firemen were ruthless, and nicknames stuck forever. This one was a kind of compliment.

"Hey, I'm no expert on that subject." John shook his head. "I don't think there's a man alive who is. You oughta be asking the women."

"Okay, Biceps, you start. What really turns a lady's crank when it comes to guys?"

"Top of the list? Honesty. Women get so sick of you guys and your bullshit. Why is it you can't just stick to the truth? We're tough, we can take it."

"Way to go, Shannon." Carolee and Marie clapped.

"Okay, write that down, guys—honesty," Spike said. "What's next on the list?"

Maria spoke up. "Laughter. A guy's got to have a good sense of humor."

"Well, we all got that in spades, right, guys?" Chug lifted his mug in a toast. "To the funny, honest guys from Jefferson Ave." They all cheered and drank and then he said, "Okay, go on. What's next?"

Carolee was mixing drinks, but she didn't even pretend she wasn't listening. She lowered her throaty voice half an octave. "Slow hands," she purred. "The reason we don't tell you guys when we have an orgasm is because you're usually not there when it happens, right, girls?"

For some reason, the women laughed harder than the men at that.

"This is getting too rowdy for me," Chug announced. "How about a game of pool?" He picked up his beer and headed toward the function room, where there were pool tables, darts and televisions. As the others followed him, Shannon decided it was time for her to head home. She took her handbag from under the bar stool and stood up.

"See you, John. I've got to go. My animals will be waiting for their dinner."

He got up, too. "I was hoping that maybe you'd have dinner with me. We could try out that roof patio upstairs? I hear the food here is good."

Her pulse kicked up a notch. She was really tempted, but maybe it was too soon. She wanted to see what he was like at work, find out more about him before she chose to spend off time with him. The rumor mill at the firehouse worked overtime. No point getting into something that might cause awkwardness if it fizzled.

Besides, she had this nagging feeling that she knew him from somewhere, and she needed time to figure out what that was all about.

"Thanks, but I really should get home."

"Okay. Maybe another time." He didn't pursue it, which impressed her. "Thanks for showing me around." He walked with her to the door, holding it open for her.

The guy had good instincts.

Get real, O'Shea. This guy has good everything. Which made her wonder if maybe he was just too good to be true. She smiled a thank-you up into his soft brown eyes, swallowed hard when she felt an unmistakable rush, and took off, once again forcing herself not to turn around and see if he was watching.

CHAPTER SEVEN

JOHN WATCHED HER JOG OFF, admiring the way her long, inky-black braid bounced, almost touching her firm round ass. She had an amazing body, a rare combination of athleticism and womanly curves. He couldn't help but imagine her naked and shivering, held tight in his arms.

"Ahh, Shannon O'Shea, you're going to be trouble, damn it all to hell," he muttered under his breath. He'd known it the moment he laid eyes on her. Tall and strong and incredibly sexy, she had eyes bluer than the California sky. And what would that thick mass of raven-dark hair look like, spread loose on a white pillow? His body responded before he could get his imagination reined in.

Back off, Johnny boy, he cautioned himself silently. *There's too much resting on this job to jeopardize it over a woman. She's not your sort, regardless of how she makes your blood boil. And you're only here for the job, so keep that in mind. You'll be gone in a few short weeks if everything goes right.*

Honesty. She'd said she wanted that quality in a man. And of course that was the last thing he could give her.

When she turned a corner, he gave his head a rueful shake and closed the door. Then he went back to the bar to pick up his half-finished mug of beer.

He'd love to head back to the motel—it had been a long, tiring day. But instead he walked into the function room where the others had gone. There were things he needed to know, and the best place to find them out was by listening as the firemen talked.

Booze loosened tongues as well as inhibitions. *Loose lips sink ships,* one of his mother's low-life lovers used to say. He'd forgotten which asshole that was, there'd been so many.

FOR A WHILE THERE, Shannon had forgotten about the mess her house was in. Climbing up the ramp to the kitchen door reminded her. At least Willow wasn't home, which was a relief. Shannon fed the dogs and was heating up a frozen casserole her mother had given her when someone banged on the kitchen door.

Cleo and Pepsi went into a barking frenzy. Shannon had to wade through them to open the door.

"Hey, Shannon." Her oldest brother, Patrick, gave her a quick hug. "What's up with the stairs? They fall off the house?"

"The stairs are the least of it. Wait till you see the rest. C'mon in. You had dinner yet? Mom gave me one of those shepherd pie things, and there's lots for both of us."

She scowled at the dogs, who were now doing their best to gain Patrick's attention. He knew Pepsi, so he neatly side-stepped when the dog raised a leg.

"Hey, Pepsi, you old reprobate. Hello, Cleo." Patrick patted each of them in turn. "I thought you'd have the black Lab from the fire living here. I saw the television clip of the two of you."

"You and the rest of the western world," Shannon groaned. "I've been in worse fires, and not a shred of publicity. But get a big old dog in the picture, and you're poster girl for the whole darn department. We named him Salvage, by the way." She opened the fridge and pulled out a bottle of wine. "Want some?"

"Sure. Wow, I see what you mean about the wreckage. Look at those counters." He loosened his tie and took off his suit jacket. "Did you just feel the need to smash something, or is there a reason for all this?"

"I made the mistake of telling Willow she could do some carpentry. She's a dangerous woman."

"I just came from a council meeting. If you think Willow's dangerous, you oughta try some of those people."

Patrick had been mayor of Courage Bay for less than a year, but already his influence was being felt. He had a way of cutting through sludge to get to the central issues, and he had zero tolerance for anything less than the absolute truth. Sometimes she wondered why she couldn't meet guys a little like her brothers.

Although sizewise, she'd met one today. She figured John Forester could hold his own quite well in a size and strength match with the O'Shea brothers.

She poured them each a glass of wine and set the table.

"I dropped by the hospital to see how Sam was doing," Patrick said. "That was bad business, that warehouse fire."

"How is he?"

"They're letting him out in a couple days. That leg injury's pretty serious—compound fracture. He's liable to be laid up awhile. He says his arm's okay, but he's got a hell of a gash on his shoulder. He and Dan are lucky to be alive, if you ask me."

Shannon nodded. "I'll say. Did he say anything about the explosion?"

"Only that it was some sort of bomb, and he suspects it was set in a deliberate effort to do away with evidence from the first fire. Sam is convinced both of them were arson."

"He have any idea who might have been responsible?"

Patrick shook his head. "Even if he did, Sam's too professional to say anything unless he's got good hard evidence."

"Which is gone now, thanks to the second fire."

The oven timer went off, and Shannon used potholders to take the casserole out. She set it on the table along with thick slabs of good bakery bread, and served them each a generous portion. There was silence as they forked up mouthfuls.

"This is delicious," Patrick said with a sigh, blotting up gravy with a slice of bread. "Mom sent me a couple of these as well, but I haven't had time to cook them. I thought I'd save them until Dylan and Fiona come back from summer camp."

"I appreciate the food. I'd like it even better if Mom wasn't such a worrywart."

"Yeah, well, sometimes she has good reason, where you're concerned. She's not the only one worrying at the moment. The fact that both my sister and brother are firefighters doesn't make me sleep too well at night when some maniac is out there setting fires and planting bombs. Promise you'll be supercareful until this arsonist is caught, kid."

Shannon felt like screaming. Now she had Patrick on her case as well as her mother? It took effort, but she kept her voice level. "You of all people should know both Sean and I are well-trained. We don't take unnecessary chances."

"Oh, yeah?" Patrick gestured at the dogs, who were lying on the small back porch. "Nobody needs to tell me you took quite a big chance rescuing that dog the other day. Mom told me some guy had to rescue both of you. And you wouldn't have needed rescuing if you weren't in trouble, right?"

"I'd have found a way out myself. He just made it easy." But even as she said it, Shannon wondered if it was true. She'd gone over the entire scene in her head numerous times, and she had to admit that she'd been in serious trouble in that warehouse. She wasn't at all sure she'd have found a way out. "Anyhow, I learned early on not to get fixated on what could happen in any given situation. You do your best, and if something goes wrong, all a person can do is learn from it, and let it go."

"If you happen to live through it." Patrick had set his fork down. He sipped his wine and gave Shannon a long, thoughtful look. He had blue eyes, like all the O'Shea kids, but his were a lighter, less intense blue than Shannon's or Sean's. At this moment, though, they were piercing. "Who was this guy who helped you find a way out? I'd like to meet him, thank him for helping my baby sister out of a jam."

"Yeah, so would I." Shannon filled in the puzzling details of the man in the silver suit. "Trouble is, nobody but me seems to have laid eyes on him, and he was pretty obvious, a good six and a half feet tall and really—"

She stopped for a moment as something hit her. The man in the silver was about the exact same size and shape as John Forester. *He'd been the man in the silver.* Which would account for the feeling she had that she knew him from somewhere.

But if it had been John in the warehouse, he sure wasn't owning up to it. Why not? And why would he have been there in the first place? Anxiety suddenly made her put her fork down. Could the man in the silver also have been the person who set the fire in the first place? And if John Forester was that person—

"Shannon? What were you about to say? Really what?" Patrick sipped his wine and studied her.

"Really—um, really strong. Big guy, huge. Sean's size. Carried the dog and dragged me along as if I was a hundred pound weakling."

"Did he say anything?"

Shannon shook her head. "Not a word." She couldn't make accusations based on guesses. "You do know Mom's convinced an angel came from heaven to save me? If she's right, I guess angels aren't much for small talk."

Patrick smiled. "If he's your guardian angel, kid, he's got his work cut out for him. But don't forget the dog. It was probably Salvage he was sent to save in the first place. You're way too wicked to warrant an angel intervention, brat."

The conversation veered then to their family, to Sean and Linda and the baby. When they'd exhausted that subject, Shannon remarked, "I think Uncle Donald has the hots for my boarder. He's taken her out to dinner tonight, and he's been helping her all day to wreck my house."

Patrick laughed. "I think you could be right. When she was staying at Mom's, Uncle Donald was there so often I heard

Dad say he ought to just move in. Except Dad didn't sound very enthusiastic about the idea."

"I'll bet. Those two argue way too much to live in the same house. I wonder why Mom never said anything to me about Donald and Willow?" Shannon missed the long, gossipy talks she used to have with her mother. Since she'd joined the fire department, their conversations invariably ended up with Mary giving her a lecture of some sort about her job.

"You know Uncle Donald's reputation with the blue-haired ladies. He's cut a wide swath through every retirement home in Courage Bay. Mom's probably afraid he'll do his disappearing act when things get serious, and leave Willow with a broken heart."

"Mom could be right," Shannon observed. "Uncle Donald's dangerous where the ladies are concerned. He's so damn charming."

"And elusive. He's been a widower for a long time. I don't think he has any intentions of marrying again."

"Well, we shouldn't underestimate Willow, either. Turns out she's no shrinking violet. Give her a sledgehammer and look out. I think she's a couple years older than Uncle Donald, so maybe she'll have a steadying influence on the old reprobate."

"I just hope they practice safe sex," Patrick said.

They laughed and Patrick cleaned off the table and they washed the dishes together. Shannon brought out maple ripple ice cream and poured chocolate syrup on it. They had it with coffee in the living room. Cleo lay on her back in the middle of the rug, waving her paws and whimpering like a puppy, while Pepsi settled down in an armchair where he knew he wasn't allowed.

Shannon gave him a look, and he gave her one right back, so she caved and left him alone. At least he wasn't urinating on Patrick's shoes.

"I'm taking Salvage to the firehouse when Lisa releases him, I think the crew will adopt him as a mascot."

"Too bad somebody wouldn't adopt Pepsi. That animal's gonna be a big drawback if you ever find a guy you decide to keep, kid. He's a rotten little sucker."

They both studied the wiry dog. He bared his teeth and growled at them, and Patrick laughed. "Although if a guy could put up with Pepsi, he's probably got what it takes. Maybe we should invest in a single-story house big enough for the dogs, my kids and you and me. And our walkers. It doesn't look as if we're ever gonna make much headway with the mating game." He sighed.

Shannon felt her heart ache for her brother. Three years ago his wife, Jane, had died suddenly, leaving him with his two beautiful kids, Dylan, now nine, and Fiona, who was five. Since then Patrick had barely looked at another woman, though Shannon knew he must be lonely.

"Don't abandon hope quite yet, big brother. Sean found Linda, which proves it's possible for the O'Shea offspring to form lasting attachments. I'm sure that's a big relief to Mom."

"Well, I got a lecture from her last week about it being high time I remarried. She accused me of being way too fussy. She's been pushing that girl from the bank my way. Nice lady, but deadly boring."

"At least Mom doesn't set me up. I'm grateful for that. In fact, she's been all for me breaking up a couple of times. Remember when I was dating that Rudy Berzutto in high school, and Mom insisted he wasn't right for me, and she couldn't see why I was going out with him? I told her he was a whole lot of fun, and she said that fun didn't count."

"Berzutto. Didn't he end up doing time for stealing cars?"

"Yeah, but that was later on. When I knew him he was only stealing horses. We got in trouble for swiping that nag from the Killarneys' ranch, remember? All we were gonna do was take her for a midnight run. I think I'd been reading about Lady Godiva at that point. Mom came down to the cop shop to get me, and Dad was mortified."

Mary had given her a stern lecture, but Shannon had had the feeling her mother wasn't unduly upset that day. They were still good friends at that time. Shannon felt lonely, remembering. She missed that camaraderie now.

"Willow knew Mom before either of them was married. She told me that Mom wasn't that keen on getting hitched. According to Willow, she wanted a career. You'd think she'd be a little more supportive about me having one."

"She's proud of you, Shannon. She's just scared for you, that you'll get hurt. She's on Sean's case as much as yours."

"How does it feel to be the golden child, Mr. Mayor? You've got the only job our mother thoroughly approves of."

"Yeah, and after council meetings like that one tonight, I start dreaming of being a news correspondent in the Middle East. And there's another meeting tomorrow morning early, so I'd better be heading home. Good luck with your renovations."

"I'm going to need more than luck. I'm liable to need a construction crew and a plumber before this is over."

Patrick left, and Shannon took the dogs around the block. She couldn't get the thought of John Forester out of her head. By the time she went to bed, she'd figured out a sure way to tell if he and the man in the silver were one and the same.

She'd be taking Salvage to the firehouse, and dogs had a sense of smell that was totally reliable. If Salvage showed signs of knowing John, she'd have no doubt he'd been in the warehouse.

She fell asleep that night thinking of the big firefighter and fervently hoping every one of her suspicions about him was wrong.

SHE WAS STILL HOPING THAT five days later when she drove to work for the first shift in her afternoon rotation. She was about to test John Forester, because Salvage was on the seat beside her. Lisa had called and said he was ready to be released. He was already running around as if the loss of his leg was only a distant memory.

Shannon parked, snapped a leash on the dog and led him into the firehouse.

The crew was in the kitchen, being briefed by the previous shift. The first person Shannon saw was John, lounging against the counter. She felt Salvage lunge forward, so she bent and unsnapped the leash from the dog's neck. Without a moment's hesitation, ignoring all the other men, the Lab went limping over to John, his tail whipping from side to side in a frenzy of excitement. He whined and sat back, balancing precariously on his bottom and putting his paws up on the fireman's chest.

"Hey, fella. Hi, there." John crouched down and rubbed the Lab's ears and throat. "Aren't you a fine dog?" He stroked Salvage and tried to ease his paws to the floor, but the canine wouldn't stay down. He tried again to jump up, and even though the rest of the crew grouped around him, patting and talking to him, the dog made it plain that John was the one he wanted to be near.

Shannon was watching closely, and John looked over at her. He smiled and shrugged as if he had no idea why the dog was singling him out, but she knew that that, too, was a lie.

Her heart sank and a mix of responses ran through her: conviction that she'd been right about John being the man in the silver at the warehouse; a feeling of betrayal because he hadn't admitted it—wasn't admitting it even now; and a sense of confusion and apprehension as to why he was being dishonest. Most powerful of all was an overwhelming sense of disappointment—in him, but also in herself.

It came down to the simple fact that she couldn't trust her heart. She'd been powerfully drawn to John, attracted to him both sexually and intellectually, and it was obvious he was absolutely wrong for her. He had some hidden agenda going on.

Well, she was determined to find out what the hell it was.

She had no intentions of confronting him in front of the other crew members, however. When the briefing was done, one of the guys took Salvage on a walk around the firehouse, and she went into the workout room for her usual half hour of exercise.

She was sitting on the bench doing biceps curls when John came in.

"Mind if I join you?" He put weights on the bench press machine and lay down on his back, raising and lowering the heavy bar over his chest as if it weighed nothing at all. Shannon could see that he was benching three hundred sixty-five pounds. Her estimation of his strength had been right on. If only her estimation of his character had been as accurate.

She felt ready to explode, and the words poured out. "You were the one who brought Salvage and me out of the warehouse. I know, because the dog recognized you, John. You were the man in the silver. Why didn't you say something when we first met? Why did you lie to me about being there?"

He set the bar in place and sat up, facing her.

"You're mistaken, Shannon." He met her eyes directly, and she couldn't detect a single indication of guile there. She felt a twinge of doubt, but she shoved it aside.

"For some reason," he explained, "dogs take to me. Dogs, older ladies and kids. I'm like the Pied Piper. Salvage just sensed that I like animals."

"That's a load of crap," she snapped. "I know dogs, and Salvage knew you. If you were in that warehouse, why don't you want to admit it? Who are you, really, John Forester?"

Are you the arsonist? That horrible thought had been plaguing her from the instant she knew that Salvage recognized him, although she couldn't quite bring herself to ask him. There were so many puzzling things about the scenario. If he'd set the fire, why was he hanging around afterward? And would an arsonist risk his life to save a woman and a dog? It didn't make any sense.

"Shannon, I *wasn't at that warehouse fire.*" He leaned toward her, looking her straight in the eye, his gaze as sincere as could be. "I didn't even arrive in Courage Bay until after the second fire. I can prove that to you. I have my airline ticket. And if you doubt my identity, I'll show you my birth certificate, my charge cards, a picture of my father—whatever it takes to convince you."

She held his gaze, challenging him. "Okay, show me."

He blew out an exasperated sigh. "Not here. I don't have my father's picture with me, or the airline tickets. Come out to dinner with me on our break, day after tomorrow. We can get to know one another better, and I promise I'll bring everything."

She held his gaze as she thought it over. If he was lying, he was doing a pretty elaborate job of covering up, and she wanted to know why. If he was telling the truth, then she certainly should give him a chance to prove it.

"Okay. Day after tomorrow, at eight."

"Good enough. Give me your address. I'll pick you up."

"Where will we go?"

"Leave that to me. I'll find a good spot."

Like a deserted road where you can murder me and dispose of the body?

That was laughable. If he'd wanted to be rid of her, he could have left her in that burning warehouse.

"Where do you live?"

She thought of the ramp leading up to her back door. She opened her mouth to suggest that she meet him instead of having him come to the house, then decided the hell with it. *She* had nothing to hide. If he wanted a date, a date it would be.

"Just come around to the back door." She scribbled her address on a scrap of paper and handed it to him, wondering if she was making the biggest mistake of her life.

CHAPTER EIGHT

SHANNON WAS STILL WONDERING that as she slid pearl studs into her ears, pulled a few more strands of hair out of the high chignon at the back of her head, and smoothed the bronze silk sheath over her hips. She hadn't worn it since last Christmas. Was she too dressed up? Was this dress too short? When you were a scant inch off six feet, there was an awful lot of bare leg exposed in a mini.

She'd decided against stockings, and she slid her bare feet into high-heeled sandals. She'd painted her toenails bronze to match her dress. It was unusual and fun to be able to wear three-inch heels without towering over her date, she reminded herself.

So, O'Shea, you gonna seduce him into telling you who he is and what he's doing here? Because you're going to a whole lot of effort for a guy you're pretty sure is a liar.

Whatever works, she told herself, and then giggled at her own absurdity.

Willow had taken off again to spend the evening with Uncle Donald, even though there was still no sign of any repairs on the house. Willow had started working at the clinic, so that was bound to slow things down, Shannon consoled herself.

She was smoothing on lip gloss in the bathroom when the dogs announced John's arrival, and her heart gave a thump, which she put down to nervousness.

Taking a deep breath, she ordered Cleo and Pepsi to lie

down and be quiet, which had no effect whatsoever, and opened the kitchen door.

"I see why you suggested the back," he said with a grin.

"I should have said it was the only option."

The dogs bounded over, sniffing at his pant legs. She tried to keep half an eye on Pepsi. His spraying tactics were so well practiced they didn't provide much warning.

"Come in, please," she invited. Wow. He cleaned up really *good*. The way it fit, his light gray suit had to be made to order, and the plain black T-shirt underneath was exactly the right dressy-casual-hip thing to wear. Very big city.

"Hey, Shannon." He gave her a thorough once-over and then whistled, soft and appreciative. "You look gorgeous." He glanced down at the dogs. "You gonna introduce me to your friends here?"

She did, and Cleo launched to her usual belly-up, aren't-I-adorable performance. John laughed and bent over to scratch her. Shannon noticed just in time that Pepsi was getting into position. He'd already sprayed a few drops when she caught him.

"Pepsi! Don't even think of it." She grabbed the scoundrel by the scruff and hauled him away. "Sorry, John, it's not just you. Pepsi's maladjusted. He pees on everybody."

John was laughing as she opened the door and herded the dogs down the ramp, intent on putting them in their run.

She'd forgotten that her heels would sink into the grass and slow her down. By the time she came back, he was in the living room, holding a framed photo she kept propped on the mantelpiece.

"Your family?"

"Yeah. My brother Sean's wedding."

John pointed at someone and raised his eyebrows, and she had to stand close to identify who was who. He had some glorious kind of aftershave that smelled like fresh grass in a meadow, and even with her heels, she barely reached past his shoulder. Bless the man. So what if he was an arsonist. He made up for it by making her feel *tiny*.

"That's my mom, Mary. My dad, Caleb. Uncle Donald, Grandpa Brian, best man is my brother Patrick, and those are his two kids, Dylan and Fiona. That's Sean, and his bride is Linda."

"And this beautiful creature is my date." His forefinger rested on Shannon's image, and he stroked it gently. Heat went shimmering down her spine, for all the world as if he'd touched her bare skin.

Get a grip, O'Shea. Who's seducing who here?

When they made their way down the ramp and out to his car, she explained about her boarder and her uncle and what had become of the steps, and he laughed.

It was so gratifying to be with a guy who thought she was amusing. And who drove a vintage Corvette.

It was black, low slung, sinfully expensive. The leather seat felt butter-soft under her bare thighs and the dash had more instruments than most small planes. How did a fireman afford a car like this? New doubts piled on top of old ones.

"Hot car, John."

As if he'd read her mind, he slid behind the wheel, smiled at her and said, "I went a little nuts and leased this baby when I landed in L.A. Always wanted to know what it felt like to drive around in luxury. Normally I get around on a vintage Harley."

She thought of Diego Larue. "I have a friend who rides a Harley. I love motorbikes."

"I'd take you for a spin on mine, but it's in storage in New York."

"You going to ship it through? Or you could ride it cross-country. That would be something."

"It would indeed. I'll give it some thought. You want to find us some music?"

A vinyl case held CDs, and Shannon flipped through them.

She had to smile, because if these were any indication, she and John had the same eclectic taste in music.

She pulled out the Kinks and slid it in the player.

"Come dancin', it's only natural.'"

She sang with the chorus, and John joined in, his soft, slightly off-key baritone blending with her contralto. It was a fine California evening. The sun was about to set over the ocean, and the sky was coral and scarlet and gold. Shannon was having trouble remembering how much she distrusted the handsome man beside her.

"Where're we going?"

"It's a surprise. I did some research, and I hope it'll be good."

It was. The Tangerine Bistro was new, situated right on the water. Shannon had heard of it, but she'd never been. It had earned an early reputation for exquisite French food and horrendous prices. They were led to a table outside on the covered balcony. John ordered wine, and soft piano music drifted out from the lounge.

When the wine came, he held up his glass in a toast.

"To you, Ms. O'Shea. Thank you for not making me arm wrestle you in front of the crew. I would have done it if necessary, but it's so much more civilized not to have to."

Shannon laughed. "Think you'd win, huh?"

"Absolutely." His smile brought out the dimples she'd noticed before. "I have my master's degree in arm wrestling."

She sipped her wine and challenged him with her eyes. "I suspect you've also got your master's in duplicity, John Forester."

The waiter came to take their order, and when he left, John reached into the pocket of his jacket and drew out a manila envelope. He placed it in front of her.

"My credentials, ma'am."

Shannon opened the envelope. First, there was a driver's license with his name, his photo and a New York address. Next was his fireman ID, social security, several credit cards. His birth certificate, giving date and place. He was thirty-two, four years older than she was. Last of all was a photograph, a faded black-and-white print. A man in a dark suit and a fedora stood in front of a roadster. His face was the same shape as John's, strong-jawed and sharp-planed.

In spite of the fact that she felt self-conscious and a little ridiculous, Shannon took her time studying the assortment. Now that she was with him, she couldn't quite convince herself that John was a fraud. And the assortment of ID certainly backed him up; true to his word, he'd even included the airline's boarding pass. She took note of the date.

It was the day of the second warehouse fire. So he'd been telling the truth. He hadn't been in Courage Bay when she'd been trapped in that warehouse. *But how come Salvage knew him?*

Stuffing everything back in the envelope, she handed it to him. He took it, brushing her fingers with his, prolonging the contact.

"So, Detective, am I still under suspicion?"

The waiter brought their food just then, so she didn't have to answer right away, and when he finally left, John changed the subject. "Courage Bay is a beautiful place. How long have your family lived here, Shannon?"

"Generations. An ancestor of my dad's—Michael O'Shea—was shipwrecked off the coast in the mid-1800s. The story goes that a beautiful native girl rode out in a canoe and saved his life. They fell in love, so our family has both Irish and Chumash Indian heritage."

"I remember the story from that documentary I watched about smoke jumping. What was the guy's name again, the one who kept the other crew members from drowning when the ship went down?"

"Michael. Michael O'Shea. And the woman's name was Kishlo'w." Shannon watched him, liking the way his brown hair waved over his forehead. He had remarkable eyes that curved down at the outer corners. His nose was a little crooked, as if he'd broken it once or twice. She knew all about broken noses. Sean had had his broken more than once. It gave a man's face character.

Character. Truth. Did she believe him? *Almost. Nearly.* She ate her lobster and sipped her wine, finished off her bread roll and reached for a second.

"I think our heritage and our environment have a big effect on what we choose as a career and the way we live our lives," John said. "Your family's lucky. You all have this symbol of great courage to inspire you."

"So what inspires you, John?" She buttered the roll.

"The job. I love my work."

"Me, too. Did you join up because of your dad?"

He was chewing a bite of steak, so he didn't answer right away, but he nodded in a thoughtful way. "Yeah, you could say my dad had a big influence on my life and my choice of career."

"How about your mom?"

"My mother?" A muscle tightened in his jaw. "Mom. Yeah. Well, that's another story. She's not well, my mother."

"I'm sorry, John. What's wrong with her?" In case he figured she was just being curious, Shannon quickly added, "I know how it feels, having your mom sick. My mother had cancer six years back. She went through chemo and surgery. We were all scared out of our minds at the time. But she's been okay, and now that five years have gone by, they figure she's in the clear. Thank God. I know how crazy it can make you when someone you love is sick."

And how you can worry about your actions causing a relapse. She still worried that going against Mary's wishes would make her sick all over again. Not that her mother had ever insinuated that. Give credit where credit's due.

He didn't really answer. Instead, he said, "I guessed from that photo that your family's close-knit. Sometimes I almost wish my mother's illness was one that surgery could cure, but it isn't. She's an alcoholic."

His tone was matter-of-fact, and Shannon could only guess at the pain behind the straightforward words. He hid it well. In the course of their job, firefighters saw the effects of alcoholism almost on a daily basis. It took an enormous toll on the lives of the people affected and on their relatives, and it often tested the firemen's patience to the limit.

"Gosh, I'm sorry. That would be tough to deal with. No one in my immediate family suffers from alcoholism, but I have cousins who've lost jobs and ended up in court because of drinking." She didn't add that as a firefighter, she'd seen enough horrible deaths that were alcohol related to last her a lifetime. John would also have seen them. "Is she in a treatment center?"

He shook his head. "Not at the moment, although she's been in and out of the best over the years. She's not able to live on her own. She has a companion, a nurse who watches out for her. She'll go months at a time without drinking, but when she does, somebody has to keep an eye on her. I did it for as long as I could, but I finally realized a stranger would do a better job."

Shannon nodded. "I can see that. Do you have brothers and sisters?"

"Nope, only child. I always wanted siblings, but it never happened. My mother never remarried after my father died." His voice was calm and very controlled. In spite of his seeming openness, Shannon felt there was a lot he wasn't revealing. There was something mysterious about this man, something she couldn't quite put her finger on.

"Do you think your dad's job had something to do with her drinking? I mean, being married to a fireman can be pretty stressful. My mother didn't want Patrick or Sean applying, and then when I did—well, she's never really accepted it." *To put it mildly.*

He shrugged. "I think you can use almost anything as an excuse to drink, if you have the disease. I've always been grateful that I didn't inherit that particular gene." He reached across and touched her arm. "Enough of that. Let's get to the important stuff. Tell me what you want for dessert."

Shannon scanned the menu the waiter produced. "Crepes with chocolate and bananas. And whipped cream."

"For two." John handed the menus back and grinned at her. "It's so refreshing to be with a woman who isn't on some strict diet."

"Are you insinuating that I ought to be?" She was teasing. She had no hang-ups about her weight or her appetite. But she was curious about the women he'd dated who were on diets. Actually, she was just as curious about the ones who weren't. Had any of them managed to ruffle that air of total control?

He shook his head and laughed aloud. "I walked straight into that one. And the answer is absolutely not, you're perfect just as you are."

"You, too. I mean, who am I to argue with dogs and elderly ladies and babies?"

They laughed, and went on to talk about books. He enjoyed the same complex English mysteries she did, although he read more nonfiction.

When the dessert arrived, Shannon took a bite and savored it. Then she said, "Who would you be if you were a historical hero, John?" It was a game she and her brothers had often played.

"Fictional or real?"

"Either."

"Robin Hood." He didn't seem to have to think about it. "I practically wore out a copy of that book when I was a kid. And you?"

What would he do if she said Maid Marion? Shannon was tempted but she didn't quite dare. "Joan of Arc. She got to play with the boys, which is what I spent my childhood trying to do. My brothers attempted to either ditch me or drown me, and I used to think a lance would be the greatest thing."

He forked up crepes and chocolate and nodded. "And there was the horse, right? Not to mention all those faithful men following wherever you led."

She nodded. "Power. Heady stuff. It would have been pretty exciting. Although I don't fancy the ending. Not with my job." She shuddered, remembering just for a moment the warehouse and the flames all around her. She shoved the memory out of her mind. "What ever became of Robin Hood, anyway?"

"Didn't he and Marion live happily ever after in Sherwood Forest? In a tree?"

Shannon hooted. "That story had to be written by a man. A woman would have explained how he built her a two-story cottage and rerouted a stream so she could have indoor plumbing."

They laughed as they finished dessert and lingered over coffee, talking about other books they'd enjoyed as children.

When it was time to leave, John gestured at the sandy beach and the moonlight streaming across the water. "Want to go for a walk?"

"Sure. I'll ditch these shoes first."

"Good thinking. I'll take mine off, too."

Outside, she slipped off her heels and he put them in the car along with his loafers. He had long, strong, elegant feet.

"Anybody ever tell you your legs are spectacular, O'Shea?"

"Maybe once or twice. But I don't mind hearing it again."

"And the rest of you matches, so that's a real bonus." He took her hand and led the way down to the water's edge. The tide was out, and the sand was wet and soft under her feet. She was very aware of his palm, and the way he'd threaded his fingers between hers. It was intimate. It was sexy and arousing. She was powerfully aware of him, of the skin on his hands, his large shape beside her, the way the length of their strides matched as their naked feet plowed through the sand.

His voice was soft and deep, blending with the sound of the surf. "So, Shannon O'Shea, what do you see for yourself in the years ahead? Do you want to be chief?"

It was a question she'd asked herself more than once. She knew the answer, but just how honest could she be with him? Men freaked when a woman started talking about love and commitment, even when it was only in general terms.

You want honesty from him, O'Shea. So give out what you expect back.

"I love what I do, but I want more than just a career. I want what my mom and dad have, what Sean and Linda found together. I want to get married, have a mess of kids and a house filled with dogs and toys and noise and pesky relatives, the way our house was when I was growing up. I want happily ever after." Funny, she'd never managed to say that to her mother. Mary's fears got to her, and then Shannon ended up spouting stuff about a firefighting career.

"You really think that's possible? Happily ever after?"

"Sure I think so. I don't think it's easy, though. I think it calls for more hard work and openness and honesty than most people are willing to give, which partially accounts for the high divorce rate. There's also the fact that sometimes divorce really is the best alternative." As it was with Willow and Steve. "I guess it's hard to know when to go on and when to end things." Shannon had waded in this far, so might as well go deeper into murky waters. "You ever seriously consider marriage, John?"

"Nope. My track record has always been shallow and short, and I don't see it changing anytime soon."

Well, that was honest enough. So she knew what to expect. She glanced up at him. He was staring out at the water. The moon outlined his profile. His jaw was set, and she thought there was something terribly lonely about him.

"I guess you could say my work is my mistress, Shannon."

She frowned. "I've heard of dedicated firefighters, but that's a little extreme, don't you think? I mean, I understand it's possible to have a life besides work."

He grinned down at her and nodded. "Yeah, but when you

say that about your work, it really impresses the hell out of the bosses."

She laughed with him, and she was still laughing when she stepped hard on something sharp that pierced deep into the sole of her foot and sent pain shooting up her leg.

"Oww." She sank down to the sand and drew her foot up, trying to see what was hurting. "Oww, I stepped on something sharp. It's in my foot."

"Let me see." He knelt beside her and pulled out a key chain with a small flashlight attached. "Here, let's have a look." He took her foot in his hand and shone the light on it. "It's a piece of glass—somebody left a broken bottle in the sand. Hold still." He held the flashlight with one hand, and with the other pulled the fragment out.

The pain was so intense it made her dizzy. "Ouch, ouch, ouch."

"All done." He held up the long, sharp shard of glass. "We need to clean the wound and put some antibiotic on it. I've got my first aid kit in the car." He pulled her up so she was balanced on one foot. "We don't want any more sand in that. It's bleeding a lot. Hold on to my neck."

He curled one arm under her thighs and swept her into his arms.

"Put me down." Shannon felt totally panicked and out of control. "I'm way too heavy for this—put me down." No one had carried her since she was a small child. She felt ridiculous and helpless and annoyed and aroused, and she fought him for a moment.

"Relax." He laughed and walked across the sand as easily as he had before he picked her up. "Unless you'd rather I used the traditional fireman's carry?"

"*No.* No, this is fine." The thought of exposing her panties while her head dangled halfway down his back made her stop struggling. She had no choice except to loop an arm around his neck. She was intensely aware of him, of the smell of his aftershave, the warmth and intimacy of his forearm on her bare thighs—why had she worn such a short skirt? Oh, hell, the damn man was a giant. He made her feel almost fragile.

He made her feel safe, the way she'd felt… The memory of the warehouse rushed into her brain. The huge man in the silver—he and John were the same size. She could swear these arms were the ones that had circled her waist that day. She shoved the thought away.

Her cheek was against his chest, and she could feel the rumble of his voice and the thumping of his heart. "Forester, you're gonna have a heart attack from packing me. Your heart's thundering like a freight train."

He didn't answer until they reached the car. He set her down, but he still held on, even after she was balanced on one leg. He drew her close, supporting her weight with an arm around her waist so that even her good foot was almost off the ground. He pressed her close against him, and she could feel that she wasn't the only one aroused.

"It's not exertion." His voice was low and rough and tender. "You're a sexy lady, and I'm just reacting to having you in my arms." He waited until she looked up at him, and his dark gaze made the blood pulse through her veins. The moment stretched and stretched, and then very slowly he lowered his head and took her mouth.

CHAPTER NINE

LORD, HE TASTED GOOD. Her pulse shot up a notch, and her resistance faded. She slid her hands up and gripped his shoulders. Her skin felt hot, his mouth was wonderful, and she eased her hands under his suit jacket, running her palms over the thin cotton of his shirt, feeling the definition of muscle and the warmth of skin. And then she was kissing him as if her life depended on it.

He held her tighter, anchoring her with one arm and using the other hand to stroke her, up and down her spine, the curve of her hips, at last using his palm to cup her breast.

"Mmm." She melted against him, into him—and yet some tiny part of her brain wouldn't let go of the fire, the man in the silver. John felt familiar, as if she'd been close to him before. She drew away from him, and pulled in a shaky breath.

"Maybe—maybe we should get in the car?"

"Yeah." He sucked in a deep, shuddering breath. "For sure we should. We're gonna get arrested out here. It's an upscale restaurant—there's probably rules about making out in the parking lot." His voice was unsteady. "Your foot sore? I'm sorry, I should have treated that for you before…"

He released her, letting the rest of the sentence fade. He made sure she was balanced on her good foot before he fumbled for his keys, unlocked the door and helped her in. "Loop your legs over the gearshift, up on the driver's seat. I'll get the kit from the trunk and dress that cut for you."

"But I'm gonna bleed all over your fancy car."

"So? I'll get it cleaned."

Her heart was still hammering, her blood pulsing through her veins, and she watched through the window as he unlocked the trunk. She was powerfully attracted to him. If only there was some way to be sure, to absolutely know without a single doubt that he was telling her the truth. Who was he, really? Why did her every instinct signal recognition, even in the face of the evidence he'd presented to the contrary?

He closed the trunk, opened the driver's side door, set the red vinyl kit on the ground at his feet. He crouched down, her foot at eye level—along with most of the rest of her. The slippery dress was barely covering her panties. First he applied antiseptic, then antibacterial cream.

"Your tetanus shots up to date?" He ripped opened a bandage and smoothed it on the wound.

"Yup." As soon as she could, she brought her legs back over to her own side, wriggling to pull her skirt down.

"Is it hurting?"

"Not bad now," she lied. "Thanks, John."

"My pleasure. Very much my pleasure." He put the kit back together, tossed it in the back seat and slid into the car. He put his shoes on and then turned and gave her a smile, reaching across, running one finger slowly down the line of her cheek before he inserted the key in the ignition and started the car.

He put a CD into the player, Rod Stewart, and the hard beat of the guitar and the raspy voice filled the space between them, singing, "Tonight's the night, it's gonna be all right—"

If only. To distract herself, she said, "Where are you staying, John?"

"At the Bayshore."

"Nice enough, but noisy, I've heard. You must be looking for somewhere to settle."

"Yeah, I am. I'm on the lookout for an apartment or a condo to rent."

"My cousin Matthew's in real estate. I'll have him give you a call if you like."

"Yeah, do that. I'd appreciate it."

John hardly sounded like someone who was leading a double life. The more she knew of him, the more confused she became.

When he pulled the car up in front of her house, he said, "Stay where you are."

He got out and came around, opening the door and helping her out of the car.

When he made a move to pick her up again, she shook her head.

"My neighbors are nosy, and they have vivid imaginations. Just help hold me up, okay?" She'd put one high-heeled sandal back on, and with John's arm around her waist, she hopped awkwardly around the side of the house to the back door.

"Oh, Lordy. That stupid ramp."

"Nobody can see you here." He lifted her again and carried her up to the door. "Got your key?"

"In my handbag. Put me down and I'll find it. Somewhere." She fumbled for it, and when she finally located it, he took it from her and opened the door, helping her through the kitchen and into the living room, where he deposited her on the sofa. He propped her foot up on a cushion. "You need a sock or a slipper on that foot to protect the bandage."

"There's socks in my sports bag, just inside the closet."

He rummaged through the bag and found one.

"Thanks." She pulled it on and stuck her feet out, one in a high-heeled shoe and the other in a gray sports sock. "Classy, huh?"

"Sexy. Put your feet back up on the pillows." He arranged them for her, and then said, "Okay, what else do you need? Want me to take the dogs for a quick trip around the block?"

"Yes, please. They've been in their pen all evening. Their leashes are hanging on the rack in the hall."

"Can I get you anything first? Something to drink?"

She considered telling him she was desperate for the bathroom, just to see what he'd do, but she decided against it. He was far too unpredictable. "With this sock on, I think I can manage to limp around okay."

"Stay off it as much as you can. It'll heal quicker."

Shannon snapped off a salute. "Yes, sir, doctor, sir. Whatever you say." She turned her tone into a growl. "Ooh, you medical guys are just so domineering. It's such a turn-on."

He gave her a warning look and his eyes darkened. "So you wanna play doctor, huh?"

There was a dangerous edge to his voice and her heartbeat sped up. Damn right she wanted to play doctor.

John leaned down and tipped her chin up. His mouth was closing in on hers when someone banged hard on the kitchen door.

Cursing softly, John straightened. "Stay where you are. I'll get it."

She heard him open the door, and a man's voice she recognized said, "Hi, I'm looking for Shannon. Is she around?"

Shannon blew out a frustrated breath and considered just letting John deal with this, but that wasn't really fair to either man.

"Hello, Diego," she called. "Come on in. I'm in here."

When the two men entered the room, she made the introductions, a little amused by the sudden tension in the air.

"Diego Larue, John Forester."

They nodded at one another, no handshake, no spoken greeting.

Ahh, so there was a testosterone thing going on here.

"Sorry to barge in on you at this hour, Shannon," Diego said, clutching his bike helmet under one arm and running a hand through his mop of blond curls. "I saw your lights and figured you were still up." He was dressed head to toe in tight black leather, and no doubt about it, he was a fetching hunk of ripe manhood.

Too bad he didn't push any of her buttons. Not the way Forester did. John had moved over to the foot of the sofa and was perched on the arm nearest her feet, making it subtly clear that he'd been there first.

Totally ignoring him, Diego said, "I just finished a long shift and wondered if you'd like to go for a ride. It's a great night out there." He noticed her foot. "Hey, what did you do to yourself?"

She raised her foot and pointed at the sock. "Stepped on a broken bottle at the beach. John got the glass out and patched it up for me."

"Want me to take a look?"

"No, I'm sure it's fine. John's a fireman—we do excellent first aid."

"Well, if it gives you any trouble, just call. You've got my cell number, right?"

"I do. Thanks, Diego."

"Okay, then." He hesitated and then finally said, "Well, if things are under control, I'll head out. Night, Shannon." He turned and gave John a curt nod. "Good to meet you."

He sounded as if it was anything but.

"And you." John's voice was cool. He got up and walked behind Diego to the door. Shannon heard it close with a little more force than necessary.

There was a pregnant silence when he came back.

"What?" Shannon frowned up at him.

"Nothing. I didn't know you liked motorbikes all that much."

"I told you, I love them. Diego's got a Harley, like you. I'm surprised you didn't mention yours." She was enjoying this little show of male antler butting.

"So what does Diego do, besides ride around at midnight on his Harley?"

"He's doing a residency in surgery at the hospital."

"Ahh. So that's why…" He gestured at her foot.

"Yeah." She was a little annoyed with him, and a little amused. She wasn't going to volunteer anything more about

Diego, but then she changed her mind. "I told you I wasn't in a steady relationship, John, but that doesn't mean I don't date now and then."

It wouldn't hurt him to think she was a man magnet. He didn't have to know she'd been trying to get rid of Diego for over a month now. The man was nothing if not persistent.

"Shannon, hey, I'm sorry." John made full use of that beguiling grin, and his dimples flashed. "I'm being a jerk here. You don't owe me any explanations at all." He sat down on the sofa and took her feet on his lap, caressing the bare toes of her good foot and sending ripples up her leg. "I couldn't figure out why some guy would be banging at your door at this time of the night. And I was pissed because he managed to do it just as I was about to kiss you."

"Coitus interruptus."

He laughed. "Not nearly close enough. Although…?" He bent his head and gently bit her toe.

Shocked, she jerked her foot back. "God, John, my feet aren't all that clean."

He lifted her foot and pretended to study the sole. "It's not that bad. There's just this little blob of something right here…" He tickled her.

"Stop that—I can't stand it." She tried to pull her foot away but he held on.

"John Forester, are you some sort of sexual deviant with a foot fetish? You can be honest here. I'm not easily shocked."

He pretended to consider her question and then shook his head. "Not by nature, unfortunately, but if that's what does the job for you—"

Shannon squealed as he sucked one of her toes into his mouth, but she had an immediate and shocking sexual reaction, as well. Heat shot up her leg and into her abdomen. She was still laughing, and he was, too, when they heard the sound of a key fumbling in the lock of the kitchen door.

John whispered, "Another one? And this guy's got a key?" He managed to look comically horrified.

"No, you idiot. That has to be Willow, my upstairs boarder. Let go of my foot. She thinks this is a respectable establishment." Shannon struggled, but was no match for him.

"An upstairs boarder, huh? You are just full of surprises, Ms. O'Shea." Instead of releasing it, he pulled her foot up and rested it on his chest, just over his heart, as Willow walked into the room.

"Hi, guys." She studied them for a long moment and then sat down in an armchair. "You having a reflexology treatment, Shannon? It's very relaxing, don't you think? Please, don't let me interrupt. I'd really like to watch your technique."

Shannon knew by the twinkle in Willow's eye that the other woman had a fair idea of what had really been going on. By the rumpled looks of her, Willow had been engaging in a touch of reflexology herself with that scoundrel of an uncle Donald.

"Yeah," Shannon said as evenly as she could manage. John was using his thumb to stroke the sole of her foot, and she could feel the reverberations in her armpits. "This nice man makes house calls. You want him to do you next?"

Willow tipped her head to the side, considering. "I'm tempted, but I've had a busy evening myself. So maybe I can take a rain check? Leave me a business card, won't you?" She wiggled her fingers at them. "Night, now. Enjoy the treatment." She headed upstairs before Shannon could introduce John properly.

"Opportunist," she hissed at him.

"Coward," he retorted.

They could hear Willow chuckling as she closed the door to her room.

"Maybe we should take a rain check on this whole production," Shannon suggested. "Damn house is Grand Central Station." She glanced around at the patched walls. "After a bomb exploded."

He considered a moment, then nodded with obvious reluctance. "I was going to take the dogs for a walk. It's probably best if I just go and do that."

"Good thinking." But she felt powerfully disappointed. What would it have been like, without all the interruptions?

THE DOGS TOOK THEIR TIME, so John was forced to as well. The ocean breeze meant that the air was cool and damp, which was a blessing, because being around Shannon had made him hot. Damn, the woman made control next to impossible.

He strolled from one streetlight to the next, studying the houses to stop himself from thinking about her. Residential, low income, in transition to being yuppified. He'd seen it happen in a neighborhood where he and his mother had lived for a while—until the time came when they couldn't afford the rent. That little problem had been a recurring event when he was a kid, after his father died.

God, even inside his head, he was starting to change fact to fiction.

His father hadn't just died, John reminded himself. He was gunned down. Johnnie Pascal was a small-time gangster who'd become transformed, for John's purposes here in Courage Bay, into a fireman, a hero, an upstanding citizen. He'd never actually married the showgirl he'd knocked up, the sad, beautiful, impossibly neurotic woman who was John's mother. Most of the time, John was careful not to confuse fact and fiction in his mind. He was an old hand at taking on a persona and making it sound authentic—one of the primary rules was to keep the cover as true-to-life as possible. The more lies you told, the easier it was to trip yourself up.

But he prided himself on staying clear as to what the facts really were. So why was it so tough, so soul destroying, to pitch the cover to Shannon?

Sure, the gap between his fictional background and the harsh reality of what his life had actually been was as wide as the East River, but so what? He'd had to be less than honest most of his life. This gig was no exception.

Except that she was exceptional. That was where the problem lay.

John had told himself he was taking her out tonight because it was obvious she didn't believe his cover, and he absolutely couldn't let her stir up doubts about him and his presence here in Courage Bay.

She was connected, he reminded himself. Her family was well-known in this little city. Her brother was the mayor, her other brother a smoke jumper, a local hero, for crying out loud. She could stir up a lot of shit for John if she chose, even sabotage the whole operation. So getting her on side and smoothing her ruffled feathers was very much a priority. And what rule said he couldn't enjoy himself while he was doing his job?

Jesus, Johnny boy, stop it. You're bullshittin' yourself again, and that's a serious thing. Con the rest of civilization, but stay honest in your head and your heart, man.

He'd planned on a great dinner, a chance to convince her once and for all that he was who he said he was—simple, straightforward John Forester, firefighter. The choice of restaurant and that walk on the beach were mistakes. He should have taken her somewhere loud, to some club where there wouldn't be the chance to talk intimately.

And of course he couldn't have guessed that she'd step on that damn bottle, or that he'd end up with her in his arms. It was only too true that the blood drained from the rational brain when other parts of the anatomy were aroused. And being around Shannon O'Shea had drained every ounce.

He tightened his hold on Pepsi's leash and tried to encourage Cleo to walk in something resembling a straight line while he told himself sternly that Shannon had to be off-limits from here on in.

You knew she was trouble the minute you laid eyes on her,

he reminded himself. He couldn't remember ever having such an intense and immediate reaction to a woman, and God only knew, there'd been plenty of women in his life, so it wasn't deprivation that was causing testosterone to go into overdrive.

So what made her different? He waited impatiently while Pepsi sized up a fence post from all angles.

"Just do it," he muttered to the ornery pooch. "It's a renewable resource. There'll be plenty left to spray my shoes when we get back."

His thoughts returned to Shannon. She was razor sharp, and that could cause him lots of trouble, because in spite of his meticulous cover documents, he was afraid he still hadn't managed to convince her that he hadn't been at that damn warehouse.

He could read the doubt in her eyes. She had the damnedest eyes, the bluest, the most arresting that he'd ever seen. Looking into them made it hard to lie. And it wasn't just her eyes. It was something about the way her entire face lit up with her smile. It had to do with her upbeat, off-the-wall attitude, her sexy, husky voice, an ingenuous lack of that big-city sophistication that could be such a pain in the ass.

And those legs, those gorgeous, mile-long, powerful legs... She'd been wearing black panties under that dress.

So she was a knockout, tall and slender and strong as an Amazon while still managing to be womanly and totally feminine— so what? He'd been with beautiful women; before, beauty per se wasn't exactly a novelty. Neither was the female species much of a mystery. A lifetime spent trying to keep his mother sober and safe had left him with few illusions about women.

So just do your job and run, Johnny boy. If things go as planned, you won't be in Courage Bay all that long, anyhow. And you'll forget her as soon as you leave town.

He wished he had a certificate attesting to that fact.

"C'mon, you two. Let's get this show on the road." Damn dogs were taking all night, and he needed to climb in the 'Vette and drive away, fast and far.

One thing was for certain: he wasn't going to kiss her again, because the job was too important to risk losing control that way. It was a good thing her boarder had barged in when she did.

"You two are not trained to heel," he told the dogs. In fact, they weren't trained at all. Cleo was glued to his pant leg, doing her best to trip him, and Pepsi nipped at his heels if he looked away even for a minute. John finally bent over and scooped Pepsi up under his arm, but the moment he did that, Cleo got jealous and rolled over on her back, waving her paws in the air and begging to be picked up, too.

"You've gotta be kidding—you're getting home on your own little tootsies," John told her. "I draw the line at packing a Saint Bernard anywhere." He finally got her moving again, but the crestfallen look on her huge face had him laughing until he got back to the house. He herded them up the ramp and opened the door.

Shannon was in the kitchen, balanced against the counter, pouring hot water from the kettle into two mugs. She'd taken off the dress and pulled on red shorts and a white T-shirt. Unfortunately for his good intentions, that outfit was every bit as sexy as the dress had been. Cleo pranced over and licked Shannon's legs.

Sometimes dogs had all the luck.

"You were gone awhile," she said, smiling at him.

"Yeah, well, these two animals could really use some obedience training." He was trying to look only at her face.

"You're right, they do need it, but I'm not much good at it," she said. "Want the job? You could have a coffee before you started."

He didn't want the coffee. He did want her, very badly.

He also wanted to accomplish what he'd come to Courage Bay to do, and he was pretty certain that Shannon O'Shea would make that more complicated than he wanted it to be. Than he *needed* it to be.

"No, thanks, I really should get going." He felt as if he were leaving paradise for a motel room with all the appeal of a second rate monastery.

"Sure, no problem. Thanks for a great evening." She was giving him a quizzical look.

"My pleasure. Hope your foot heals fast. Do you want me to put these two out in their pen?" He didn't trust himself to get close to her, or touch her, or God help him, kiss her again.

"They're fine in here."

"Okay. Good night." He turned and bolted out the door, and it was one of the more difficult things he'd ever forced himself to do.

CHAPTER TEN

THE DOOR CLOSED BEHIND him, and Shannon shook her head in bewilderment.

"What the heck did you two do to him, anyway?" She scowled at the dogs and poured both cups of coffee down the sink. "Before you got hold of him, he was coming on strong. Leave you guys alone with him for half an hour and he runs for cover."

She was trying not to let it get to her, but the way he'd bolted was puzzling. She glanced at the clock. Okay, long after midnight, certainly time to be on his way—if he wasn't going to stay.

And it wasn't the fact that he'd left, she lied to herself. It was the way he did it, as if he couldn't wait to get out of her house. If his actions were any indication, he wouldn't be asking her out again anytime soon. So there went her chances of finding out more about him.

Finding out about him, hell. The truth was, she'd wanted him to kiss her again. She'd wanted to let him help her down the hall to her bedroom, maybe even carry her. How many times would she meet a guy who could actually lift her?

She didn't do one-night stands, but she'd wanted him to at least want one with her. Oh, screw it. She wasn't making sense even to herself. And she felt far too restless to go to bed, because she'd never sleep anyhow.

Too late to call Lisa. And Shannon's foot was way too sore to go out jogging, which wasn't the best idea anyhow, considering it was the middle of the night.

"C'mon, you guys. Let's see what's on TV."

Backdraft was on the movie channel. She'd seen it four times before—the guys at the fire station rented it regularly so they could rewrite the script the way they figured it ought to have been written the first time. She watched it, paying scant attention, letting her mind drift.

She definitely had a jones for Forester. But physical attraction aside, she just couldn't let go of this thing with the warehouse and the man in the silver. Intuition told her that it had been John inside that place. And she couldn't for the life of her figure out why he'd go to such lengths to deny it.

There had to be a way to find out more about him. It was the age of computers, where no one's secrets were safe. Maybe there was a way to search him out on the Net. That would be a great idea, except she'd never been interested in learning much more about computers than how to enter shift data on the one at the fire station.

She didn't own a computer, nor did she have a clue how to go about searching the Net for personal information about someone. And she wasn't about to ask the computer nerds at work for help, not with this. Word would go out in a millisecond that she was in love with a member and doing a background screen on him, and the next thing she knew, John would find out all about it.

Her brother Sean might know how to get such info. He and Patrick were way more computer literate than she was. In fact, maybe Patrick was a better bet than Sean. He had contacts all over the country because of his position as mayor. He could use some political clout and do a background check for her. She'd pay him a visit first thing in the morning.

Well, maybe not first thing. It was almost three, and she was as wide-awake as she'd ever been. She'd go see Patrick whenever she managed to drag herself out of bed. There was a coffee shop near his office—he could buy her breakfast. And maybe he'd do the search for her right away, which would settle things one way or the other.

For all the grief they'd put her through when she was growing up, there were times like this when having brothers was a blessing.

"NOPE, SORRY, there's no way I'll do that for you, Shannon." Patrick shook his head and smeared butter on a pecan muffin. "Absolutely not. You're asking me to do a search on someone based entirely on feminine intuition. You say you've seen the guy's ID, his birth certificate, everything except his dental records, for cripes' sake, and everything checks out, right?"

"Yes, but—"

"No buts about it. There's absolutely nothing to link Forester to the warehouse fire except your gut, and we both know your hunches have been wrong before."

"They've also been right. Remember that Marylou Grainger you were dating? I told you she was just trying to get you in the sack so she could find out if that rumor about you was true."

Patrick scowled at her and finished off his muffin in one huge bite. "Forget Marylou, that was years ago. I was just a kid."

"You weren't a bad kid. But now you're the mayor, and you won't do a single simple thing for someone who actually voted for you."

"Keep your voice down. Other people in here might have voted for me as well, you know." But he was grinning. Patrick didn't give a tinker's damn for politicking in the usual way. He relied on brutal honesty and sensible action, which Shannon had to admit were fine characteristics—except they weren't working in her favor just at the moment. She tried another tack.

"So what happens if somebody gets hurt—maybe even murdered by this arsonist—and it turns out to have been Forester? You'll feel awful if that happens, Patrick, you know you will. Especially when you could have prevented it. Especially if it turns out to be me or Sean who dies in the process."

It felt like blasphemy to even suggest John was involved. How could the same gentle man who'd bound up her foot, who'd kissed her brains out, be an arsonist? Patrick didn't stop chewing. "Don't use guilt on me, kid. It won't work. Even Mom's given up trying. You have no proof whatsoever that Forester was the guy in the silver. You also have nothing that says the guy in the silver was the one who set the fire or had anything to do with the bomb. You're on really flimsy ground here. And in my opinion, the person you should be talking to about all this is your captain, Joe Ripani."

Shannon poured maple syrup on her pancakes and then slid the side order of eggs on top and sliced the whole thing into neat bites. "What good is having a mayor for a brother if he won't even do a small favor for you?" She tried to make her voice pathetic, but it was tough going. Patrick was impervious to guilt. Why did he have to be the only politician in the western world who couldn't be corrupted?

She took a huge bite of pancake, savored the combined tastes of whole wheat, fresh eggs, pure maple syrup and strawberries, and decided she'd drop by and see Sean.

She'd enjoy the rest of her breakfast—which she'd decided Patrick was definitely buying—and then she'd pay her other brother a visit.

SEAN AND LINDA HAD BOUGHT a new house on a sloping lot with trees at the back and a view of the harbor in front. Shannon pulled up in the spacious driveway and hobbled up the steps to the front door just as her sister-in-law opened it.

"Hey, Shannon, I saw you drive up. What happened to you? You're limping." Linda gave her a hug and drew her into the house. "C'mon in the kitchen. Sean's making lunch—tuna sandwiches."

"With pickles?"

"He won't let me have pickles. Says I'm taking in too much salt. I'd eat them on porridge these days if he let me, not to mention ice cream. And I was the one who said loud and clear I didn't believe in cravings, they were an old wives' tale. Now, what happened to your foot?"

"I stepped on a piece of glass at the beach the other night."

"Obviously you were barefoot at the time. What were you doing, skinny-dipping?"

"I wish." They'd reached the kitchen, and Shannon limped over and gave Sean a hug. She was reminded all over again of John. The two were alike, sizewise at least—big and brawny and solid as rock. She wondered if the time would come soon—please, goddess—when ten minutes could go by without her thinking about John.

"Hey, sis, good to see you. Sit down and I'll make you a sandwich."

"Thanks, but I just ate my way through a huge breakfast and stuck Patrick with the bill."

"So, were you alone on the beach when you cut yourself?" Linda sat down at the table and Shannon joined her.

"Nope, I was there with a guy."

"You were out on a date? Good going, sister. Who with? Do we know him? Is he cute? Thanks, sweetie." Linda smiled up at Sean as he set her sandwiches down and poured coffee all around.

"The new guy at the firehouse, John Forester. He said he's met you, Sean."

"Yeah, I did meet him. He seems like a really good guy." He gave Shannon a teasing look. "He must be, if he talked you into a date this fast. He's only been at the station a week or so, and we all know how fussy you are."

"Yeah, well, I sort of had an ulterior motive this time." Shannon explained about her conviction that John was the man in the silver who'd rescued her and Salvage. "The dog knew him, I'd swear to it. But he consistently denies being at that warehouse fire, and all his documents back him up. Still, I can't go against the way I feel. I just really think he was the guy in the silver. And I can't come up with any reasonable explanation for him to deny it, the way he's doing." She took a sip of coffee. She was going to be wired all day with so much caffeine.

What the hell, she was wired from a lot more than caffeine. The memory of John's kisses had threaded through her dreams when she'd finally managed to get to sleep.

"Unless he had something to do with starting the fire, why would he be there, and why would he disappear the way he did? Unless he has something to hide. And what's with him getting the posting at this fire station, anyway? You know, Sean, there's guys who live here who had their applications in, perfectly competent guys, too. But no, they parachute in somebody from New York who nobody knows."

Linda was giving her a thoughtful look, and Sean was chewing on a mouthful of sandwich, his face impassive. "The bosses don't exactly explain themselves to us," he said. "Maybe they wanted a seasoned guy instead of a probie."

"Did you see his face at all, Shannon, at the warehouse?" Linda asked.

"Nope. You know those silver suits cover up every inch of the body. And they have that dark face mask that you can't see through. They're sort of spooky. They look like what astronauts wear. And he didn't say anything, either, so voice recognition is out." She looked over at Sean. "I was wondering if you could run a check on Forester somehow, maybe on your computer? Because if the guy's lying, somebody should find out and go after him about it. I mean, if we've got an arsonist going around setting fires—"

Sean set down his sandwich and scowled at her. "Let me get this straight. You went out with John Forester last night, and now you figure he's an arsonist? What the hell did the guy pull to make you think that, Shannon?"

"He didn't pull anything—it's just a feeling I have." Sean's face had taken on the grim look Shannon recognized. All the O'Shea men got that narrow-eyed, tight-jawed, bullish expression when they figured one of their women needed protection.

Which was the joke of the century, because every single O'Shea female was more than capable of taking care not only of herself, but also of any male who happened to be around. Linda fit the pattern perfectly.

Sean didn't look convinced, so Shannon sighed and said, "Honest, he was a perfect gentleman. He took me for dinner at the Tangerine Bistro, that new place on the beach, and when I stepped on the glass, he carried me back to the car and did a professional job of patching up my foot. Then he drove me home and took the dogs out for a walk for me."

Linda whistled. "*Carried* you, huh? I'm impressed. As tall as we are, it's not easy to find a guy with enough brawn to actually pick us up." Linda was only an inch or so shorter than Shannon. "It's one of the things about Sean that tipped the scale for me, the fact that he could actually lift me. Not that he's made the effort all that often. When we went up the mountain and the horses bolted in the lightning storm, you made me walk every single last step of the way back, remember that, Sean?"

"How could I forget? You keep bringing it up all the time." Sean gave her a look and went straight back to the issue at hand. "Sis, do you have a single shred of actual evidence to link Forester to the warehouse fire?"

"Yeah, I do. The dog, Salvage? Like I said, he recognized John, I know he did. When I brought him to the firehouse, he went straight over to him, put his paws up and licked his face, as if he was saying thanks for getting us out of there."

Linda nodded as if she was convinced, but Sean looked exasperated and shook his head. "I meant something besides your famous women's intuition."

Both Shannon and Linda glared at him, and he held up his

hands. "Hey, I'm not knocking it. God knows, in lots of cases women can be right, but in this one, we're talking about a fellow firefighter. I'd need a lot more than a dog making friends before I'd do a background check on a brother. Sorry, Shannon."

He stood up and put his cup in the sink. "I've got to take off. I've got a meeting to attend." He bent down and kissed Linda, placing one big hand on her flat belly. His voice was so tender it brought tears to Shannon's eyes when he added, "You and Speedbump take it easy, okay, darlin'? Don't do anything, just rest and read. I'll bring food home and make dinner, so don't even think about cooking."

He gave Shannon an affectionate tap on the shoulder and a peck on the cheek. "I think your imagination is running away with you, kiddo. But if you come up with anything concrete, be sure and let me know."

When he was gone, Linda heaved a sigh. "If he could manage it, he'd have me spend these next seven months in a wheelchair. He's making me nuts. Lord knows what he'll be like when I finally go into labor."

"Try and do it when he's not around. Mom or I will get you to the hospital safely and then we'll call him."

"Good thinking." Linda got up and rummaged in the pots and pans cupboard. She extracted an extra-large jar of dill pickles, then set it on the table along with a box of oatmeal chocolate chip cookies that she'd stashed in the tea towel drawer. She took out a pickle and rested it on a cookie, took a bite and closed her eyes.

"Mmm, ambrosia. Believe it or not, this combination settles my stomach. Thank God he's gone. I hate the very smell of tuna on whole wheat. Now, let's have ourselves a healthy little snack and you can go over this whole Forester thing again for me." She shoved the cookies Shannon's way. "Sean may not believe you, but I do. And I can do searches on the computer. Just write down everything you know about this guy and we'll put a trace on him. As soon as we finish these cookies."

An hour and a half later, the cookies were gone, and Linda had been through one search engine after the other. If the computer was to be believed, John Forester didn't exist.

"I don't get it." She sat back and frowned at the screen. "There ought to be something somewhere. I mean, the guy must do banking or something on the Net, and yet there's no record of him. Nothing on those military sites, no health records. How can that be?"

"Nothing in these newsletters from the fire departments in New York, either." Linda had printed them out and Shannon had carefully read each one, searching for John's name or one that could belong to his father. "He didn't say exactly when his dad died, but you'd think there'd be something here. They always have write-ups on any fireman who dies."

"The plot thickens," Linda said. "Have you thought of asking your captain, Joe Ripani, about him?"

"I'm considering that. Patrick suggested it, too. But I think first I'll call the Brooklyn Fire Department on some pretext or other and see if anybody there knows him. He said his father worked at Hall Seventeen."

"Let me." Linda's eyes sparkled with excitement. "I can say I'm a local reporter for the magazine section of the Courage Bay newspaper, and I'm interested in doing a piece on John Forester, because he's new in town, and we need some background info— heard that his father was a local hero or some such blarney."

"Do it." Shannon handed Linda the phone.

And fifteen minutes later, they were back where they'd started.

"They didn't say they'd never had a Forester work there, which would at least give us something to go on." Linda sighed. "The guy I talked to said that they weren't at liberty to disclose any information without written permission."

"Who from?"

"Next of kin. I was gonna do the sister routine, but I didn't think it would fly."

"Good thinking. He told me he's an only child, so you'd have gotten caught in that little white lie."

"Damn and blast. Men are so *suspicious*."

They both thought that over and then burst out laughing.

"There's always a way—we just have to figure it out," Linda said. "When I came here to do that documentary and wanted to know more about Sean, I called you up and asked if we could have lunch, remember? And then you invited me for Sunday dinner at your parents' place, and I fell in love with your entire family. As well as Sean."

"They all fell hard for you, too."

"Well, maybe that's the answer."

Shannon shook her head, puzzled. "You've lost me. John doesn't have any family here. His dad is dead and he said his mother's an alcoholic who spends a lot of time in hospitals. I don't think I could—"

"Nope, other way round. Bring him home to meet the O'Sheas. We're all good judges of character, especially your mom." Linda's eyes twinkled. "She liked me right away, so there you go. And I love that whole Sunday dinner family thing. It's like something out of a Norman Rockwell print. Let us have a go at your Johnny Be Good. Maybe you're too deep in the forest to see the trees."

"Good thinking."

"And if I know your brothers, they'll want to interrogate him, anyway, seeing you were out with him. How about I drop a little hint in Sean's ear that maybe he ought to invite John for Sunday dinner, get to know him a whole lot better? Takes the pressure off you that way."

Shannon thought it over and nodded. "Mom's got a first class bullshit detector. I wouldn't mind hearing what she's got to say about him. And having somebody new for dinner at least gets her off my case for a few hours."

"Mary's a worrier. I know for a fact she's read up on every single thing that could go wrong with me and the baby."

"Doesn't that make you crazy?"

"It would if I didn't know that she's doing it out of love. It doesn't bother me the way it would if it was my mother doing it. But Mom's too involved in getting her medical degree to have time to worry about me, so it's kind of comforting in a way that your mom does."

"I'd take your mom's approach any old day."

"Speaking of approaches, have you considered the up close and personal one with your Forester fellow?" Linda winked at Shannon. "When you said the guy had picked you up in his arms and then fixed your foot, it sounded as if he wasn't exactly Quasimodo, am I right?"

"He's nothing short of gorgeous," Shannon confessed.

"And while he was packing you around and fooling with your toes, you wouldn't have left out any little detail like a kiss or two, huh? Maybe on your foot, to make it all better?"

"How did you know? Lips, toes—I can tell you, as a kisser he's world class. He made the nape of my neck sweat."

"Uh-uh, I figured something like that. Your eyes went sort of glazed there. So why not capitalize on that animal attraction and get real close to him?"

"You mean…"

"Yup. As close as humanly possible. Down and dirty. Naked, if that's what it takes. That way, you can watch his every move. You said he's on the same shift as you, so that takes care of the work part of it. Tie him up at night, either literally or otherwise, and he won't have much time for plotting arson. Rotten work, but someone has to do it."

"Anything for my career," Shannon said, making her eyes wide and putting one hand over her heart. "Thanks for the advice, Linda. And I promise I'll take it under advisement. It's so refreshing to deal with someone who trusts instinct over reason."

"Sex is their vulnerable area. Knowing that is one of our strengths as women. It's what makes us dangerous."

Shannon knew they weren't being entirely serious. But she also knew that for all sorts of reasons, getting close to John could be dangerous. Maybe not for him, but definitely for her.

CHAPTER ELEVEN

WHEN SEAN O'SHEA INVITED him to his parents' house for Sunday dinner, John came dangerously close to turning the invitation down. He'd pretty much made up his mind to keep his distance from Shannon, and tough as that was proving to be, he'd been sticking to his decision. He'd seen her at work, but he'd managed to keep things strictly professional between them.

"This is the first Sunday in a long time that Shannon and I have both been off—we usually work alternate shifts," Sean explained. "So the whole family will be there."

Meeting her extended family didn't seem the best way to go about getting her out of his system, John thought, although there were also powerful reasons he ought to accept Sean's invitation.

Shannon's brother Patrick was the mayor. Sean was a fellow firefighter, extending the brotherly hand of friendship, and unless John came up with an airtight explanation as to why he couldn't attend, it would look downright surly to refuse.

And what kind of excuse could he come up with, anyhow? All he had planned for Sunday was a visit to the nearest Laundromat.

"Thanks, Sean, I'd love to come," John said. "Sure your mother won't mind?" He wouldn't in his wildest nightmares consider bringing a guest home for dinner with his own mother. The idea was so ludicrous it almost made him laugh. If the guest was male, she'd do her best to seduce him. Female, and his mother would find a way to humiliate her. Naomi couldn't abide competition, and neither could she cook.

"Sunday dinner's a tradition with my family," Sean said. "Mom's a great cook and she loves it when we bring someone new home."

"Give me time and place, and I'll be there."

John scribbled the address down on a paper. "We eat early, around five, so come an hour or so before and meet everybody."

AT QUARTER PAST FOUR on Sunday, after two trips around the block to work up his courage, John finally pulled up in front of the rambling two-story frame house on one of Courage Bay's quiet, old residential streets. He'd faced loaded guns and a switchblade with cool confidence, but the knots in his gut right now were a direct result of pure terror.

Get over it, Johnny boy. Just go in there and act your socks off. It's only dinner, for crying out loud. How tough can it be?

He delayed for a moment, studying the house.

Well cared for was what came to mind.

The front lawn was closely trimmed, as was the box hedge. A riot of late summer flowers bloomed in neat beds, and a hanging basket by the front door spilled scarlet geraniums and white baby's breath. Lavish blossoms that John didn't recognize filled huge pottery planters that bordered the paving stones leading to the front door.

What did he know about families? He'd grown up living with his mother in apartments, some not bad, but then as her drinking got worse and money became a major issue, they'd started moving from one low-rent dive to the next, until at last they were living in rat-infested dumps. He'd known he had to get through school at all costs, so he'd worked at anything he could find until he graduated.

As soon as he started making real money, John had invested in a condo for himself and an adjoining apartment for his mother. He'd paid an astronomical amount to have both places professionally decorated, but because of his job, he was hardly ever home, anyway.

His mother regularly hocked most of the apartment furnishings for money for booze and drugs, so he'd started using less expensive modular pieces to fill in the blanks.

So much for his nice middle class upbringing. This whole white picket fence, American family bit was foreign to him. Few things made him nervous, but families were one of them. He had no idea how they operated.

Well, you got yourself roped into this, so get your ass in there and pretend to have a good time.

With the bottles of wine he'd thought to bring tucked under his arm, he made his reluctant way to the entrance and rang the bell. The door opened almost instantly—and it was apparent that the tall, heavy man balanced on the step was on his way out.

"You must be John Forester. Come on in." The big bald guy smiled and held out a massive hand, and after a moment's hesitation, John set the bottles of wine on the hall runner and shook hands.

"Pleased to meet you, John. I'm Sean's father, Caleb. I'm just on my way to the convenience store. Been sent on an errand by the wife. She forgot to get whipping cream for the banana cream pie. Can't have my favorite pie without cream." He chuckled, a low, friendly rumble, and John found it easy to smile into his arresting blue eyes. So this was where Shannon and her brother had inherited those startling eyes, and also where their height came from.

Caleb was eye to eye with John and probably fifty pounds heavier, which would put the older man at six-five and in the low-three-hundred range.

"Mary," he bellowed over his shoulder. "Mary, sweetheart, come and take charge of this young fellow while I get the cream."

"For heaven's sake, Caleb, stop hollering." But the reprimand was accompanied by a smile every bit as welcoming as Caleb's had been, and the tall, big-boned woman with the halo of long, wild white curls grasped John's hand in both of hers and held it. Here, too, he could see traces of Shannon—in her mother's high cheekbones and long, graceful neck.

"I'm Mary O'Shea, Caleb's wife," she introduced herself. "And of course you're John Forester. Welcome to our noisy home, John. It's a wonder the neighbors haven't made us muzzle him, he's that loud," she said as her husband planted a noisy kiss on her cheek and headed out the door, slamming it behind him.

"We'll have to just wait here a minute—he'll be back for his car keys," Mary confided with a wink. "I've got them in my pocket."

Sure enough, the door burst open an instant later.

"Where the hell are my—"

"Here you go. I found them on top of the microwave this time."

Caleb took them with a sheepish shake of his head and left again.

Mary laughed. John retrieved the wine and handed it to her, and she thanked him. "I love this wine. You have great taste, John. We'll enjoy it with dinner." She set the bottles on the small entrance table. "I'll open them and let them breathe in a minute, but right now, come this way and meet the gang." Holding John's hand in one of hers, she led him down the hall and into a spacious living room that seemed filled with people and loud voices.

A quick glance told John that Shannon wasn't there, and he felt a sharp stab of disappointment. The fact that she would be here was the single thing about this invitation that had been appealing.

"Hey, John, glad you made it." Sean was standing behind a tall, beautiful lady, his arms looped around her shoulders. He kissed her cheek, released her and came over to John, drawing him into the group.

"You've met Mom, and this is my wife, Linda." His voice resonated with pride.

John extended a hand, and Linda took it. She was a confident-looking woman, and she had a firm handshake and a wide smile.

"Pleased to meet you, John."

He had the distinct impression that her astute gray eyes were doing a fast and expert assessment of everything from his clothing to his haircut and shoes.

"Shannon told me you patched up her foot the other night."

Her words had a mischievous undertone, and John wondered how much else Shannon had told her. He was debating whether to ask where Shannon was when an older man appeared beside Sean. Sean slung an arm around his shoulders.

"This is my grandpa, Brian O'Shea. We just celebrated his eighty-fifth birthday last week, and we're trying to talk him out of learning skateboarding. Grandpa, this is John Forester, the newest member of the Courage Bay firefighting team."

"Good to meet you, John." Brian's grip could have been that of a much younger man. "These young whippersnappers just want to stop me from having any fun," he complained. His wide smile was mischievous and young, although the heavily veined hand John held trembled slightly. "No one offered you a beer yet, young man? Got to watch this crowd—they're territorial about their beer."

"Just about to give him one, Gramps." Sean held out an icy can, and John took it gratefully as Sean indicated an older man who looked very much like Caleb. John immediately recognized the woman beside him, although they hadn't been formally introduced.

"This is my uncle Donald O'Shea—he's Dad's big brother. And this is Willow Redmond. Willow, John Forester, the new guy at the firehouse."

"We've sort of met," Willow said with a wide and wicked smile. "Almost. Good to see you again, John. How's it going with the reflexology?"

"I think I need more training." He remembered exactly how

it had felt to hold Shannon's foot against his chest, and when Willow looked at him, John could tell from the amusement dancing in her eyes that she was remembering the same scene.

"Reflexology?" Donald frowned. "That something else you're into, Willow?"

She turned and put her hand on his arm, stroking it a little. "Not really, Donnie, it's just an interesting alternative therapy."

"You'll have to show me sometime," he purred, looking at her with a fond expression.

"Absolutely," Willow said, winking at John, who was studying Donald O'Shea.

Donald and his brother Caleb could be twins, they looked that much alike. Both were tall, well built and moderately overweight. They had even both chosen to shave their heads, and it suited them.

Willow seemed impossibly fragile next to Donald, small-boned, slim and dramatically elegant. Her silver cap of hair shone; her black silk pants and matching top looked sophisticated. Silver bracelets jangled when she extended a long graceful hand, and John thought he detected the clipped syllables and rapid speech of the native New Yorker, a clue that had escaped him the other evening at Shannon's. But then, he'd been otherwise occupied.

Her words confirmed it. "Sean says you're from New York, John. I've lived in New Jersey most of my adult life, but my family are native New Yorkers from ages back." She smiled warmly. "What made you decide to leave the big city and come to Courage Bay?"

He needed to be careful here. Instinct told him that this woman might trip him up if he wasn't careful.

"Oh, I needed a break from the city, and I saw a documentary about smoke jumpers and Courage Bay," he said in a casual tone. "This place intrigued me, so when an opening came up in the fire department, I applied."

"We must get together and have a talk about the city," Willow said. "I've always found that sooner or later, New Yorkers discover they know some of the same people. It's amazing. It's happened to me over and over."

John very much doubted that it would happen with him. Unless he was badly mistaken, there wasn't a chance in a million that he and Willow Redmond's paths had come within a mile of one another, much less crossed. All the same, he was relieved when Sean said, "And here's the mayor, late as usual. Patrick O'Shea, John Forester."

Black, well-cut curls, those trademark blue eyes and a wide, engaging smile had probably helped get Patrick O'Shea elected. All the O'Shea offspring were distinctively attractive. John watched as the two brothers exchanged friendly high fives before Patrick turned and extended a hand in his direction.

"Hello, John, welcome to Courage Bay. I'm pleased to meet you."

But the heartiness in his voice wasn't matched by any warmth in his penetrating blue gaze. It was obvious Patrick O'Shea was putting John on probation, for whatever reason. How to best set him at ease? John was working on that one when he felt a gentle touch on his shoulder.

"Hey, Big Bad John, how's it going?" Shannon had come up behind him, a white butcher's apron covering her abbreviated green shift. Her face was flushed; her long legs and feet were bare. He knew the cut on her foot had healed without incident, and he noticed that she now had brazen red polish on her toes. Having her close to him had the usual effect—his heart rate increased and he had to force himself not to stare at her lips.

"You been introduced to this whole crew?" she asked.

"Yes, Sean did the honors, thanks." John couldn't stop looking at her. Her midnight hair was again pulled up into a messy, shiny knot at the crown of her head. Bits were floating around her ears and down her neck, and her blue eyes with those amazing long, curling lashes sparkled at him.

John's pulse picked up another several notches. God, she was beautiful.

"Sorry I didn't come and say hi sooner, but I was trapped in the kitchen. Mom made me stir the gravy—it's really high maintenance." She motioned to several brown stains on the front of the apron and wrinkled her nose. "Darn stuff spits at you, too. No gratitude whatsoever."

John watched her, mesmerized, as she turned her attention to Patrick. "Hello there, big bro." She gave him a quick, hard hug and a smack on the cheek, and John noted the softening of Patrick's expression as he held her close for an instant. These people cared deeply about one another, and they weren't afraid to show it.

Observing them gave him a feeling that might have been emptiness. Or maybe he was just hungry.

"So," Shannon said to Patrick, "you and John talking politics and religion already? I've heard that's the very best way to get a party going."

"We only just met," Patrick said, glancing over at John with that considering look. "No time yet for controversy."

"Well, don't start, because Dad's back and Mom says dinner's ready, so come and sit down." She raised her hands high over her head and clapped them as she announced in a loud voice. "Dinner is served in the dining room, ladies and gentlemen. And the cook is temperamental, so don't waste any time. Just follow me—one, two, three, *march.*"

Laughing, talking, arguing, everyone did as she ordered.

In the spacious dining room, John found himself seated between Linda and Willow. He felt a tiny stab of disappointment when Shannon, her apron gone, sat down across from him, a brother on either side of her like protective bookends. Caleb was at the head of the table and Mary at the foot.

The long dining table, covered in snowy-white linen, was laden with a mouthwatering array of food. A standing rib roast decorated with scarlet crab apples sat in the middle, surrounded by bowls of buttery mashed potatoes, a platter of asparagus, beets and carrots, a huge ceramic bowl of green salad scattered with oranges, plus various small pots of relishes and pickles. John drew a deep breath and realized he was ravenous. Breakfast had been a very long time ago, and nervousness had made him skip lunch.

He filled his plate as the food was passed and the wine was poured. He was about to lift his fork when Mary said, "Caleb, would you ask the blessing?"

After a quick glance around, John bent his head along with the others, and both Linda and Willow reached over and took one of his hands in theirs.

"We thank you for bringing friends and family together on such a beautiful afternoon," Caleb said. "We ask your blessing on this wonderful food that Mary and Shannon have prepared for us. Thank you for bringing John and Willow to share it with us. Protect each and every one of us as we go about our daily lives, and give us peace and joy and love in our hearts. Amen."

Everyone murmured amen.

Intellectually, John knew that many people said grace, but this was the first time in his entire life he'd been a part of such a group. Religion hadn't figured in his upbringing. It gave him the strangest feeling to have Caleb mention him by name, and suddenly he felt deeply ashamed of deceiving these good people. When the grace was over, he looked up and met Patrick's eyes, and it seemed to him that Patrick knew, that he could sense just by looking at him that John wasn't being honest.

Get hold of yourself—the end justifies the means, John told himself, but the old mantra didn't have much power today. The food lost a tiny bit of its appeal, but his hunger dictated that he eat, and every bite confirmed how delicious it all was.

"So, John, tell me exactly what neighborhood you grew up in in New York? What did your father do for a living?" Willow took a bite of roast and waited expectantly as he swallowed his own mouthful.

Her words fell into one of those silences that come about in groups, and he could sense that everyone around the table was listening, waiting expectantly for his answer.

"My dad was a fireman. He's dead now." That much was accurate, as far as it went. There had been a fireman named John Forester, and he was no longer alive.

"We lived in Sunnyside, Queens," John lied, feeling a sudden and disturbing reluctance about embellishing the mixture of fact and fiction that was his cover story.

"Queens," Willow said. "Nice neighborhood. Did your house have a view of the New York skyline?"

"We lived in an apartment building—one of those six-story brick jobs," he said, relieved beyond measure that he'd taken the time to scout out the area he'd chosen as his fictitious home.

"What station was your father at?" Willow asked. "My mother's family had a number of firefighters. Mother's people are Irish."

Willow was like a bulldog, John thought—grabbing on and never letting go. "Hall Seventeen, in Brooklyn," he replied.

"Really? I had an uncle with the Brooklyn Fire Department. He might even have been at Hall Seventeen, I'm not sure. He knew everybody. He was the head of the union, so he might have known your father. Sorry, but what did you say his name was again? My brain is a sieve sometimes."

"Same as mine." John could see Patrick paying close attention as his tongue took him further and further from the truth. "John Forester."

"John Forester," Willow repeated thoughtfully. "I'll ask my uncle if he knew him."

John thought about coincidence. What were the odds of meeting anyone in a small city on the West Coast who'd have personal knowledge of a fire station in Brooklyn? Yet here he was, sitting next to the second person he'd met so far who did. Somebody, somewhere, had a weird sense of humor.

As soon as he could, he turned toward Linda and asked her questions about the documentary she'd helped make about the smoke jumpers. Here, at least, he was on firm ground, because he'd watched the video enough times that he could talk about it with confidence.

"I especially enjoyed the story the interviewer told about the sacred pool up in the mountains," he said to her. "And the footage you had of it was spectacular. It really conveyed a sense of timelessness. Have you made it back there again?"

"No, unfortunately not. It was a magical place… I still want to go back someday." She looked over and caught Sean's eye, and the intimacy of the look they exchanged made John feel uncomfortable again. "We'd planned to go back to the sacred pool on our honeymoon, but Sean was called out to a fire in Montana, and I had an assignment in Mexico. By the time we were back, we'd both had enough of roughing it, so we went to Hawaii. And while we were there, I found out I was pregnant. I haven't felt up to mountain climbing."

John knew less than nothing about pregnancy. The whole idea made him feel queasy, and he averted his eyes from Linda's flat middle.

Of course he knew where babies came from. He just hadn't been around very many women who were growing them.

"You travel much, John?"

"Some. A couple trips to Mexico, a few to Europe, and last year I had a job—uh, took a trip to Ireland." He was still concentrating hard on not looking at her midsection, and the question had caught him unawares.

Pay attention, he warned himself. *You slipped there. A fireman probably wouldn't have money enough to go globe-trotting, idiot.*

Get her talking. It was safer that way. "How about you, Linda? What are you working on at the moment?"

"Until very recently, I worked as a television photographer based in San Diego. I traveled most of the time. When we got back from Hawaii, I landed this super job at the local station. I'll be filming interviews, covering sports events. I never thought I'd be content to settle down in one place, but that was before I met Sean."

"So you don't miss it, the globe-trotting?"

"Not so far." She smiled across at her husband. "I guess falling in love changed me. Living with Sean is all the excitement I can handle these days."

"Works for me," Sean declared.

Had he ever met a couple who appeared to be this happy? John wondered. *This visibly in love?*

"How about you, John?" The question came from Mary. "You think you'll be able to settle down here in Courage Bay after all the excitement of the big city?"

"Oh, for sure. Courage Bay has a lot to offer—no traffic jams, no crowds." He remembered that he was supposed to be living on a fireman's wages. "No exorbitant rents, either, I hear."

"John's looking for a condo or an apartment to rent," Shannon said. "I called Matthew. He said he'll be in touch, John."

"My nephew's an honest Realtor," Caleb assured him. "He'll find you something at a fair price."

The talk veered to real estate. When everyone was finished eating, Shannon got to her feet and began to collect the plates.

Linda started to get up to help, but John said, "Why don't you let me?"

He stood up, gathered plates and cutlery and followed Shannon into the kitchen. He noticed that Mary and Willow also started to help, but at some signal from Linda they sat back down.

He was grateful, because he was sweating and felt as if he'd been through an ordeal. He and Shannon repeated the clearing process several times, and after the final trip to the kitchen, Shannon said, "So, Forester, you rescue injured ladies on the beach, walk dogs, help with dishes. Do you do windows as well?" She set the last load of plates down and started scraping food into the garbage container and then stacking the dishwasher.

He did the same. "Only when there's a fire and the windows need breaking. I'm not exactly what you'd call an expert in the kitchen." He smiled at her, admiring the way her simple dress skimmed her body, hinting at the slender curves underneath. "Willing but inexperienced, that's me. Cooking is pretty much a mystery."

She gave him a curious look. "You must have had to cook at the fire station when you were a probie."

Jesus, Johnny boy, get a grip. "Yeah, of course. I'm just not much good at it."

Damn. He was slipping and sliding all over the place today. It wasn't like him.

"Well, stick around here and we'll get you whipped into shape." She was bent over, rummaging in the fridge. Her dress hiked up to the top of her thighs, and he took full advantage of the view.

"Speaking of whipping…" She looked at him over her shoulder and caught him staring. He raised a suggestive eyebrow, and her dimples appeared as she laughed. "Sorry to disappoint you. It's the cream we're working on here."

He longed to take the container out of her hand, back her up against the cabinets, press her tight against him and kiss her senseless.

There's danger here.

"Here's the mixer." She handed it to him, dumped the quart of thick cream into a large bowl. "You do that, and I'll make coffee."

He'd never whipped cream before, but how hard could it be? He plugged in the mixer, shoved the blades in and turned the machine on high.

Cream spattered across his face, his shirt, his jeans, the curtains, the wall. He yelped and then swore, and Shannon burst into giggles.

"Your technique needs work. You have to hold the beaters straight up and down, like this," she demonstrated, moving in close and taking the machine.

Her hair brushed his arm. She smelled like coffee, like cream, like vanilla, like everything delicious he'd ever tasted.

"Now beat this until it's good and thick, but not too thick, because it'll turn to butter, and we'll be sunk. Put a spoonful of sugar in once it starts to thicken, and then add the vanilla and mix it just a tiny bit more. I'll slice these pies and put the pieces out on serving plates, and you scoop up a good-size dollop of cream and plonk it on each one."

"Plonk? Is that a cooking term? I thought it was cheap wine." He was enjoying himself. He was enjoying her. He was wondering how long they could spin this out.

"Get busy, slave."

He did, and this time, he actually managed to turn the thick mixture into whipped cream. Together, they ladled out generous portions of pie and cream. When the last was done, Shannon ran a forefinger around the bowl, scooping up the remainder of the cream, and stuck it in his mouth.

"Good, huh?" She gave him a teasing, mischievous grin, and those blue eyes seemed to dare him.

Her smile faded and she gasped when he sucked lasciviously on her finger, holding her hand so she couldn't pull away. Then he tugged her close and kissed her, hard and fast and very thoroughly. She tasted like something elusive that he'd been searching for all his life.

"We'd better get this pie in the dining room before my dad comes looking for it," she said when he let her go. But he noticed that her voice wobbled and her hands were trembling when she started loading the plates on a huge wooden tray.

He lifted it, and he was on his way out when he heard her say in a soft tone, "I can't quite put my finger on what's going on with you, John Forester. But I'm going to find out…you can bank on it."

Now why didn't he find that reassuring?

CHAPTER TWELVE

LATER THAT EVENING, Shannon somehow found herself alone with her mother, a situation she tried hard to avoid.

John had been the first to leave, and then it was like lemmings heading over a cliff. Uncle Donald and Willow hurried off to attend a movie. Linda was tired, so she and Sean had gone home, and Patrick took Gramps and her father to the marina to look at a boat he was thinking of buying.

After dessert was eaten, everyone had helped clean the kitchen, so there wasn't much left to do except strip the cloth off the table, put it through the laundry and carry the garbage out. While Shannon was doing that, Mary made another pot of coffee and set two mugs and a plate of oatmeal cookies on the kitchen table, which made it pretty difficult for Shannon to stage the quick getaway she'd planned.

"I like your young man," Mary said, pouring cream into her mug.

"Mom, John is *not* my young man."

"Oh, so you let just anybody kiss you like that in the kitchen? I wasn't spying. I was just coming to see what had become of the pies."

Rats. Busted. And how on earth could she explain now that she figured John might be an arsonist, and she was just trying to get at the truth?

"I don't think he's been around families like ours a whole lot. He seemed a little on edge. What do you know about his background, Shannon?"

Good question. The answer: not half as much as she'd like to know.

Shannon shrugged. "Just what he told everybody at dinner. That his father was a fireman, that he's dead now. And he did tell me he's an only child and his mother's alcoholic—she's been in and out of hospitals. I gather that John takes care of her."

Mary nodded. "He's a kind man. It shows in his eyes."

And by the way he drags dogs and women out of burning warehouses?

Time to change the subject. "Mom, you used to know Willow really well, didn't you?"

"Well, yes, long ago. We were friends before either of us married. We toured with that little rock band. But years passed, and we lost touch. People change, I can't say I know her all that well anymore." Mary's voice took on her usual worried tone. "I just hope Donald isn't going to break her heart. He's so careless about women's feelings." She sighed and then brought her attention back to Shannon. "Why do you ask, dear? Isn't it working out, having Willow board with you?"

"I'm not exactly sure yet." Shannon explained about all the things Willow had ripped out at her house. "I just wondered if you knew how good she is at finishing things she's started."

To Shannon's surprise, Mary laughed. "If that isn't just like her. I remember her taking a dress of mine apart one afternoon. I wanted it for the show we were doing that night and she insisted it needed to be taken in and hemmed. She went to the store for thread, and darned if she didn't go flitting off with some boy she met there. I was furious with her. I don't think she ever fixed that dress for me."

Shannon tipped her head back and groaned. "That's what I was afraid of. Willow the total whacko, the human wrecking ball. I'll bet she drove her husband nuts, ripping their house apart. I'll bet he's relieved she's gone."

Mary looked uncertain. "I doubt that. I never met Steve

Redmond, and she's never really said it in so many words, but I think Willow was in an abusive marriage."

"Oh, no. Oh, Lordy, Mom, why would she stay with him so long?" It was something Shannon never understood. There'd been calls she'd gone on where it was obvious the woman had been beaten. A month or two later, another call, same woman. What was that about?

"I'm only guessing, but I'd imagine it was because of her son. Aaron had to have numerous operations on his leg when he was growing up, and Willow had no career apart from playing the guitar. She couldn't have supported Aaron and herself all on her own. Things were different back then...laws weren't as strict about support. And I've read that women who are beaten always believe the man is going to change."

"Yeah, right, like that's gonna happen. Why are women so gullible?"

"I guess we all want to believe in happily ever after."

Shannon remembered something Willow had said about Mary refusing Caleb's marriage proposals. "Was that what you wanted, Mom? To get married and live happily ever after?"

Mary studied her coffee cup for several long moments, and then she slowly shook her head. "No, it wasn't. As a matter of fact, I didn't want to get married at all. You know there were fourteen kids in my family. I grew up changing diapers and baby-sitting and sleeping in a bed with at least two of my sisters. I decided early on I wanted a singing career instead of that."

"So what changed your mind?"

Mary raised her eyes and met Shannon's. "I got pregnant, and I didn't believe in abortion. So your father and I got married."

Shannon was stunned. She stared at her mother. "You never told me that before."

Mary's smile was wry. "It's not exactly something I broadcast, dear. Don't get me wrong, I couldn't be happier about Sean and Linda. Attitudes were very different when I was a girl."

Shannon was doing math in her head. "But—was that—were you pregnant with…with Thomas?" Of course she knew that Mary and Caleb had lost their first son when he was only two. He'd caught some virus and died within twenty-four hours. But the dates still didn't add up. Shannon figured they'd been married a couple of years before Thomas was born.

"No, no. Not Thomas. I lost that first baby when I was six months pregnant. She didn't live."

"But you were already married."

"Yes, of course. Your father had proposed time and time again. When he found out about the baby, he was overjoyed. We got married right away. And then I had the miscarriage. In those days, they didn't let you see the baby, but I insisted. She was so beautiful. I called her Angela, because she was already with the angels." Mary's hazel eyes filled with tears. "I got pregnant again almost right away. With Thomas."

Who'd died at age two. Shannon reached across the table and took her mother's hand.

"Mom, I'm so sorry. I had no idea."

Mary squeezed Shannon's fingers and let them go so she could get up and find a box of tissues. "Of course you didn't." She sat back down and blew her nose. "How could you? It's not something I ever talk about."

Shannon didn't know how to phrase the next question, but she very much needed to ask it. "Were…were you sorry you'd gotten married, Mom? I mean, you lost the baby. You still could have gone ahead with your career—"

Mary shook her head. "Never. I grew to love your father more after we were married than I had before. He was heartbroken when we lost the baby. Sometimes love happens fast, like it did for Sean and Linda. Other times, it grows slowly, like it did for me with Caleb. One kind is no better than the other, as long as you recognize it and treasure it. And I've been so lucky. You and Sean and Patrick are all healthy, thank

God." She paused, and Shannon knew what was coming. She got the usual sinking feeling in her stomach.

"Although I guess I'll never get used to you and Sean having such dangerous jobs." Mary sighed, a familiar sound, and her face took on the expression that Shannon thought of as her martyr mask. "I know you think just because you're young and strong, nothing can happen to you, but it's not true, Shannon. Your father's lungs are damaged from breathing in smoke. Sean has had I don't know how many close calls. I've told you before I think it's foolhardy and thoughtless of you to work on the trucks the way you do. You could transfer into dispatch or become a medic. Why won't you see reason, honey?"

This was the point where they usually got into a heated argument. This time, however, Shannon didn't feel the usual irritation and impatience with her mother. She hadn't realized before how vulnerable Mary must feel about her children. Losing two babies was enough to make anyone paranoid. And she'd also lost her dreams, regardless of how much she denied it. Instead of anger, Shannon felt compassion.

"You and Dad raised us kids to be brave, Mom. From the time we were little, we heard the story of Michael O'Shea getting saved by the Chumash princess." Her voice was soft, and she struggled hard to find the words that would help her mother understand.

"It's in our blood, Mom, this need to help people. Sean and I do it one way, and now Patrick's chosen another. I'm doing what I love. I feel so lucky every working day to have a job I enjoy, one that challenges me to the max. It bothers me that…" Damn, her eyes were filling up. Was she going to bawl here? She cleared her throat, but the tears came anyway, dripping down her cheeks. "It bothers me that—that you aren't proud of me, Mom. I always wanted to make you proud of me." She was sobbing in earnest now, and she hated to cry. She hardly ever did. It made her furious. She reached out and grabbed a handful of tissues and blew her nose hard.

"Not *proud* of you?" Mary was horrified. "Oh, sweetheart, I have always been so proud to have you for my daughter. And even though I worry, I also tell everyone I meet that you're a firefighter. How many women could do your job? Never, ever think for one moment that I'm not proud of you, because it's just not true. That's like saying I don't love you." She got to her feet and pulled Shannon out of her chair, wrapping her in a fierce, long hug. "My beautiful, strong daughter," Mary said through her own tears.

They stopped crying eventually, and drank coffee and ate cookies and talked about Linda and the baby and John and Willow and Donald, giggling together the way they had when Shannon was younger.

And by the time she headed home, the wound in Shannon's heart had begun to mend.

It felt good to be on better terms with her mother, but other things weren't going as well. John didn't call the way she'd hoped he might. And Shannon was beginning to think that her relationship with Willow was also on the downswing.

Her house still looked as if a missile had hit it. Granted, Willow was working long hours at the clinic, but even on the weekend, she hadn't made any appreciable effort at putting Shannon's place back together again. Shannon was wondering how best to deal with the problem when Lisa called from work.

"I need to talk to you about Willow," she said after they'd exchanged pleasantries.

Shannon got a sinking feeling in her gut. "How's that working out?"

"On the whole, really well." Lisa didn't sound too certain, though. "She's a crackerjack with people, and she's excellent with the patients. But I wondered—have you noticed any problems with her and anything electronic?"

"Electronic? Not as far as I know. What's going on?"

"Well, Agnes left things in such a mess here, and Willow

said she knew exactly how to sort it out, but in the process she deleted the files on the computer. *All* the files. It's sort of a disaster because all our tax info was on there. We now have no idea where we stand financially, and even our friendly computer nerd can't retrieve anything. He says that by trying to fix it herself, she somehow fried the motherboard. The machine was almost brand-new. Then the autoclave we use to sterilize the instruments stopped working, and without consulting anyone, Willow tried to fix it, but it blew up. Thank goodness no one was hurt. And now this morning our X-ray machine's out of commission. She said it wasn't working properly and she adjusted something on it and it gave out."

Same story, different page, Shannon was thinking.

"In other ways, Willow's such a good employee," Lisa added. "She's here on time every day, she works really hard, she has a great attitude. I just wondered if you'd noticed anything?"

Give it up, Shannon. Lisa deserves to know about Willow's not so little quirk.

"I haven't noticed anything with appliances or electricity, but there is a major issue around here with steps and decks and plumbing and stuff. She pretty much wrecked half the house, promised she'd fix it all, and hasn't. I'm going to have to speak to her about it."

Lisa sighed. "That's what I'm going to have to do, too, I guess. But what do I tell her? I can't forbid her to touch the machines. Using them is part of her job."

"Well, I'm definitely going to say that I don't want another single thing torn out until the rest of this stuff is fixed."

"And I'll have to make a rule about not repairing anything on her own. I don't for a moment think she screws things up deliberately. Her intentions are the best. But the end result is the same, deliberate or not. By the way, your uncle Donald takes her to lunch almost every day. They're out together right now, and he picks her up after work. He's such a sweet guy. They make a cute couple."

Shannon rolled her eyes. Uncle Donald, professional heartbreaker, and Willow, demolition expert, didn't exactly strike her as a match made in heaven. "I really hope it works for them," she managed to say.

"Me, too. And speaking of work, how is Salvage making out at the firehouse?"

"Oh, the guys love him. The only problem is he's gonna gain way too much weight. They keep bringing him treats and bones and leftovers. He now has his own doggy bed, more toys than most kids and his own grooming tools."

Lisa laughed. "He's hit doggy heaven."

"I'd say so."

"Gotta go here, Shannon. Somebody just brought in a snake with a bellyache. Let's get together soon."

"For sure." Shannon hung up the phone. It probably wasn't funny for Lisa or the snake, but she couldn't help smiling. Firefighters had some strange calls, but they'd never encountered a snake with a bellyache. She'd have to tell the guys about that one when she went to work the following afternoon. She was starting her night shift rotation, six in the evening to six the next evening.

MAYBE THE SNAKE WAS a portent, because the next day, Shannon hadn't been on shift even an hour when the first call came in.

"Engine One, Rescue One. First alarm to 199 Main Street—report of woman lodged in tree," the dispatcher related in her usual flat monotone.

The shift sergeant was Marty Rodriguez, a grizzled, tough veteran all the probies were afraid of. He was straight-laced, and as far as anyone could tell, had absolutely no sense of humor.

"How the hell could a woman get lodged in a tree?" he growled. "And what's she doing up there at this time of night?" Marty was infamous for heading for bed at eight-thirty if he could get away with it. It was still light outside, but Shannon was as puzzled as the rest of the crew as they hurried to the truck and headed out.

When they reached the destination, however, it all became clear. Wayne, a tall, stooped man with a woebegone expression, met the truck in front of a small suburban bungalow and led the crew around to the back. He pointed up a tall old cherry tree where an extremely large, redheaded woman was perched on one branch, her arms wrapped around another. She was wearing blue shorts, and one massive bare thigh was stuck between two other branches.

"It's about time you got here, you lowlifes," she bellowed down at them. She had the kind of shrill voice that would carry for blocks. "A person could die up here, waiting for you frigging slackers to turn up. You better bloody well get up here and do something before this goddamn branch lets go, or so help me, I'll sue the ass off the city."

Shannon exchanged glances with John. She could see he was also trying to keep a straight face.

"Bunny's stuck up there," Wayne explained unnecessarily. "She went after Sammy. Sammy's her cat. He's way higher up—see him?"

They all craned their necks, and sure enough, Shannon could just make out a ginger cat, clinging to a branch near the top of the tree.

"Bunny got that far and then she slipped and got her leg stuck between those two branches," Wayne told them. "And I tried my best to get her down, honest. Tried to get Sammy down first, but he wouldn't come. So Bunny, well, she's got a short fuse, like. She got mad at me and went up herself."

Bunny was now calling the entire fire department names that would have made a stevedore blush. Short fuse was an understatement.

"I can't get either one of them down," Wayne declared, wringing his hands. "And I'm scared that branch she's sitting on is gonna let go any minute," he added in a plaintive tone. "So I called you guys. I didn't know what else to do."

As Bunny went on mouthing off, Shannon thought that in Wayne's situation, she might have been tempted to go inside, turn the volume up on the television and let nature take its course.

There was no way to get the truck close enough to use the lift, so they decided on a ladder. By the time it was in position, Bunny was screaming and swearing as the branch supporting her gave yet another ominous creak.

"You better go up first, O'Shea," Marty ordered in a low tone. "Miss Manners up there is trouble. If I send a man up, she's liable to charge him with sexual assault. Do what you can. You need help, Forester will back you."

Shannon climbed up and did her best to calm Bunny down while she figured out how to extricate her. It wasn't going to be easy. Bunny's substantial right thigh was pinned good and tight between two large branches.

"Okay, here's what we're gonna do," Shannon decided. "I'll get off the ladder and onto that limb over there. I'll support you from behind in case the branch you're on breaks, and John will come up the ladder with the saw and cut off the branch that's got your leg trapped—"

Bunny started to scream like a rusty saw blade. "You'll cut my leg! You're all assholes! Nobody's coming near me with any bloody saw!"

"Calm down and stop hollering," Shannon ordered. "We're absolute experts with saws. We won't come anywhere near your leg with the blade."

By the time John climbed the ladder with the saw, the backyard was filled with neighbors, most of whom were finding the situation amusing. Shannon could hear their subdued laughter, and so could Bunny, who screamed invectives down at them, ordering them off her property and threatening to charge them with trespassing, which had no effect. Nobody moved. It was far too good a show.

Shannon's arms barely made it around Bunny's sweaty and substantial middle, and she was finding it tough to subdue her own hysterical giggles as John fired up the power saw and Bunny screamed bloody murder.

The situation struck Shannon as hysterically funny, and from the frozen expression on John's face and the look in his eyes, she suspected he was struggling not to laugh. The two of them managed not to make eye contact. Shannon was convinced they'd both lose it if that happened, and Bunny would call a press conference to protest the heartlessness of Courage Bay's fire department.

After a few tense moments and shrill screams from Bunny, John managed to slice off the tree limb and free the human one. Bunny sagged backward into Shannon's arms, and as she did so, the branch holding her gave one last creak and began to give way.

"Grab her, John, I can't support her—"

John made a frantic lunge for Bunny, barely managing to keep her and Shannon from falling. Bunny, thoroughly terrified by now and still screaming and swearing in turns, wrapped both her arms and legs around John in an octopus hold, nearly upsetting the ladder. If he'd been a smaller man, the two of them would have toppled.

Over Bunny's shoulder, Shannon saw the expression of stupefied horror on John's face, and she lost it. Helpless tears rolled down her cheeks as she tried to muffle the laughter that exploded out of her as John somehow got Bunny and himself down the ladder.

When they were finally on the ground, Bunny planted an openmouthed, extended kiss square on John's lips. He turned magenta and struggled to dislodge her, but she took her own sweet time letting him go.

Shannon, finally in control of herself, was halfway down the ladder when Bunny, in a tone worthy of a drill sergeant, ordered, "Hey! You get right back up there, bitch, and get my poor Sammy down."

Shannon hesitated. A glance upward confirmed that, sure enough, the orange cat was precariously clinging to a thin branch a lot farther up the tree.

"Lady," Shannon heard Marty say in a no-nonsense tone, "get this through your head. We're not rescuing your cat from this tree, you understand me? To do so would endanger O'Shea. Cats come down by themselves. I've never seen a cat skeleton in any tree, have you? Anybody here ever seen a cat skeleton in a tree? There you go." Without waiting for Bunny's answer, he bellowed, "O'Shea, get down here. We're done."

Shannon did, grateful about not having to scale the tree again. She knew they'd rescued cats and even a baby parrot from trees before, but it was at the discretion of the shift boss. Rodriguez had obviously had it with Bunny and her mouth, which now went into overdrive. The woman spewed out curses and threats and pleas, in the midst of which the crew made a hasty escape. So did the neighbors. Shannon gave Wayne a sympathetic glance. No wonder he looked so haggard.

The moment they were safely in the truck, everyone except Marty Rodriguez burst into laughter, and they went on laughing hard as the truck made its way back to the station.

Shannon figured later that was probably why no one noticed the smoke billowing from under their truck.

At a stoplight, a young guy on a bike banged on the side of the cab and hollered, "Hey, your fire truck's on fire."

Rodriguez pulled to the curb, swearing, and everyone jumped off.

Sure enough, the bottom of the truck was shooting out flames and smoke. A quick call brought the pumper truck, and the fire was extinguished, but not before photographs were taken of the fire truck on fire and the frantic crew doing their best to put it out.

A disgusted Rodriguez went straight off to bed, and for the rest of the evening, the story of Bunny combined with the burning fire truck went the rounds, amid gales of laughter and lots of ribaldry aimed in John's direction as a result of Bunny's kiss.

Shannon was brushing Salvage later that night when John joined her.

The dog whined and wriggled away from Shannon, doing his best to balance on his one back leg and his bottom so he could put his front paws up on John's leg.

"Hey, fella, aren't you looking good? Gaining a little weight here, I see. Gonna have to watch the old gut." He patted the dog's sides and turned his attention to Shannon. "Your cousin called me—thanks for the referral. I spent yesterday afternoon with him looking at condos."

So they were going to discuss real estate. "Did you find anything you liked?"

"Unfortunately, no, but he's going to see what else is out there. By the way, I wondered if you'd seen this yet? They were just unloading the magazines when I dropped into the drugstore today." He handed one to her.

She glanced down at it and groaned. It was this month's copy of *California Woman*, and her photo was spread across the cover. She was in turnout gear, one knee on the cement, the other balancing her helmet. Behind her was Engine One.

"Oh, no, they went and put me on the cover." She felt her face flame with embarrassment. "I look like a total dork. And now I feel like one, too. The interviewer told me that this was going in as a rush story. I never dreamed they'd make it this prominent."

"You look beautiful and dignified." John's quiet voice made the words sound matter-of-fact. "And the interview is top-notch. The person who did it obviously really liked and admired you."

"You don't know the half of it," Shannon muttered, flipping the magazine open.

There were more photos of her accompanying the article. She scanned it quickly, and had to admit that Melissa Child had written a fairly balanced, albeit flattering, story. But Shannon could feel her insides shrivel at the thought of the number of people who would be reading the magazine.

"Maybe nobody buys this thing," she said hopefully.

"They had four bundles of it at the drugstore. I'd say it's pretty popular." John grinned at her. "Face it, O'Shea, you're a celebrity." He brushed the dog hair off his trousers. "I think I'll join the guys. They've rented *When We Were Kings*. You gonna join us?"

She shook her head. "It's a great movie—I've seen it twice before. I'm gonna make some fresh coffee and a sandwich."

She hoped he'd offer to keep her company, but he didn't.

"See you later, Shannon."

"Enjoy." She watched him walk off, admiring the way his back narrowed to a slim waist. He had the best ass. He had the best everything, damn his deceitful hide.

Salvage was also watching him walk away, and whined regretfully.

"You know him, don't you, boy? I'm not hallucinating here. He hauled us out of that warehouse, I'm positive he did." She went back to grooming the dog, wondering how best to put into action the plan she and Linda had concocted, the one that involved seducing the truth out of him. It was going to be tough if John stuck to this avoidance routine he seemed to be on.

That night was relatively quiet. There was a call-out at three in the morning to an apartment where a man was bleeding. It turned out the guy had hemorrhoids. Shannon was able to go straight back to sleep when they returned to the station.

The rest of the shift was routine until four the following afternoon. The crew was just about to sit down to an early dinner when the alarm sounded.

"Engine One, Rescue One. First alarm. Report of man trapped in a car with his penis chained to the steering column. Police request assistance. Gravel road off of Fisher Street."

Mystified, they looked at one another and waited until the dispatcher repeated the information.

"Must be some mistake, or somebody playing a joke," Rodriguez insisted in a dour tone as the truck left the station, and the rest of the crew agreed.

But when they arrived at the location and Shannon got out of the truck, she saw a battered old green car with a half-naked man in the driver's seat. The car's side doors were open, and two young police constables were standing by. The man was about forty, mostly bald and sporting a pronounced potbelly. He was wearing a black T-shirt, white athletic socks, navy runners and nothing else.

A large empty bottle of rum was on the seat beside him. He was sipping from a second, half-full bottle. What looked like a short bicycle cable was looped tightly around his penis and testicles and secured with a locking device. Another bike cable was strung through the first, its two ends threaded through the car's steering wheel and then fastened together.

Rodriguez took a long look and then shook his head in disgust. "What bloody next?"

"We've been trying to figure out how to get him out of this," one of the young policeman said, obviously trying to sound professional, but the scandalized expression on the shift sergeant's face did him in. A burst of laughter quickly became a cough.

"Those locks have a tubular key," he added when he'd regained control. "Waldo here says he threw it into the bush somewhere over there." The officer gestured toward the thick undergrowth at the side of the road. "We've looked for it, but we can't locate it. We called a locksmith. He says he could pick an ordinary lock, but these special tubular keys aren't doable."

Shannon heard him let out another snort of suppressed laughter.

"Craziest call I've ever been on," he said. "A guy hiking along this road came across him and called us. Waldo says he's been here since about three this afternoon. Had a fight with his girlfriend."

"Now, why would you go and do something like this, Waldo?" Shannon heard John say in a reasonable tone to the man in the car.

The guy turned his head and looked up at John with sagging basset hound eyes. His voice was slurred and he burped long and loud before he said, "I've hurt too many women with this thing. This's the only way I can think of to stop myself."

"Oh, yeah? Well, it seems just a little extreme to me, Waldo," John remarked.

"Extreme?" Rodriguez was building up a head of steam. "Extreme? Try totally bonkers. What kind of a dumb prick—" He caught himself and swore under his breath. "Okay, let's go find that so-and-so key so we can get back to supper."

Shannon joined the others, crawling around on her hands and knees in the underbrush in a futile search for the lost key. Every so often she got the giggles, and she could hear the others trying to muffle their laughter, as well.

Finally, after some discussion between Rodriguez and the policemen about how to proceed, John got a hacksaw out of the tool kit and started to work through the end of the cable attached to the wheel, amidst curses and squeals of pain from Waldo.

"Just hang in there, sir," John kept saying, which made it harder than ever for the firefighters and the policemen to stifle their laughter.

When Waldo was finally free of the steering wheel, they gently loaded the unfortunate victim, along with the cable still circling his swollen privates, into the back seat of the cruiser. The police had offered to drive him to Emergency at the hospital.

Shannon tried to stop laughing and couldn't. "How do you think the docs in the E.R. will handle this one?"

"Probably give him a sedative and elevate the injured member until the swelling goes down," Spike said. "Or they could call somebody who's into S and M, This sort of thing must happen now and again."

When the police car drove away, hilarity swept through the crew of firefighters, and it was all they could do to load the tools back into the truck. Rodriguez shook his head, swore under his breath and never cracked a smile, which added to the whoops of laughter that erupted all the way back to the station.

CHAPTER THIRTEEN

SHANNON FELT GIDDY by the time the shift ended.

"Who's for a beer at the B and G?" someone asked.

She felt half-drunk already just on laughter, and she could see that John did as well. Each time they caught one another's eye, they broke into guffaws.

"Beer sounds good to me," he agreed. "You're coming, aren't you, Shannon?"

"Absolutely. I just have to call and make sure Willow feeds the dogs."

Willow was home, and she assured Shannon she'd already fed Cleo and Pepsi, so Shannon changed into her street clothes and joined the group heading to the Courage Bay Bar and Grill.

Inside, everyone grouped around the bar, and the story of Penis Man went the rounds. Several of the policemen had already heard about it from their buddies, and soon everyone was retelling war stories.

Shannon sipped her beer, listening and laughing. She'd noticed that John claimed the bar stool beside hers. After a while, he leaned over so his lips were close to her ear, and under the noise he murmured, "I'm hungry—we missed dinner. How about joining me upstairs?"

"Sounds good." She slid off the stool and he followed her as she threaded her way through the crowd over to the stairs that led to the rooftop patio.

It was midweek and the place wasn't crowded. They were given a table with a spectacular view of the ocean. The three-piece orchestra was just setting up and the air was balmy and fresh, scented with the odors of the flowers in the pots all around the patio, and the breeze from the water.

As she sank down into her chair, Shannon smiled across at John. "How perfect is this?" She still felt giddy, and buoyant, and excited. Maybe she'd only imagined that John was keeping his distance?

"I special ordered the ambience just for us."

"You should have warned me. I'm not really dressed for the occasion." She had jeans on with a sleeveless blue blouse, and runners on her feet.

"You look just fine to me." The way he said it sent goose bumps down her arms.

The waiter came and John ordered a bottle of wine, and together they studied the menu. "I'm having filet mignon," he said. "Join me?"

"Sounds like a great idea." She sipped her wine and felt herself relax fully.

"I had no idea firefighting would be so much fun," he said.

She gave him a sharp look. "What, you mean it wasn't fun back in New York?"

"We had our moments, but not like today."

The band started to play something slow and romantic.

"Dance?" John held out a hand, and when she hesitated, he said, "Your foot's not still sore, is it?"

"Not the least bit. But I can't do this with runners on." She bent over and took off her shoes.

"Me, either, come to think of it." John took off his own runners.

When he stood up, she slid into his arms.

"No broken glass in sight," he assured her. "And I'll try not to step on your bare toes with my bare toes."

He didn't. He was a great dancer, smooth and easy to follow, definite about leading. Being in his arms reminded her of kissing him, of being held against his chest as he'd carried her that night on the beach. She let the music fill her, moving instinctively in whatever direction he did. He was incredibly graceful.

She looked up at him. "You took lessons in this. You're really smooth."

"My mother taught me when I was a little kid." There was a sad note in his voice.

"She must have been an exceptional teacher."

"She was. She…she did a lot of dancing when she was younger. She wanted to be an actress."

"That's so funny. Well, not laughably funny, but a coincidence, because *my* mother used to sing in pubs and restaurants all up and down the coast. That's what she was doing when she met my dad." Shannon rested her head against him, letting the music take her for a while. "What's your mother's name, John?"

"Naomi."

"That's lovely—Naomi Forester. And you said your dad was John."

"Yup. I was named after him." Had there been the slightest hesitation there, or was she imagining things? *Relax, O'Shea. Enjoy the moment.* She cuddled up to him, resting her head against his chest again, loving the way it felt to be folded in his arms, enjoying the feel of the smooth floor beneath her bare toes.

They slow danced to a Sinatra number, and then the tempo picked up. They looked at one another and sat down. Fast would spoil the mood, and their salads had arrived. Shannon was hungry, and they ate for a while without saying anything.

"That story in *California Woman…*" John began.

"Oh, no," Shannon groaned.

"You were pretty evasive about your love life."

"I should think so," she said forcefully. "Who needs their entire romantic history spelled out for everyone to drool over?"

"That juicy, huh?"

She knew he was teasing. "Scandalous. See, I had this massive crush on one of my teachers, Mr. Carlisle, in the third grade. But that didn't go anywhere, alas, because he only liked older women. Then my first kiss came along when I was eleven. One of Sean's friends caught me when we were playing tag, and planted one. That didn't turn out too well, either, because before I could really get into it, Sean caught us and socked the poor guy in the head, and my admirer never so much as looked at me again. And he must have warned his friends, because hardly anyone came near me most of my teens. When some brave soul actually did, my brothers intimidated the hell out of him."

"There must have been *someone* brave enough to take on the O'Shea brothers." John reached across and filled her wineglass. He wasn't joking anymore when he said, "You ever get serious about anybody, Shannon?"

Truth or dare? She decided on truth.

"Once, yeah. *Only* once. Back in college. Jared was a really great guy, a graduate student from France. He had the looks, the accent, the brains. I really fell for him—brought him home at spring break to meet my family. He was charming, they were charmed."

"So how did he break your heart?"

"Wow. I didn't think the scars were still visible. It was a long time ago."

"They're not. But he must have done something, or you'd still be with him, right? You don't strike me as a love 'em and leave 'em sort of lady."

"It was nothing, really. A little temporary amnesia, is all. He forgot to mention that he had a wife and two kids back in Perpignon."

"How did you find out?"

"Believe it or not, I found a photograph. In his dresser drawer. I was looking for something else—" condoms, she remembered clearly "—and there it was."

"I hope you set your brothers on him."

"I was too ashamed." Even now, the memory embarrassed her. "There were signs, I just didn't pay any attention." She finished her dinner and laid her fork down. "How about you, John? You ever fall in love?"

He nodded. "Like you, just once. She was a friend of my mother's, thirty something. I was sixteen. I asked her to marry me and she refused. Broke my heart."

Shannon studied him to see if he'd give some indication that he was joking around, but there was something about his expression that told her he wasn't. So she nodded and didn't ask if the woman was his first sexual partner. She could guess. "And since then?"

"Nope. Footloose, that's me. Barefoot, too, at the moment." The waiter appeared. "You want dessert, Shannon?"

She had a moment before, but the word *footloose* seemed to have some negative effect on her appetite. "No, thank you. I should be getting home."

"Got your car?"

He knew she didn't, the sneak. "Nope. I'll just put my shoes back on and jog. It's not far."

"It's dark. Better let me drive you." John was suddenly too busy scribbling his name on the credit card receipt to look at her, and she knew that this was the moment of decision. She could accept the ride home, invite him in, get naked and proceed with her devious, dirty plan for getting at the truth, or she could run like hell—literally—away from him.

Run, O'Shea. Any sane woman would. "Thanks, John, but I…"

Was she losing her nerve? Was she a woman or was she a wimp? What about those fine high-minded vows she'd made about finding out who this guy really was? *Screw your courage to the sticking post, Biceps.* Did she have decent underwear on?

"Yes, please, I'd like a ride." *Round and round and round*

we'll go and where we'll stop— Well, it wasn't the stopping she was contemplating. It was the going.

While he was tying his shoes, she went over the routine in her head. Let's see, she hadn't done this in a very long while. How did it go again?

You started by saying in a throwaway tone, "Would you like to come in, John? How about some coffee?" And music— mustn't forget music. Something slow and moody, with a heavy back beat. Seduction took time, and grace, and deliberation. Did condoms come with an expiration date? The ones she had were probably antiques.

Except John kissed her before he even started the car, and she had trouble getting her breath when he finally revved the engine. She could feel the tension building as they drove the short distance to her house.

She was breathing hard, and she needed to touch him, so she put her hand on his thigh—lightly, just in case he lost his place—but she probably wouldn't have had to. He put his hand on top of hers and moved it farther north. One thing about the guy, he was nothing if not single-minded. And he was wonderfully aroused.

In front of her house, he turned off the car and was kissing her again before the motor even died. They pretty much kissed all the way inside, which made walking hazardous. Shannon had to walk backward and he had to lean forward, which wasn't up to anybody's safety standards, especially around corners and on that cursed ramp at the back door, but God, it felt good.

With the tiny part of her brain that was still functioning, Shannon realized that Willow was probably home, because the dogs were in. As soon as she got the kitchen door open, they barked and pawed at her legs and competed with John's mouth for her attention. Shannon ignored them and went right on kissing.

She broke off long enough to lock the kitchen door and curtail Pepsi from trying to chew off the laces in John's shoes, but she figured since there was no question they were eventually heading for the bedroom, she might as well skip the whole coffee, music and conversation thing and proceed with the main event.

Now he was running his hands all over her. Walking backward and leading the way down the hallway to her room, she tripped on Cleo, but John caught her before she fell. He sort of lifted her up and over the damn dog so she was barely touching the floor all the way into her bedroom.

Pepsi managed to get in ahead of them. He jumped up on the bed and nipped Shannon's hand when she picked him up. She yelped, then grabbed him none too gently and dumped him in the hall.

"I'll deal with you later," she warned, and he bared his teeth and growled at her. Cleo was now in the bedroom, lying on her back in the middle of the rug, waving her legs in the air.

"Can you move her? She won't walk when she gets like this." Shannon knew she sounded breathless. She felt irritated and hot and sexy and impatient as hell. She was definitely going to send these animals back to Lisa. Later.

"Can do." John took Cleo's paws, but the dog was deadweight. Shannon grabbed Cleo's back legs, and with considerable effort and some grunting on both their parts, they towed her out the door. Both of them scurried through the bedroom door and Shannon slammed it shut and locked it for good measure.

John drew her close and kissed her again. She tugged his shirt up and out of his jeans and ran her hands up and down his back, trying to figure out where the condoms were. Probably in the bathroom. A lot of good they'd do there. Although they were likely full of moth holes, anyway.

"Mmm, you have such great...skin." Her hands were trembling.

"And you." He pulled her shirt over her head without unbuttoning it, and ran his hands from her shoulders to her waist and back up. "Nice bra."

He was being sarcastic. It was a white cotton sports model.

"Nice pants." She reached down and rubbed her hand across the front of them.

He drew in a breath through his teeth and backed her up against the door, kissing her, running his mouth down her neck and using his tongue where her bra covered her nipples.

"I really like that," she gasped, aware that the dogs had started howling and pawing at the door panel, but more aware that John was unfastening her jeans and sliding them down her legs and off.

The door was hard against her back, and it sounded as if the dogs were going to come right through the paneling.

"Bed?" she suggested, and he growled in agreement. She stripped off her bra in one easy upward motion.

"I'm crazy about you," he said, taking off his pants and shirt and boxer shorts, and breathing as if he'd been running. He extracted something from his pants pocket. "What the hell is the matter with those dogs?"

"Jealousy." She could see he was ferociously aroused. He was the most beautiful man she'd ever seen naked. Maybe even clothed. Her voice was shaky now as well as her hands, but she tried to stay rational and relate to what he'd said before the bit about the dogs.

"Crazy is good. I like crazy—" Her breath caught and her words stopped because his fingers had slid under her panties and inside, making her shudder and forget how words joined together.

He lowered them onto the bed and kissed her again, hot and frantic, and she nipped at his lip and wrapped her legs around his naked hips and moved, wanting speed instead of technique. But he resisted. He moved his mouth down to her right breast and suckled as if they had all the time in the world.

God, he was slow. She struggled with her panties, slithering out of them.

Cleo and Pepsi howled and scratched as John's lips moved from her mouth to her throat, to her ear, and then to a place on the side of her neck she hadn't even known was there.

The dogs whined and started a barking contest as he did enticing things to her nipples with his tongue. She closed her eyes and writhed against him because she was burning up. This put a whole new meaning to spontaneous combustion.

"Condoms," she groaned. "I don't have—"

"I do." He held up an economy-size pack.

"When did you…?"

"Drugstore."

She opened her mouth to ask him if he'd actually been planning this since yesterday, but he stopped her with a kiss that made her toenails curl.

And then, finally, he was inside her. Heat and a feeling of incredible fullness gave way to friction, to unbearable sensation, to long shuddering slides that drew her up and up until at last she broke, an instant before him.

It took her a moment to figure out that it was the dogs howling, and not her and John.

Still short of breath, she said, "So help me, I'm gonna take those two back where I found them. They're going to have the neighbors calling the cops on us."

"Or the fire department."

That struck both of them as funny. Unfortunately, their laughter made the dogs worse.

"I'll just go and put them in the kennel." She started to get up, but John stopped her with a kiss.

"Stay here. I'll go." He pulled his pants on and shoved his feet into his shoes.

Shannon heard him outside the door gentling the dogs, talking softly to them as he led them down the hall, into the kitchen and out the door. It was dark in the bedroom, and she lit a candle she kept beside the bed and then flopped back down on the pillows, stretching a body that felt boneless and satiated. How nice not to have to get up and do everything herself. How nice to feel this satisfied and peaceful and content.

He was a strong, tender lover. She had a hunch he had way more moves that could surprise her. They'd gone pretty fast. She heard the back door close, and she waited, half-asleep.

When at last he appeared in the bedroom doorway, he had a tray with two glasses of orange juice and a bag of her mother's oatmeal cookies that Shannon had stashed in the cupboard. He cleared a spot and set it all down on the bedside table, then pulled off his pants and hung them over the chair. His wallet fell out, and he set it on the dresser.

"Wow, a guy who makes fantastic love and feeds me as well," she sighed, devouring him with her eyes.

"You're a lucky woman, just keep that in mind," he said, handing her the juice. "Drink this. And have a cookie or two."

She propped herself up on one elbow and yawned. "I'm way too drowsy to want to spoil it with a sugar high."

"Eat. You're going to need all the energy you can muster before morning comes," he warned, putting his empty glass back on the tray and lying down beside her. He looped an arm across her and kissed one breast and then the other.

She came close to spilling the juice on the sheets.

He raised his head and smiled into her eyes. "Trust me on this, O'Shea."

CHAPTER FOURTEEN

BY DAWN the following morning, she believed him. The man had incredible stamina. And now he was asleep, and she would be, too—as soon as she used the bathroom.

Shannon eased out from under his arm and slid out of bed. The candle in its glass holder still burned, the soft light illuminating the huge male form sprawled across her bed. He snored a little and then turned his head to the side. She blew the candle out. The first gray light was already creeping through the blinds, throwing ribbed shadows across her sleeping giant.

Her heart ached with tenderness as she watched him. He'd sung to her when they weren't making love, sentimental Irish ballads she remembered her father singing when she was a little girl. John couldn't carry a tune, and that made the effort even more endearing.

It wouldn't take much to fall in love with you, Big Bad John, she told him silently. And when the image of the man in the silver popped into her head unbidden, she felt like groaning aloud. She didn't want to think about any of that right now.

She turned away from the bed and started toward the bathroom. She was passing the dresser when John's wallet caught her eye.

She couldn't. It was a huge breach of everything they'd just shared. Only sluts in B movies went through their lovers' wallets.

Did she dare? *Should* she dare?

She had an obligation, she assured herself, not just to herself but also to her fellow firefighters. Maybe to the entire community. It was her civic duty.

Come off it, O'Shea. Who are you fooling here? You need to know for you, plain and simple. You need to know if this man you're more than half in love with is lying to you. You have to know if he has something to hide. You have to know if you can trust him with your heart.

Checking again to make sure that he was asleep, she reached over and gingerly lifted the wallet. Then, feeling like a criminal, she scurried into the bathroom, eased the door shut and locked it. Then she switched on the light, blinking in the sudden glare. She couldn't meet her own eyes in the mirror.

Her heart was hammering and her fingers shook. She felt like the worst sort of traitor as she opened the soft leather wallet and started taking out the cards neatly tucked inside the slots.

Remember the order, O'Shea. A thief needs a good memory. Or was that a liar? Probably both. Crouching on her haunches, making mental notes, she laid the plastic cards one by one on the white bath mat on the floor. Here was the New York driver's license he'd shown her, the birth certificate, the fire department ID, his gold Visa card. Three hundred and sixty-two dollars—wow, he carried around a lot of cash. He even had a money clip. She'd never met a guy before who actually used a money clip.

When the wallet was empty, she examined it again, turned it upside down, gave it a shake. Nothing. Except—there was one area where it didn't seem to bend the way soft leather should. She opened it up again and probed the spot with her fingers. A loose flap lifted, and, heart pounding, she pulled out another driver's license.

This was also issued in New York. The photo on it was unmistakably John, but the name on the license said John Sebastian McManus.

McManus? Shannon stared at it, and every cell in her body

seemed to shrink. She sank down to the floor, breathing fast and shallow, as waves of desolation rolled over her. She'd been right. Oh, Lordy, she hadn't wanted to be right. She hadn't wanted real proof that he'd been lying to her. Now she knew for certain that every suspicion she'd had about him was accurate, and it made her feel as though she was dying inside.

John wasn't the person he was pretending to be. Who the hell was he, then? Who was this John Sebastian McManus person? What resemblance, apart from physical, did he have to the man sprawled across her bed—the man who'd said, "I'm crazy about you"?

But did it really matter? Everything else he'd said was a lie. Undoubtedly that was just another one. She felt like throwing herself flat on the cold tile and howling the way the dogs did.

It took a good ten minutes before she started thinking anywhere near straight, and then the only conclusion she could come to made her sick to her stomach. There could only be one good reason for the detailed lies he'd told, the elaborate cover-up he'd perpetrated.

Much as she hated to countenance the idea, John had to be the arsonist.

She ought to feel vindicated. She ought to feel pleased that she was right.

Instead, she felt sick to the very depths of her soul. Her body still ached in all sorts of places from his lovemaking. She could still taste him, smell him on her skin. She knew every inch of his body, as he knew hers. She felt shattered and heartsick as she carefully slid each card, each bit of his phony cover, back in his wallet.

The only thing she kept back was the driver's license she'd found in the secret compartment. Several times, she'd seen John talking to their captain, Joe Ripani. They'd looked to be deep in some serious discussion, which at the time she'd put down to the transfer of pension benefits or the political situation. Now she was rethinking those conversations. She'd always liked Ripani, respected him—but what if he and John were working together? What if both of them were involved in this mess? She couldn't take that chance; the stakes were too high. She came to the conclusion that she had to go over Ripani's head on this one.

There was no choice. She'd have to take the license to the battalion chief, Victor Odom. The very thought of confiding anything to Odom made every hackle rise. In her opinion, the man was a sexist opportunist with wandering hands. But he was also the top of the heap as far as line of command was concerned. There didn't seem to be anything else to do.

At last, she got stiffly to her feet. One thing for sure, she couldn't go back and climb into bed beside John. And it was still way too early to call Odom's house and ask him to meet with her. But she couldn't spend the next two hours locked in the bathroom, either.

Finally she slid the incriminating license underneath a basket of fancy soaps Linda had given her, and splashed her face with water. She'd have to creep back into the bedroom to get her jogging clothes. She'd have to pray that John didn't wake up, because she had to return the wallet to the top of the dresser. Then she'd come back in here, put the license in her pocket and go for a run. She needed the release of physical exercise more than she ever had before in her life.

In another hour, she'd contact Odom and get him to meet her somewhere. *Somewhere very public.* The thought of being alone in a deserted spot with the man made her flesh crawl.

Her heart was hammering against her ribs as she crept along the hallway and back into the bedroom. She stood just inside the door, holding her breath, studying the man in her bed, trying to determine if he was really asleep. An insane part of her longed to rip the duvet back, grab his shoulders, jerk him out of sleep and demand an explanation.

Yeah, O'Shea, go totally nutso. That's a really smart move.

He was snoring a little. She set the wallet back as close to where it had been as she could determine, and inch by inch, opened a dresser drawer. She grabbed the first running shorts that came to hand, and pulled out a sports bra and singlet as well. Thank heaven she kept all her sports gear in one messy drawer.

Holding the clothes, she backed an inch at a time toward the door, watching the bed for signs of movement. There were none. A board squeaked when she stepped on it, and she froze.

John mumbled, turned his head to the other side and went right on sleeping. She breathed again and eased her way into the hall. After a quick detour into the bathroom to dress and tuck the incriminating license into the zippered pocket in her shorts, she crept along the hall to the kitchen—and came perilously close to screaming at the sight of her uncle Donald, shoes in hand, also sneaking out the door.

He was as surprised as she was. His blue eyes went huge, and his face reddened with embarrassment. He rubbed a hand across his bald head and opened his mouth to say something, but Shannon put a finger to her lips and violently shook her head. She opened the door as silently as she could, retrieved her runners from the mat by the door, and together they tiptoed down the ramp like thugs escaping a building they'd just burglarized.

The dogs saw them, of course, and started barking, loud enough to wake the neighborhood.

Shannon groaned.

"I'll get them for you," Donald offered, and started for the pen. Of course he thought that Shannon would take them with her, but she grabbed a handful of his rumpled cotton shirt, and when he turned around, she shook her head again. Violently.

"But what…?" Uncle Donald gave her a puzzled, questioning look as she shushed him.

"I'm going for a run by myself," she whispered to him, pulling on her runners and tying them. "Wait until I'm gone and then *you* take the dogs around the block. And don't tell John you saw me."

"But honey, why…?"

"Don't ask. Just do it. We'll talk later." Her insides were shaking. She drew in a shuddering breath and forced her legs to move. After half a block of fast walking, she broke into a jog.

Just as she'd known it would, running calmed her. She went a couple of blocks and then headed east toward the mountains, away from the city. She needed space and air, needed the healing silence of the deep woods. Breathing deeply, forcing everything but the rhythm of her body out of her mind, she ran away.

JOHN HAD COME AWAKE as soon as she moved out from under his arm. Groggy, he opened his eyes a little, and was about to lift his head and say something to her when he saw her stop beside the dresser. He feigned sleep, sensing that she was watching him closely. And then, through slitted eyelids, he saw her reach out a hand and take his wallet before she slipped out the door.

He felt disgusted with himself. He'd been uncharacteristically slack, and in his business that was unforgivable. *And dangerous.*

But he also felt reluctant admiration for Shannon. Obviously, she'd outsmarted him, using the oldest female trick in the book to do it. But most of all, he felt incredible disappointment and an overwhelming sense of loss that took him by surprise. He hadn't realized how much he'd wanted her to trust him.

He lay unmoving, every muscle tensed, waiting.

It took a very long time before she crept back into the room, and he knew by the rapid way she was breathing and the stiffness of her posture that she'd found the damn license. Why hadn't he hidden it somewhere else? He wasn't usually this careless.

Again, he feigned sleep, and again, she stood watching him for a very long time. He must have done a good job of appearing comatose, because she silently replaced the wallet, inched open the dresser, pulled out handfuls of clothing.

Even now, he noted the elegant shape of her as she stood there naked. Her lovely breasts were high, firm and full, rising and falling with her quickened breath. Beautiful arms and strong shoulders tapered to a narrow waist, swelling just slightly into trim hips, long lovely legs.

She had powerful muscles in her thighs. He knew because those legs had been locked around his waist only a short time before. They'd made love with intensity and abandon, with laughter and teasing, and yes, a depth of tenderness he'd never experienced before.

And now she was on to him. It was irrational as hell, wanting her to believe in him, to give him the benefit of the doubt—even though he'd been lying to her. He wanted her trust. He wanted her to have faith in him, to realize he was only doing what he had to do.

And how idiotic was that? But his feelings for Shannon weren't connected to his brain; he'd been learning that ever since he'd met her. Neither were they entirely hooked to his penis, although sex was definitely a factor. So what did that leave?

Your heart, Johnny boy?

And your ass in a sling if she takes that license to the wrong person. Joe Ripani would be a stroke of luck. But if it's Odom...

He waited until he heard the front door open and then gently close.

In one lithe movement, he was on his feet, grabbing for jeans and shirt, socks and shoes. From here on in, it was damage control all the way. He had to catch her before she jeopardized the entire operation.

He tore down the hallway, out the kitchen door and around the corner of the house—and almost tripped on the dogs and Donald O'Shea, who seemed to be trying to get Cleo up off her back, while simultaneously warding off a snarling attack on his pant legs from Pepsi.

"Which way did she go?" John had no time for polite small

talk. She was in excellent shape. He'd be damn lucky to overtake her, even with just a five-minute head start.

"I guess if she wanted you to know, she'd have told you, right?" Donald gave him the hairy eyeball.

Every moment wasted would make it that much harder to catch her in time. What the hell could he say to change her uncle's mind? And what had Shannon already told him? It couldn't have been much; there hadn't been time.

"Look, Donald, I'm in love with your niece, and I need to tell her so." It was the first thing that popped into John's head, and amazingly enough, it worked.

Donald looked him straight in the eye for one long, tense moment and then pointed down the street. "There's an alley to your right. Follow it to the end. It leads to a path up the mountain."

John didn't wait to thank him. He felt guilty about lying to Donald, but at this stage, one more whopper didn't really seem to matter much.

SHANNON JOGGED SLOWLY until her muscles warmed up. She had to struggle with the constant urge to cry. Her chest hurt in the region of her heart, and it wasn't from running. This was a different sensation, a feeling of loss and betrayal and of terrible waste for what might have been.

For the first time, she admitted to herself that she had fallen in love with John Forester—except, she reminded herself harshly, that wasn't his name.

His name was John Sebastian McManus, and she had no idea whatsoever who he really was. She only knew how he kissed, and that he seemed to know all the spots on her body that reacted to his lips, to his touch. How could she have shared that kind of intimacy with a man who was a total phony? She'd always trusted her instincts, but this time they, too, had betrayed her.

As the incline became more pronounced, a sob that she

couldn't hold back rose in her throat, and energy seemed to drain out of her body. Had she made a mistake, running away? Maybe she should have stayed and confronted him.

She stopped and turned, looking back the way she'd come. Courage Bay lay below her, spread out along the shore like a toy village. It was still gray out over the ocean, and that grayness seemed to permeate her thoughts. She felt a desperate and unreasonable longing for the sun. Maybe daylight would help her think straight. She caught a glimpse of blue, moving down below her, and she watched until she saw it again. Another jogger was following the winding path she'd taken, and a bolt of fear shot through her.

Although she hadn't seen his face, she knew it was John.

He was still a long ways behind, but she had no illusions about his stamina or his physical condition. After last night, she was intimately familiar with every muscle on his body. He was after her, and unless she moved fast, he'd soon catch up.

And then what? What would he do?

He wasn't out for a casual morning jog—he wasn't dressed for it. He had to be wearing the same clothing he'd worn last night—jeans, blue golf shirt. Trainers. He did have trainers. He'd taken them off to dance, just as she had.

For a moment, she had an overwhelming desire to stand right there, wait until he caught up, and confront him. She ached to vent her anger and outrage at his deceit.

Yeah, and maybe that isn't the smartest idea in the world. He's awfully big, O'Shea, and he knows you took that license. Why else would he be coming after you?

She turned and fled.

He had longer legs, but she'd run this mountain route all her life. She was lighter; she could take him on distance. And distance was exactly what she planned to put between them.

CHAPTER FIFTEEN

JOHN'S CHEST WAS BURNING and his throat was parched. His breath came in short, heaving gasps, and still he pushed himself to go faster up the steep, winding path.

He'd assumed he could overtake her without much effort; after all, he was half a foot taller and physically as fit as he'd ever been—he'd had to train hard to impersonate a fireman. But although he was closing the gap, he was beginning to think it was touch and go. She was still running full out, and the path was steeper here. He was getting winded.

Face it, Johnny boy, you're getting trounced by a woman.

He was also getting angrier with each labored step, although he had no breath left for curses. Somehow this had become a contest, an arm wrestle, and he was determined that she was not going to get the better of him. He used the anger as fuel and forced his legs to pump harder. The gap between them shortened, and shortened again.

His lungs were on fire. He couldn't get the oxygen he needed, and he could feel his muscles starting to burn, to give out. Gasping, he used every ounce of willpower he could muster and increased his speed one last time.

He burst around a corner, and there she was, scant yards ahead. He lunged, reached out an arm, grasped a handful of her singlet, tripped, staggered.

She screamed, but just when he thought they'd both tumble to the hard-packed earth, she caught herself, turned and slugged him square on the jaw. Hard.

The shock was severe, but so was the blow. She had one mean upper cut, and he was already off balance. He grunted, bit down hard on his tongue, and the pain made him lose his grip on her shirt. He managed to grab one of her forearms, and she pivoted and tried to knee him in the groin. She missed her target by mere inches, and now he was furious.

"*Stop*. Damn it, Shannon—" His mouth was full of blood, but that didn't affect his volume any. He was hollering and she was punching again, so he grabbed her other arm and shoved her backward as hard as he could. His weight over-balanced both of them, and this time they went down together. She landed on the hard earth, flat on her back with him on top of her, and he heard the air whoosh out of her lungs.

Her blue eyes were wild and frantic and there was naked fear in them. It dawned on him that she actually thought he was going to deliberately hurt her. That made him angrier than ever, and he straddled her, pinioning her with his thighs, holding her arms flat at her sides as he struggled to speak. It wasn't easy to hold her. She was incredibly strong. She was also winded, desperately trying to draw air into her lungs.

"You—bloody—fool," he finally gasped out.

She struggled in his grasp, and it was all he could do to hold on, even though she was still making rasping noises in her throat.

"Listen—to—me. *Stop this*—and just—listen." Drops of sweat were running down his cheeks and dripping off his chin, landing on her face and neck. He had the insane urge to lean down and lick them off, but the coppery taste of blood still filled his mouth. Besides that, she'd probably bite him if he got close enough.

She was trembling, and so was he. And in spite of the lack of oxygen, she was still fighting. Jesus, the woman was a warrior.

He tried again. "Will—you—stop? And let—me—explain?"

This time he got through to her. She quieted, but he didn't

dare release her. Not yet, not until he was certain she wasn't going to sock him again. Or hit him smack in the balls.

"You found the license, right?"

She jerked her chin up and down, and now there was contempt in her blue eyes. "John—Sebastian—McManus," she spat at him as she got her breath back.

"Right. FBI." He watched her expression, and he knew right away that she didn't believe him. Well, why the hell should she? He had to admit he hadn't really given her much reason to trust him.

"Liar. Let—me—go."

"If you promise to bloody well sit still and listen, okay. Otherwise, I'm hanging on. And I also want your word that what I tell you stays between you and me."

Her eyes were still brimming with sparks and her expression was mutinous, but after a long moment, she nodded. He guessed that it had dawned on her that she wasn't in much of a position to negotiate.

"Say it." He didn't trust her one bit. That knee had come way too close to its target, and he could feel his jaw swelling. It was a wonder he hadn't lost a tooth.

"Okay." She threw the word at him like a weapon. "Okay, I'll listen. Okay, I won't breathe a word of your lies to anyone else. Now…*take your hands off me."*

Very gradually, with extreme caution, he did. She scrambled up to a sitting position, wincing once or twice as she scuttled a good three feet away from him. He started to worry that maybe he'd broken her ribs, they'd gone down so hard, but he saw her draw one deep, shuddering breath and then another, so he figured she was okay in that regard.

He sat back, resting his elbows on his bent knees. He was soaked with sweat, the knees of his pants were filthy and his hands were stinging about as much as his mouth was.

She rubbed her arms and he could see scrape marks there. She had scratches on her legs. Neither of them had come off unscathed. He turned his head away and spat out blood, feeling with his tongue to make sure his teeth really were intact.

"Show me your identification, if you're FBI."

He gave his head a frustrated shake. Trust her. "I don't have it with me, for God's sake. I'm undercover. I shouldn't have had that damn license in my wallet."

She was scowling at him. "You were in that warehouse fire. You were the man in the silver, weren't you?"

"Yeah." He nodded and sighed, longing for a glass of water. "Yeah, I was."

Anger flared in her eyes. "So you lied when I asked you, and then you went right on lying to me over and over. *Why?* How could you do a thing like that, be so dishonest? Unless you're the one who started that fire. Unless you're the arsonist."

That surprised him and then made him laugh. "C'mon, Shannon, you can't really believe that."

But he could see from her expression that she actually wasn't sure. For God's sake, she really thought he was a criminal? Now, *that* hurt his feelings.

"I'm FBI," he repeated. "And as soon as I get a chance, I'll prove it to you. I have documents back at the motel. I'm here in Courage Bay on a major case, Shannon."

How much could he tell her? How much *should* he tell her? Caution and training and the need for secrecy warred with his desire to be totally honest with her. *What the hell.* Desire won.

"There's a major Freon smuggling operation based here in Courage Bay," he began. "The perps were storing the stuff at that warehouse. They'd moved it out just before the first fire, but we're not sure yet if the fire had anything to do with the Freon."

"Who's we?"

"Joe Ripani and me. Joe's the only one who knows who I really am and why I'm here. And now you do. Joe told me that Sam Prophet recovered parts of the triggering device used for that first fire, and he hasn't seen anything like it before. He thinks a cell phone wired to explosives had been jammed behind a supporting beam. When the number was dialed, the connection set off the explosives. It's damn clever, whoever did it."

And he'd had to get his boss to call off the investigation the police were conducting because it jeopardized his own investigation.

She was listening hard, but he couldn't tell what she was thinking. After a minute, she shook her head and his heart sank. She still didn't believe him.

"I don't get it. If they'd moved the Freon out like you said, why blow up the warehouse?"

"I don't know for sure." That was only one of the things that puzzled him. "Maybe to destroy evidence because they'd been careless? In fact, I know they'd left some things behind. They must have been in a hurry to get the stuff out of there. They used heavy straps to secure the metal canisters the Freon is stored in, and that's what I was doing in the warehouse. I needed to recover those straps as evidence."

"That's when you found me and Salvage."

He nodded. "I heard you call out. It was sheer coincidence that I had the silver. The company that makes the suits for the Aeronautics and Space Association wanted a new version tested for use by commercial firemen. My boss at the Bureau is a friend of the guy who runs that department, and he asked if I'd try one out if I got a chance. The warehouse fire was a good opportunity."

"So you were already in Courage Bay when that fire happened. The airline ticket you showed me was a fake."

"Yeah, it was. I'd flown in on a private jet the day before the fire. In order to maintain my cover, I couldn't be seen in that silver or at the warehouse. Joe knew I was there. He got me out and away without anybody knowing, except for you. And Salvage." John shook his head and gave a rueful smile. "Damn dog did his best to bust me."

"I knew all along that Salvage recognized you. And what about the second fire? Did it start with that same cell-phone thing?"

John frowned and shook his head. "The weird thing about that fire is that Sam figures it was started with a fuse and liquid accelerant. And the question is, why would the perp change his pattern? For that matter, why torch the warehouse a second time?"

"Yeah, and another question is, why couldn't you have told me all this in the beginning? Why make me feel like an idiot, blabbing to everybody about a guy in a silver that nobody else had seen? You were lying right, left and center about everything. You made a fool of me."

"Shannon, cut me some slack here. I didn't know you. For all I knew, you could have been in on the operation. In fact, when I saw you in that warehouse, I figured at first you might have been the one who set the fire. You were at the exact spot where I found the straps."

Now she looked outraged. "Of all the stupid suppositions, that takes the prize. I was only trying to get Salvage out of there alive."

"I know that now. I know that you wouldn't be involved in anything like this Freon thing. Or anything else the slightest bit illegal or—or immoral—or wrong."

He swiped at the sweat running into his eyes. He really wasn't doing a good job of this at all. He tried to figure out how to phrase what he wanted to say and couldn't, so he blurted, "I—I guess I'm trying to say that I trust you now, that I...well, I guess I sort of...I care about you, Shannon." It was tough to verbalize his feelings, and he soon realized he'd botched that along with everything else.

She narrowed her eyes at him and her voice dripped with sarcasm. "You sort of *care* about me? Gee, that's so reassuring, John. What's that supposed to mean, exactly? Let's see now..." She used her fingers to tick the points off. "You care about Salvage. You care about little kids. You care about old women, and your job, and your car, and no doubt your damn motorcycle, and—and football. All guys care about football. And then there's—"

There was only one sure way to shut her up. He lunged to his feet, grabbed her hands and dragged her up by sheer force when she resisted.

"You don't make anything easy, do you?"

Her blue eyes were startled and he could feel the stiffness in her body as he wrapped his arms around her.

"What do you think you're—"

He bent his head and kissed the words away, trying to show her that the way he cared for her had nothing whatsoever to do with those other types of caring. He wasn't sure himself exactly how his feelings for her were different, but they were. So he went on kissing her until her body went soft and pliant in his arms, and he only winced a little when she got very involved in the kissing and it affected his jaw and his cut tongue.

"You taste funny," she said after a while, pulling away a little and scowling up at him.

"Blood. You busted my chops, remember?" He kissed her again, with less urgency and more attention to his wounds this time. *Due care and attention.*

"Blood? Yuck." She pulled away and made a face.

"You have a mean right hook, lady." He rubbed a hand gingerly over his jaw and was reminded that he hadn't shaved yet. A powerful odor from his underarms made him add showering to the list. And he hadn't so much as swallowed a single damn glass of water, never mind breakfast.

He was probably on the verge of dehydration. After all the energy he'd expended during the night, plus sprinting at top speed halfway up this steep mountain, he was pretty much running on empty. In fact, he didn't think there were even fumes left.

He could hear the plaintive tone in his voice, and he didn't care. "Can we go back to your place and clean up a little? Please? Then I'll take you out for breakfast and we can discuss this some more."

"I've got eggs and bread and coffee. We can eat at my house. Maybe Uncle Donald has already made breakfast, the old sneak. Although I hope not, because I've still got a million questions I need to ask you."

DONALD AND WILLOW WEREN'T there, but the questions had to wait, because when they walked in the front door, the phone was ringing.

Shannon answered it, and it took a moment for her to recognize her mother's trembling voice.

"We're at the hospital," Mary said, and Shannon's hand tightened on the handset.

"It's Linda. She's losing the baby—can you come, dear? Something's gone very wrong."

"I'll be right there." She hung up and turned to John. "That was Mom. Linda's miscarrying. I need to get over there now—" She glanced down at herself. "Oh, God, look at me. I can't go like this.'

"Go have a quick shower. I'll get my stuff from your room and I'll drop you there."

In ten minutes, she was in the car, and in another six and a half, during which she gained new respect for John's driving talents, he was pulling up in front of the hospital.

CHAPTER SIXTEEN

JOHN BRAKED THE CAR and turned toward her.

"Do you want me to come in with you?"

She looked at him. He was bruised and dirty and sweaty. His pants were torn at the knee, his shirt had seen better days and there was blood on his chin. She gave him a shaky smile and shook her head.

"Thanks, but no. You need a shower and some food. Mom's here, and my dad, and my brothers. I appreciate the offer, though." She leaned across and gave him a quick, hard kiss. "Maybe just say a little prayer for Linda, okay? She and Sean were so excited about this baby."

He nodded. "Do you have a cell phone on you?"

It was in her handbag. She recited the number and he repeated it. Then she got out and raced into the hospital, where she was directed to the surgical floor. Her mother and father were there, in the waiting area. Caleb's arm was around Mary, holding her close to his side.

Shannon hurried over to them. "What's going on?"

"Oh, Shannon, I'm so glad you're here." She could hear the tension in her mother's voice, and when she touched her arm, could feel her trembling.

"Sean was on shift at the fire hall. Linda called him and she was hysterical. She was in terrible pain, on the verge of passing out. The doctor believes she had an undiagnosed ectopic pregnancy, and the fallopian tube may have burst."

"Oh, no." Shannon knew how dangerous that was. A ruptured tube was life threatening.

"Sean got the call transferred to a cell phone," Mary continued. "He kept her talking, and he and the rescue unit got there before the ambulance." She drew in a sobbing breath. "She's in surgery. Sean's pacing the hallway, waiting to hear." Mary looked at Shannon, her hazel eyes brimming with tears. "It's very serious, isn't it?"

Shannon nodded. She couldn't think of anything comforting to say. She recalled vividly the rescue training they'd had dealing with ectopic pregnancy and the severe hemorrhaging that could result. She'd been relieved to hear that such pregnancies were rare, and she remembered hoping she'd never in her life have to encounter such a situation.

And now her brother had had to face it, with his own wife. She felt compassion for Sean, but she also felt pride in his strength and knowledge.

Wordlessly, she put her arms around her mother and then her father. Suddenly they both looked older, and she could feel them trembling in her embrace.

"All we can do is wait," Caleb said.

"And pray," added Mary.

Shannon knew they were all three doing that already. They sat in a row on the hard plastic chairs with their hands joined, and after a long while Patrick came racing in.

Shannon told him what had happened.

"How serious is it?" Patrick asked.

She hesitated, but there was no point in soft-pedaling. "Very serious."

Patrick's face blanched. "Do they know yet…?"

She shook her head, and he sat down beside Caleb, looping an arm around his father's shoulders.

The hands on the clock moved through a full, slow hour before Sean finally walked in. He wore his fireman's blue uniform. His face was greenish-white and somber.

Shannon's heart gave a sickening lurch. They all got to their feet, surrounding him, afraid to ask.

"Linda's still in surgery," he said in a choked voice. "She's—" His jaw was clenched hard as he struggled to hold back tears. He stopped and wiped a hand across his face. What he wasn't saying hung like a sword over them.

"The doctor says she'll live, but they aren't sure yet if they'll have to do a hysterectomy." Sean swallowed, and it was obvious he could barely speak. "She wanted this baby so much. And now, if—"

"Don't even think it," Shannon said. She and her mother wrapped their arms around Sean in turn, and Caleb awkwardly patted his back. When the women released him, Patrick gave his brother a hard hug.

No one said anything. Shannon could feel fear like a dark presence surrounding them in the neon-lit room, and she knew they were all praying silently in the endless interval before a doctor walked in.

He'd obviously just come from the operating room. A mask hung from his jaw and his green scrubs were spotted with blood.

Linda's blood. Shannon felt sick, and utterly terrified.

"Linda's going to be fine, Sean—we didn't have to perform a hysterectomy," the doctor said immediately. "We were able to remove the damaged portion of the fallopian tube and reconnect it. We repaired the uterus, so future pregnancies shouldn't present any problem. Linda won't be waking up for another hour or so, but you can sit with her, Sean. She's in Recovery. Come with me—I'll take you there."

Mary started to cry, and Caleb wrapped an arm around her. "We'll go home now, son," he said to Sean. "We'll be back a little later, when Linda's able to have company."

When they were the only ones left, Patrick turned to Shannon. "I haven't had any breakfast. How about if we find the coffee shop?"

They took the elevator back to the lobby and headed for the hospital cafeteria.

Neither of them said anything until they'd filled their trays and sat down at a table in a secluded corner.

Patrick lifted his sandwich and then set it down again. "God, that was scary. Sean came close to losing her, didn't he?"

Shannon found her appetite had disappeared, even though she hadn't eaten yet today. Her eyes filled with tears and her voice quavered. "Yeah. Very close."

"I never really thought about the risks of pregnancy when Janie and I had our kids. I think I'm glad I didn't."

"Me, too," she said. "If you had, you might have deprived me of my beautiful niece and nephew."

"No way. I can't imagine my life without them." Patrick took a bite of his chicken sandwich. "You ever talk to your boss about your concerns with Forester? Because now that I've met him, Shannon, I have to say I agree with you. On the surface he comes across as a straight up guy, but there's something not quite right about him, although I can't put my finger on exactly what it is. So I've decided to do what you asked…pull some strings and do some checking on him. I have a friend who runs a private detective agency in New York. He owes me a favor."

Shannon had started eating her sandwich, as well, and now she almost choked. She swallowed hard and reached for her water.

"*No.* Patrick. Don't do that. Please, that's not a good idea anymore."

"What d'ya mean?" He frowned at her. "Last time we talked about him, you practically begged me to find out more about him. And now, when I figure you actually have a point, you don't want me to? What's going on, Shannon? What's changed?"

"Nothing. Everything." Damnation, there was no way she could confide in Patrick. She trusted her brother implicitly, but she'd promised she'd keep John's secret, and she couldn't break that promise. "Listen, Patrick, you have to just trust me on this. Don't go digging. Leave things the way they are. Take my word for it—John's absolutely a good guy. Promise me you won't contact your friend."

Patrick studied her with narrowed eyes. "I get it. You've gone and fallen for him, haven't you, kid?"

"*No.*" She knew right away the denial had been way too vehement. "Well, maybe. A little. Nothing terminal. I need, umm, time," she stammered. "On my own with him. And I don't want you interfering, okay? I know now that I was way off base asking you in the first place."

Her brother gave her a dubious look. "Now, why doesn't that comfort me? My kid sister falls ass over teakettle for some guy I don't trust, and wants me to promise I won't try and find out anything about him? Shannon, that doesn't make sense. Not when you had doubts yourself just the other day."

"But I don't now, honest. Let me handle this my own way, Patrick. Please?"

He was facing the doorway, and now he looked over her shoulder, his blue eyes suddenly turning cool. "Well, it looks like your own way is on his way over."

Shannon twisted around. Sure enough, John was weaving his way through the crowded tables. He stopped behind Shannon and put a hand on her shoulder.

"Patrick," he said with a friendly nod.

"Hi, John," she said, smiling up at him. "Sit down."

He did, and Shannon saw that he'd showered and changed into fresh jeans and a white sweatshirt. There was a slight swelling on his jaw where she'd punched him, and she longed to lean over and press her lips to that place, but she could imagine what reaction Patrick would have to that.

Her protective big brother would be on the phone to his private investigator friend within the hour, asking for a full report on John by tomorrow morning. The guy probably wouldn't be able to find anything—after the search she and Linda had done, Shannon figured the FBI went to great pains to protect their operatives—but John didn't need that kind of interference. She hadn't had a chance yet to really think about all that he'd told her, but she did know she believed him. Believed *in* him.

John had taken the chair between her and Patrick. "I tried your cell number, Shannon. It wasn't responding. Is Linda okay?"

"I saw a notice that cell phones aren't allowed in hospitals, so I had to turn it off. Linda had a very bad time—scared us all half to death. But she'll be okay."

"I'm glad." John glanced at Patrick and got to his feet. "In that case, I should be going. There's a meeting I'm supposed to attend."

Shannon got up, too. "I'll walk you to your car." That was well done, and on an almost empty stomach. She cast a longing look at her half-eaten sandwich and reached for John's hand, aware of a decided, stiff-lipped chill emanating from Patrick.

Better rescue her cowboy and get the hell out of Dodge before the sheriff tied him up and used hot irons to extract the truth.

ONE THING FOR CERTAIN, Patrick wasn't his new best friend, John decided. In fact, he had the distinct notion that Shannon's big brother had a real urge to pop him one.

"See you," John said in his direction.

Patrick gave a curt nod and returned to his sandwich.

"Linda had an ectopic pregnancy—you ever heard of that?" Shannon was saying as she hurried him away.

"Nope. I've never been around pregnant women much." *Much* was a gross overstatement. Apart from seeing swollen ladies on the street, he had no knowledge whatsoever of pregnancy or its complications. He listened closely while she explained the finer points of the condition.

Jesus. The details made him feel queasy and light-headed.

He felt incredible admiration for Sean. Faced with a similar emergency, John wondered what he would have done.

It didn't take a moment's thought to figure it out, though. Through ignorance, he'd probably have let the woman die. John shuddered as an icy chill shot up his spine. There was so much he didn't know.

"Lucky your brother knew what to do."

"Yeah, well, they touch on situations like that one when you take advanced first aid. If you'd actually taken fireman's training instead of just pretending, you'd know all that stuff."

They'd reached the lobby. Shannon seemed to know all the staff, and now one of the nurses at the admitting desk waved and called to her.

"Hey, Shannon, I heard about your sister-in-law. I'm so sorry about the pregnancy. But I'm glad she's gonna be okay."

"Thanks, Miranda. And your sister just had a baby. Congratulations."

Miranda beamed. "Thanks, she had a girl, I'm so happy to be an auntie." Her expression changed, and she said, "Sorry, Shannon. Linda just lost her baby, and here I am gloating about being an aunt."

"Don't feel that way, not for a moment. Babies are a miracle. Sean and Linda will try again. How much did your niece weigh?"

"Almost twelve pounds. She's a bruiser. Hey, she's in the nursery at the moment, getting some drops in her eyes. You wanna come up and see her?"

"Can we, Miranda?"

John could hear the naked eagerness in Shannon's voice.

"Sure, I can sneak you in. Everybody knows who you are."

"I'll just head out to the car—" John began, but Shannon had hold of his hand. She tugged him along to the elevator.

"Just come in here," Miranda said when they got off. She led the way into a small room, empty except for a hospital bed and a straight-backed chair. She left, and in another moment came in carrying a baby wrapped in a yellow blanket. She placed her carefully in Shannon's arms.

"I'll be back in a minute. I'll just tell the staff what's going on. It's against the rules, but I need to show her off." She hurried out.

"Oh, John, just look at her. Oh, Lordy, isn't she precious? Look at her little hands, these tiny fingernails. And her eyelashes…she's got the longest eyelashes. Oh, she's adorable."

John kept his distance while he peered at the baby. It was incredibly tiny, and *adorable* wasn't the precise word he'd have used to describe it. The kid had a red, scrunched-up face, and her eyes were closed so tight they looked glued shut. She had a pink toque on her head, which seemed a little too small because scraps of wild red hair stuck out from under the edges. John thought she seemed pissed off at the world and exceedingly strange looking, but he wasn't about to say so. He figured a comment like that could earn him worse than a pop in the jaw, judging from the awed expression on Shannon's face.

Besides, he didn't exactly have personal experience with this, so he had nothing to compare the kid with. Maybe they all looked this way at first. How the hell would he know?

He did know for sure that being this close to something that small and new made him feel uncomfortable and out of control. It was the same feeling he'd had the Sunday he'd met all of Shannon's relatives, as if he'd been parachuted into a foreign place where he didn't know the language or the customs.

He'd lived his life in a certain way, a way that was familiar to him, where the rules were clear-cut. There was him and there was Naomi. There was no guesswork about who had to make decisions or take charge; he'd been doing all of it since he was nine. There were no prayers over Sunday dinner, because there was no Sunday dinner. The idea of Naomi going misty-eyed over a baby was laughable.

These O'Sheas were a different tribe. The men knew how

to save their women's lives. An emergency like the one today brought each and every family member racing to the hospital, even when there was nothing concrete they could accomplish.

He looked at Shannon's face and a shiver wound its way down his back.

She was perched on the edge of the bed now, cradling the baby against her chest. There was a rapt, intent look on her face as she stared down at the infant, an expression of yearning and tenderness and absolute enchantment, and he felt shut out, excluded.

He had an overwhelming urge to drag her away from here, to blatantly use the powerful sexuality between them to distract her, to make her forget this flannel-wrapped, minute bundle.

All morning, ever since he'd left her, he'd been trying to figure out how this thing between them would play out, where the end would be. His time in Courage Bay was determined by how long it would take to complete the investigation and—he hoped—take the perps into custody. Then he'd be heading back to New York, back to his own life.

In his deepest soul, John considered himself a loner. In New York he was anonymous. Sure, there were restaurants he frequented where the waiters knew him. He spoke to people at his gym; he played games of handball with guys he knew or sometimes with guys he didn't. He met the same people jogging in the park and said good-morning. He had occasional dates with an ever-changing, yet similar array of sophisticated women.

None of those women had ever gotten under his skin—or inside his head—the way Shannon O'Shea had done. To the best of his knowledge, none of them lusted after a twenty-inch-long, blanket-wrapped bundle. Those women wanted a good time. They talked politics and Broadway shows and fashion, gossiped amusingly about people they knew. He'd never met any of their mothers or brothers or in-laws or uncles, and he'd had no desire to do so.

Shannon was as different from those women as John was from the O'Shea family. The Sunday he'd spent with them had been as much a mystery to him as visiting an ashram in India might be. Sure, he knew people who got married, had babies, bought houses, lived some version of the American dream, but it had never been something he thought much about, because from the time he was a small boy, his entire life had been centered on survival.

As he grew older, he'd become adept at it, until now he thrived on danger. He got an adrenaline rush out of getting in and out of life threatening situations. *Was he in one now?*

"Look, John, she's yawning."

He watched Shannon's lovely face instead of looking at the baby, and he was taken totally unawares when she suddenly plopped it into his arms. "Support her head with your arm...that's the way."

Utter terror gripped him. "No—hey, take it back, Shannon. I don't know how—I've never—here, take it back, please." Frozen in place, he didn't dare move to hand the bundle over. Shannon was laughing, and she'd moved several steps away. John was too afraid to walk, certain that if he moved at all, he'd drop the baby. There was nothing to do but hold on.

The infant squirmed and stretched, tiny hands reaching up and out. Its eyelids opened and it looked up at him with navy-blue, long-lashed eyes that looked ancient and wise.

He felt as if he'd touched a live electrical wire. This wasn't an *it*. He was holding a living, breathing human being. She was already a person; size had nothing to do with it. She was helpless, she was totally dependent on him at this moment, and he didn't even know how to hold her properly.

The enormity of the thing overwhelmed and terrified him. He took one slow, precise step, then two, and carefully passed her off to Shannon as if the baby were a live grenade. He was sweating. He had to get out of here. He had to clear his throat before he could even talk.

"Shannon, do you need a ride home? Because I've really got to go now. I have a—a meeting."

She barely looked up. "You do? Oh yeah, you said you did." She nodded, her attention centered on the baby in her arms. "Thanks, but I'll stick around here. Patrick will drive me home. But I want to get together with you. There's still a ton of questions I need to ask about that stuff you told me this morning."

"Sure. Absolutely. Whenever." His hand was on the door, and the urge to bolt was overwhelming.

"Maybe later today?" she suggested.

"Sure," he said again, but the truth was he wasn't sure at all. The way he felt right now, if he could hop the next plane back to New York, he'd be on his way to the airport. He wanted the safety of knowing what the hell was going on, even if it was just dragging Naomi out of another bar. That was clear, straightforward. Here, nothing was. Around Shannon and her family, everything kept shifting. He was in over his head, and he didn't know how or when it had happened.

She walked over to him and stretched up to plant a kiss on his lips. "Thanks for coming, John."

With the baby between them, the kiss was a perfunctory effort, but just being close to her muddled his thinking.

"You want to come over to my place tonight?" She must have seen something in his eyes, because she added hurriedly, "Just to talk. We've both got work in the morning. We can make it an early night."

"Good thinking." He knew she'd expected something more from him. They'd spent the previous night locked in each other's arms, and part of the morning locked in violent confrontation. He knew he was letting her down in some fashion by not taking another step ahead, but the way he felt at this moment left him no room to maneuver.

"See you this evening." He opened the door and stepped out. It closed behind him. He strode down the hallway and impatiently punched the elevator. When it didn't immediately respond, he headed for the stairs, taking them two at a time. In the parking lot, he unlocked his car, slid in and expelled the breath he'd been holding.

Freedom, at last.

In seconds, he was accelerating out of the lot, onto the street. He headed for the highway exit and got himself on the freeway heading south toward L.A. He needed speed and distance. He needed to get a long way from Shannon O'Shea, get the smell and the feel of her out of his system.

What the hell was going on with him, anyway? He felt as if somebody had taken the top off his head and stirred his brains with a spoon. He'd made up his mind at least once before that getting involved with her wasn't a good idea, so what had he done?

Seduced her. *Smart move, Johnny boy.*

Well, maybe the seduction was more a mutual thing, although he hadn't exactly been the soul of restraint in that whole episode, had he? And it wasn't as if one night with her had cured him, either. It had made him want her more. How was that possible?

He couldn't remember lusting after any woman this much since he was sixteen and in lust with Fleur. She'd done a great job of introducing him to sex, and he'd always been grateful to her for that. She'd taught him how to please a woman. He'd thought himself in love, but looking back, he recognized the feeling as lust.

He lusted after Shannon, too, but it wasn't just sex he wanted with her. He wasn't exactly clear on what he did want. Friendship? And sure, sex. Conversation? And sex. Camaraderie? And sex.

Jesus, he was one sick puppy. Granted, she was one hell of a package. Brains, strength, humor, sensual appeal—the whole nine yards. They could have a wonderful time while he was in Courage Bay, but the trouble was, he'd somehow taken on a package deal. It included her entire family, a whole cast of characters so interwoven in her life that it was hard for him to tell where the boundaries were between them all. Or if there were any boundaries.

This business with Linda, for instance. The whole family had turned up at the hospital. He'd never given it much thought before today, but wasn't all this stuff pretty private?

One thing he knew for sure, he couldn't adapt to this group mentality idea. Not even short term. Not that he was contemplating anything long term—of course he wasn't—so why the hell was he stewing over it?

He might get around to thinking about a permanent partner when he was a lot older. He'd seen those old people walking down the street together hand in hand, and there was something about it that appealed to him. But for now, his life was perfect the way it was. Right?

Well, maybe not perfect exactly. Nobody ever got a certificate that entitled them to a perfect life, did they? There was his mother. She was an ongoing pain-in-the-ass problem and would be until she died, but he'd learned to cope with that. Money made things easier, made it possible to afford a full-time companion for her, an apartment, the best drying-out clinics. Not that any of them had had any lasting effect. But having the money to send her was something.

The money had been pure dumb luck. Before he signed on with the FBI he'd moved in some questionable circles. One of the guys he knew from that life, a little weasel named Waldo Bronoski, had gotten himself in a tight spot and needed help at one point, and John had provided it.

Bronoski went straight after that little scare, and it turned out the guy was a genius at investing. John had given Waldo a few thousand here and there over the years to invest for him, and Waldo had turned it into a sizable fortune, to the point where it wouldn't be long before working would be a choice rather than a necessity.

John had pretty much figured out what he wanted to do at that point.

There was this place in the Virgin Islands called Tortola. He'd had to go there a few years back to roust out a Mafia type, and he'd fallen in love with the island. When he retired, he'd go there, start a little business taking tourists sightseeing, something like that.

Just thinking about it made him calmer. He had to remind himself when he was around the O'Sheas that he had a life of his own, a long-range plan, a future. He had to keep in mind that Courage Bay was only a job. Sure, getting to know Shannon had made it one hell of a lot more interesting. But he wasn't misleading her in any way, was he? He sure as hell wasn't talking rings or weddings or happily ever after, God forbid.

He'd been clear as air about relationships. He remembered saying straight out that he was footloose and fancy free. But just in case, he'd bring it up with her again tonight, so there was no question about her getting the wrong idea.

Speeding along in the fast lane, he'd been lost in his thoughts and pretty much driving by rote. Now, for the first time, he looked around. He took in the vista of hills and ocean flashing by beside the freeway. A sign came up saying he'd soon be in the outskirts of L.A. It was past time to turn around and head back.

He found an off ramp, got himself a burger at a drive through and turned around so he was heading north again. He really should find out what time Shannon was expecting him tonight. After fishing his phone out of his pocket, he punched in the numbers he'd memorized. She answered on the second ring.

"Hi, John. How'd your meeting go?"

For an instant, he couldn't figure out what she was talking about.

"Oh, it got put off. Hey, I was wondering. You want me to pick up some pizza before I come over tonight?" He hadn't thought about that until this very minute.

"That sounds great. I'm just leaving the hospital parking lot now with Patrick. Linda was awake, so we were all able to give her our love."

"Well, that's good. That's fine. So what kind of pizza do you like?"

"There's this place called the Flying Wedge. It's down on Washington Avenue and Twentieth Street. They make the best pizza in town. They've got one with pine nuts and zucchini and tomatoes."

"Okay. Six sound good?"

"Great. See you then."

He hung up, smiling a little. He liked the way her voice sounded on the phone, husky and full of relief.

He'd gotten bent out of shape over nothing. All he had to do was stay clear, stay focused, stay in control. Stay honest. She'd gone on about honesty that night at the pub. As long as they were both on the same page with this relationship stuff, what harm could it do to enjoy one another?

CHAPTER SEVENTEEN

SHANNON WAS ENJOYING the pizza. She bit into her third slice, chewed and swallowed.

"This has to be the best ever." She was sitting on the floor on pillows. John was on the couch. The coffee table was between them, with the two large pizzas he'd brought. She'd wisely locked both dogs in the kennel before he arrived, and so far there was no sign of either her boarder or her uncle.

Delicious as it was, however, pizza wasn't the foremost thing on Shannon's mind.

Tonight, John had brought along FBI identification. "Just in case you still think there's any question about who I am," he explained, handing the documents over.

She studied them, even though she no longer doubted him. But there were still things that puzzled her.

"I don't understand how you know Joe Ripani. You didn't trust *me* at first, fair enough. But why the heck would you trust him? Why would you tell Joe that you're here undercover with the FBI?"

"Because Joe has a cousin in the Bureau. Which is partly why it was decided my cover would be as a fireman. Joe came to New York and coached me on exactly what I'd need to do and know in order to fit in here."

"Okay, I get that part. But why here? Why Courage Bay? Is this the only place Freon is being stockpiled or smuggled or whatever? I don't think so. I mean, we're not exactly the crime center of the California coast."

He hesitated. Shannon could see him wondering whether he ought to answer her, and she sighed with exasperation.

"Look, John, you know that anything you tell me stops with me. I gave you my word on that. But I need the full meal deal here. I need to get my head around this so I can understand exactly what's going on. You never know, I might be able to help in some way."

That wasn't the smartest thing she'd ever said, because he scowled at her and shook his head. "Get that out of your mind. This could be dangerous, Shannon. There's no way you're getting involved in any of it, you got that?"

"I am already involved. And like they say, a little knowledge is a dangerous thing. So why Courage Bay?"

"Because we traced the shipments, and the suspect lives and works here."

"No kidding, *duh*. I'd pretty well figured that much out on my own. So who is it? It has to be somebody connected to the fire department. Otherwise you'd have gotten a job at the library or the animal shelter."

"Jesus, Shannon, you never give up, do you? I'm breaching security by telling you anything at all."

"Well, it's done already, the breach of security, so you might as well spill the rest of it. Who's your suspect? Maybe I know this person. Maybe I can tell you more about him. It is a guy, right?"

"Right. And yes, you do know him. It's the battalion chief, Victor Odom."

She'd been chewing, but forgot to swallow. *"Odom?"* The name came out in a spray of half-chewed pizza.

Now that's attractive, O'Shea.

"Sorry." She brushed the mess off the couch and washed the rest down with soda before she tried again. "I should have guessed. Odom's a total jerk, everybody knows that. He's the only guy who's ever made overt sexual advances to me on the job."

John looked interested. "Oh yeah? What'd he do?"

"Put his hand on my rear a couple times. Made sure he brushed against my chest. Came into the shower room when I had the sign turned around. He's a total creep, but because of his position, I figured it would cause me more grief to report him than it would just to stay out of his way. But I never figured he was a criminal as well as an asshole. Wow, it feels so good to know that. How'd he get onto this Freon thing in the first place, do you think?"

"The kind of Freon being smuggled is known as Halon 1301, which was used in firehouses as a fire suppressant before the ban on Freon. When that happened, the Halon was sent to Venezuela, where the stuff is legal for another decade."

"What do they use it for?"

"To service and maintain existing air-conditioning units and refrigeration equipment. Air-conditioning systems on cars or trucks older than 1994 require Freon. Odom, of course, knew where the stuff from the fire station had been shipped to. That made it easy for him to arrange to have it smuggled back into the U.S. Unfortunately, there's good money to be made here on the black market."

"So is he doing this all on his own? Wouldn't you think he'd have to have partners?"

"It's a good guess there's somebody besides him involved. How much do you know about the guy?"

Shannon shook her head. "Only fire hall gossip. He divorced his wife a couple years ago. Apparently he's living with some bimbo. To hear the guys talk, she's pretty hot, but I've never met her. Never even seen her. Like I said, I keep my distance from the creep."

"Her name is Rachel Gruber. She has a criminal record— pretty minor stuff when she was in her teens. Escalating to break and enter in her twenties, theft and finally assault with a deadly weapon. Gruber did time on that one, eighteen months, and was released four years ago now. She's a hot number, likes the good life, and consequently she's also high maintenance. Odom would never be able to afford her on his department salary."

"So you FBI guys have been keeping an eye on the two of them?"

"For quite some time now. Odom and Gruber have made frequent trips to Venezuela, and some discreet inquiries prove that Odom lives well beyond his means."

"If you know for a fact he's smuggling, and she's in it with him, why can't you just arrest the two of them?"

"We could get him on tax charges, failure to report income, but we'd rather nail them both on the Freon thing. There's an ongoing federal initiative to crack down on trafficking in chemicals, but we don't have enough evidence yet for a clear-cut case."

"So how can we get it?"

He got that mulish look on his face that she was becoming all too familiar with. He slowly set his pizza plate on the coffee table and leaned forward. "Shannon O'Shea, read my lips. There is no *we* in this thing. I'm a federal agent, doing my job, and you are absolutely not going to be involved. It's dangerous, it's risky, it's foolhardy. It's not going to happen."

She shrugged. "So? My job as a firefighter can be dangerous. It was risky and foolhardy to rescue Salvage, but that didn't stop either of us. C'mon, John, we'd work well as a team."

He narrowed his eyes at her. "I seem to remember having to haul both you and the dog out of that inferno."

"I'd have managed on my own." Damn, she was such a bad liar. "Probably. Maybe. And that's the only time I've ever gotten in a tight spot. You can't disqualify me for one little slip."

"Yes, I can. And the answer is no."

"Just no? No reasons, no hard and fast rules, no exceptions?"

"Not where you're concerned." He took another slice of pizza and munched away at it. He was about the only guy she'd ever met who actually looked good chewing.

"So it's just me, is that it?" She wasn't about to cave on

this. "Plain old sexism at work here, looks like to me. What about Joe? Isn't he helping you?"

"Of course he is, but that's different."

"How so? Because he's a man? In case you haven't noticed, he and I have the same basic training. I can't believe you'd be a chauvinist about this, John. At least tell me how you plan to trap Odom."

"I don't have a plan, not yet. But I'll come up with one."

She'd been hoping he'd say that. "I already know one that'll work."

He pursed his lips and blew out an exasperated breath. "And I don't want to hear it."

"Of course you do. You need all the help you can get. You may be a chauvinist and sexist, but you're not stupid, right? And it's a great plan. Wait till you hear it."

"O'Shea, you're giving me a headache."

"Really?" She pitched her voice low and sexy. "I know this great cure for headaches." She slithered around the table and put her hand high on his thigh. She felt the muscles contract and heard him draw in a hissing breath.

"You wouldn't seriously be considering seducing a federal agent to get your own way, would you, Ms. O'Shea?"

"My motto is Whatever Works."

"Much as I'm tempted by the offer, I have to tell you I never use sex or condone the use of it as a bargaining tool."

"Smart man. So why not listen to my idea first, and then we can just use sex for any old reason that comes along? Like fun, for instance."

Her hand was still stroking, and he was looking the worse for wear.

"How many poor men have you driven berserk so far?"

"You don't wanna know. But trust me on this, you do want to hear my idea."

"Okay, okay, lay it on me. And move your hand—I can't listen when you do that. But all I'm doing is listening, remember."

"Boy, you're stubborn. When's your birthday, anyway?"

"What's my birthday got to do with anything? It's May fourth, over for another year, and if we have to wait for the next to implement whatever your scheme is, I'm afraid the time frame's just a little off."

"Idiot. May, huh? I think that's Taurus the bull, which explains a lot about your nature, like why you're so stubborn and bullheaded. But Willow knows all about astrology and stuff. She'll be able to analyze your personality for me and then I'll know everything about you."

"Willow, eh?" He sat up a little straighter and glanced toward the door. "I forgot about her. Where is your bodyguard this evening, anyway? Shouldn't she be arriving anytime now to spoil our fun?"

"She's out with my uncle Donald again, I believe they're having their sleepover at his house this time. He needs to be more careful after what happened when he tried to sneak out of here this morning, the slippery old slider."

"How so?"

"Uncle Donald's what used to be called a rogue. He's dated any number of ladies of a certain age, and as soon as they start thinking long term, he dumps them."

"Not the marrying kind."

"Definitely not. He *was* married years ago. She took off with the mailman, if you can believe that. Fortunately, they didn't have any kids."

"That's enough to put you off the postal service for life."

"Yeah. Well, obviously it put Uncle Donald off long-term commitment."

John gave her a look. "Lots of men don't do long term."

"Like you, right?" Might as well have him say it again.

"Yeah, like me."

He'd told her before. Why did she have to keep nudging him to say it again? It was like picking at a scab. She knew what was underneath, knew it would sting, but couldn't stop herself.

Okay, so much for that. She'd do a Scarlett O'Hara and think about that another time. Right now, it was back to the business at hand.

"Here's what I think we should do."

He opened his mouth to say something, but she reached up and put her fingers over his lips. He promptly put his hand over hers and pulled her little finger into his mouth and sucked, which came very close to derailing her. Sexy, sexy.

"Nice try, Forester. Or should I say McManus?"

"Stick to Forester. It's too easy to slip otherwise."

He was right. She reluctantly removed her finger from between his lips and organized her thoughts. "I think we ought to just go ahead with what I was planning to do anyhow, before you confessed. It makes perfect sense. Of course, I won't take that incriminating license along, but I'll go to Odom and tell him I'm suspicious of you, that I'm certain you had something to do with the fire at the warehouse. You can bet he's heard about all the commotion I made concerning the man in the silver. It's become a joke—they call you my asbestos angel. So it won't come as a huge surprise that I'm suspicious of you. I'll talk about Salvage, how he recognized you, and I'll get creative and tell him I've been spying on you. I can even say that I've seen you poking around at the warehouse since the fires. I'll tell Odom I got you to confide in me. With his nasty little mind, he'll just assume I seduced the info out of you."

"Actually, that would be pretty much the truth."

"Actually, it wouldn't. What I did was wrestle it out of you up on the mountain, remember? Or is that just too humiliating to admit?"

"And here I thought I won that contest."

"Dream on, Sebastian. Anyhow, I'll tell the dear man that you seem to think there was something hidden in that warehouse before the fire, something worth a lot of money."

"And what exactly are we going to gain from all this? He's

liable to start wondering if I'm an undercover cop or FBI or some such ridiculous thing."

He'd said we. So she was winning the battle. A tiny voice reminded her that she was also probably losing the war, but she ignored it.

"He won't, because I'll tell him that you're desperate for money, that you have gambling debts, that I'm pretty certain you—I don't know—snort coke or something on your time off. I could throw in that you're a sex addict."

"Stick to fiction, it's safer that way."

"Okay." Her mind was racing, because she hadn't actually figured out the finer points of all this until now. "I'll say my theory is that you were in that warehouse wearing the silver because someone paid you to set the fires. If Odom did hire someone, he'll know that isn't true, but he'll also get nervous and do his best to get you off the trail. He might just be antsy enough to do something that'll incriminate him."

"And here I thought you were just a pretty face."

"Shows how wrong you can be. So what d'ya say? Are we partners?"

The humor suddenly went out of his voice. "Why the hell do you want to be involved in this, Shannon? It could be dangerous, it's bound to get nasty. There's no logical reason for you to be part of it."

"Oh, yes, there is." She was clear about this. "I'm proud of what I do," she said fiercely. "I'm proud of the hall I work at. How do you think it makes me feel, knowing that the battalion chief from my station is a rotten crook? That he's actually bringing stuff into the country that can destroy the ozone layer, and he's using insider info to do that?" Her voice hardened. "And then there's the little matter of my private vendetta with the slimeball. He deliberately took advantage of his position to come on to me, knowing that I probably wouldn't fight back, and I didn't. So other female firefighters will be up against the same thing with him—or worse. Believe me, I've got a whole list of reasons why I want to see Odom busted, John."

He looked at her for a long time, then reached out and stroked a finger down her cheek. "You're a fine piece of work, Shannon O'Shea. A bona fide original."

She didn't say anything. She'd already covered every argument she had. Now it was up to him.

It took a while. She was thinking it was game over when he finally sighed and said, "Okay, Shannon."

"Yes!" She punched a fist in the air, narrowly missing his nose.

He jerked back. "Go easy on me, okay? My jaw is still aching from the last time. Now here's how it'll go. We'll play Odom your way, because I think it actually might work. But there are conditions, and you have to abide by them."

Wouldn't you know? Male ego, front and center. "What conditions?"

"I guess you won't just make me a solemn promise without me spelling them out?"

"You guess right. Why would I? A person always has to read the fine print."

"You're a hard woman, O'Shea."

"No. I just drive a hard bargain. There's a difference."

He smiled at that, but the smile faded fast. "These are the rules. If and when a situation comes up that I feel has the potential to be physically dangerous, you're out. No arguments, no discussion."

She opened her mouth to debate that and shut it again when she recognized the steely glint in his eyes. "Okay. And?"

"And it's my way or the highway when it comes to decisions. No second-guessing me."

She snorted. "Talk about a typical alpha male." But again, the look in his eyes told her that there was only one acceptable answer. "All right. You Tarzan. Me Jane."

"One more, and it's a biggie. You don't make any moves without checking with me first."

There was no need to swear in blood, was there? "Right. So when do we start?"

"We're both on shift tomorrow. When you get a chance, ask to talk to Odom in private, and make sure the meeting happens in daylight, in a public place, preferably with me nearby."

She blew out a breath. "I'm not physically afraid of that little worm. I could easily knock him senseless if I had to."

"Probably. And here's your first directive as my partner. Nobody can win against a weapon, Shannon. Keep in mind that this isn't an arm wrestling contest. Odom and Gruber are dangerous, and they have no morals. What they probably do have is guns or knives or explosives. So absolutely no heroics, understood?"

"Gotcha." She traced a finger down the seam of his jeans and back up again. "So, are we all done with the work part now?"

"I'd say so." He reached down and pulled her up on the sofa beside him, wrapping her close in his arms. "What did you have planned for recreation again?"

"I know these really great Pilates exercises." She put her mouth on his and outlined his lips with her tongue, and then kissed him until she couldn't get her breath. "Only problem is," she gasped, "we have to do them naked."

He heaved a beleaguered sigh. "Well, I guess if we have to, we have to. Anything for physical fitness." He undid the buckle of his belt and then paused. "Where are the dogs, by the way?"

Remembering the fiasco they'd created the last time, she smiled. "Locked in the dog run."

"And you're certain your upstairs boarder is up to no good with Uncle Donald?"

"Nearly positive. But just to be safe, let's move to my bedroom, where there's both a door and a lock."

"Practical and smart, what a lady."

"Guess again, Sebastian. I'm no lady."

CHAPTER EIGHTEEN

FORTY MINUTES LATER, Shannon collapsed into the curve of John's arm. Her breath was none too steady, and neither was her voice.

"Lordy. We'll have to try that again on a slower speed."

"I kept saying whoa, and easy does it, but you weren't listening." He pulled her down and snuggled her tight, wrapping strong arms and legs around her. "There's always the next time. Just give me a moment here. I'll recover and then I'll try to do better."

"Practice. We need lots of practice."

"Mmm." He was quiet for such a long time, she thought he'd drifted off to sleep.

"Shannon?"

"Yeah?"

"Are you okay with this?"

"Pretty much. Your leg's a little heavy, but hey, I can live with it."

"I meant with us. You and me. Being together this way."

She knew exactly what he was asking. "You mean this hot sex, short-term, no holds barred, no-promises thing we've got going?"

"Exactly."

"Apart from lying about everything else, you *have* been honest about your lack of intentions." This was taking fortitude. "You told me up front you weren't a forever guy. Here today, gone tomorrow is pretty much how I interpret it. Am I right?"

The silence this time was much longer. "Yeah. Right. That about sums it up, I guess. Not that I'm gonna walk out on you without a word, or never call again. That's not the case at all. It's just that because of my job, I won't be in Courage Bay very long. I'll be going back to New York. I just wanted us to be on the same page with this, Shannon. No misunderstandings."

"Absolutely not." She understood, of course she did. That didn't mean she felt good about it. In fact, she felt pretty rotten all of a sudden, the kind of rotten that needed privacy. She rolled away from him and stretched, pretending to get a glimpse of the bedside clock.

"My lord, look at the time. We have to get up in a couple hours if we're gonna make it to work on time."

"Maybe I ought to head back to the hotel, let you get a little sleep."

So now even spending the night was too much of a statement for him. "Yeah, that's probably the most practical idea."

He rolled out of bed and located his clothes. When he was dressed, he leaned over and kissed her.

She kissed him back. She couldn't help herself, and besides, it wasn't his fault.

"Don't get up," he whispered. "I'll find my own way out. I'll use your keys to lock the door and then leave them in the mailbox."

"See you at work." She waited until she heard the kitchen door close before she let out a stream of curses. They didn't make her feel any better.

She swung her legs over the edge of the bed and wrapped her arms around her naked belly. This was pathetic. It was such a cliché, falling for an unavailable guy. What was wrong with her? Besides letting herself love John Sebastian Forester McManus, of course. But then, did anyone plan that sort of thing?

He has no intentions of doing anything more than giving you a really good time in bed, she reminded herself. *He's said so, twenty times to Sunday. So get over it.*

Except she didn't know how to get over it. She didn't have the energy. She was tired, no question there. It had been an eventful day. She went over it, deliberately doing a freeze-frame when she reached the part where she got to hold the new baby.

I want one of those, she thought, and a mental image of a baby girl with John's gentle smile appeared in her mind. Jesus, Mary and Joseph, as her father was fond of saying. It was obviously time to break out the pecan ice cream and the chocolate sauce.

WHICH WAS PROBABLY WHY her stomach was upset the following day—or could it be from being in the same space as Victor Odom? Shannon wondered.

The same *small* space. They were in Joe's office, and the door was firmly closed. Odom was lolling back in Joe's chair, and she was across the desk from him, thank goodness for small mercies. Even so, his weaselly eyes were running all over her like greasy smoke. She'd need another shower when this was over.

"I saw the article in *California Woman.* Congratulations, O'Shea. Too bad they didn't do a centerfold." He tipped the chair back and smirked at her. He had the kind of smarmy voice she associated with dishonest politicians. "Now, what exactly did you want to see me about?"

"I needed to talk to you privately about the warehouse fire, the first one. Maybe the second, too, I'm not sure."

She watched closely, trying to discern the slightest reaction, but Odom's pale gray eyes weren't giving anything away except his lecherous nature. They were focused on her breasts, and she resisted the urge to cross her arms over her chest.

"Oh yeah? What about the fires?"

"I have good reason to believe that John Forester was the man in the silver who pulled me and the dog out of the warehouse after that first fire. And I think—I'm almost certain— that he was the one who started it."

Odom frowned, and now he looked at her face. He had quite a line etched between his eyebrows. Smuggling must be a high-stress job. Had he heard of Botox?

She amused herself by imagining him getting an overdose of botulism.

"That's a pretty serious accusation, O'Shea. What do you have to back it up?"

She launched into the story she and John had agreed on, detailing her suspicions about John doing drugs, emphasizing that he'd confided in her about his need for money. She hinted that she'd taken John to bed and he'd told her that something of value had been hidden in the warehouse.

"So if he figured there was something there worth money, why the hell would he torch the place?"

"I think he was deliberately destroying evidence, maybe for somebody else. Whatever was stored there was illegal, and he burned the warehouse to hide the evidence. And I've followed him a couple of times. He was poking around there again after the second fire, too. Maybe he started that one as well."

Odom pursed his fleshy lips and narrowed his eyes even more. "Doesn't sound as though you have anything concrete to go on, O'Shea. I'd recommend keeping your mouth shut about all this unless you have definite proof. You talked to anyone else besides me?"

"No, sir. I felt it best to come straight to you."

"Smart thinking. Leave it with me. You can be certain I'll look into it." He got to his feet and was around the desk before she made it out of the chair. Damn, he was fast as a snake, even without the venom. She sidestepped him, but there wasn't a lot of space to maneuver, and by the time she got to the door, he had his hand on the knob.

"Thank you, sir." She waited for him to open the door, and when he didn't, she gave him a questioning look.

"You can come to me anytime, O'Shea. I want you to know

that." His smile sent a shudder through her. She reached for the doorknob, but he went right on holding it.

"Next time maybe we oughta meet somewhere more private."

She put her hand over his and wrenched at the door. He slowly drew his arm back, managing to touch her breasts before she got the door open.

When she bolted out, she saw John kneeling only a few feet away, supposedly checking and repacking first aid kits. Odom walked away without giving any sign that he'd noticed or recognized him.

Shannon saw the look that John shot after the battalion chief, however, and once again a shudder went up her spine. John's brown eyes, usually filled with humor, were icy cold, and the expression on his face was murderous.

HE'D KILL THE BASTARD.

John saw the way Shannon bolted out of the office, and how close Odom was to her. It didn't take much imagination to figure out that the man had had his hands on her again.

It took every ounce of control John could muster to keep from springing to his feet and grabbing the asshole by the neck. *Somewhere, sometime, you'll pay for that,* he silently promised Odom.

The PA system came on just then, and they were called to a rooming house in a run-down area of town. An old man had died in his bed, and the other residents hadn't realized anything was wrong until the smell of his decomposing body began to permeate the entire upper floor. There was nothing the firemen could do except wait for the police, and they were back at the fire hall before John had an opportunity to talk to Shannon in private.

They met in the workout room. Shannon was using free weights, and John retrieved a set and sat down beside her.

"I think he believed me," she said in a low voice. "But he's a really good actor. There wasn't the faintest sign that he knew what I was talking about, or that it upset him in any way. In fact, I had the feeling he *didn't* believe me. Maybe it wasn't the best idea after all," she said in a forlorn tone.

"It was a great idea, and I'll bet you twenty bucks he'll be on my case before the day is over." John hefted the weights, working on his biceps. "What did he do to you, anyhow? You came out of there like you were shot from a cannon." He managed to sound simply curious.

"Nothing, really. Just his usual, copping a feel whenever he's within arm's reach, stripping me with his eyes." She shivered.

"Nice guy, our Mr. Odom."

"I hope you win the bet, John."

One of the other men came in just then, and there was no more opportunity to talk. But after supper John was called to the phone.

"Battalion Chief Odom here. I'm in my car, black Olds, parked up the street. I want a very private word with you, Forester. Now."

"What about, sir?" John tried to combine respect with a good dollop of nervousness.

"Don't ask questions, just get your ass out here, and don't broadcast where you're going."

"Yes, sir." John hung up and walked out through one of the bays into the darkness, making his way to Odom's car. He opened the passenger door and slid inside.

Odom was smoking, and it was obvious he smoked a lot. The leather interior of the luxurious car smelled like an overflowing ashtray.

"You wanted to talk to me?" Again, John tried to sound both nervous and respectful, one of the toughest acting jobs he'd ever taken on. One of Odom's pudgy hands was resting on the steering wheel, and John imagined those sausagelike fingers touching Shannon, and then allowed himself to visualize slowly bending them back until they snapped. Violence was a thing he'd always detested, but at this moment he could see its advantages.

"I hear you might have some interesting news about the two warehouse fires."

"Where did you hear that?" Belatedly, because it almost choked him, he added, "Sir?"

"There are no secrets around a firehouse, Forester. You must know that by now. Let's just say a pretty little bird whispered in my ear that you might have pyro tendencies." He snickered.

The bloody creep. He didn't even have enough loyalty to protect Shannon. If John really were the arsonist, Odom would be deliberately putting her in danger.

"So how much of what she says is true? *Did* you set those fires, Forester?"

"No." John did his best to sound outraged. "Why the hell would I do a thing like that?" He pretended to segue into anger. "I never set any fires. But I'm pretty sure something valuable was stored in that warehouse before it was torched. I figure that's why it was torched."

"Oh, yeah? Valuable like what?"

John paused, waiting until Odom looked directly at him. "Like Freon. Before I came here, I'd heard via the grapevine that there's a shitload of money to be made on the black market by bringing that stuff into the country."

"Yeah? Who told you that?"

"This guy I met from Venezuela. He said his brother was making big money smuggling it in. He mentioned Courage Bay. And then after I got here, I overheard one of the firemen saying there used to be a lot of it around our hall, that it was used as a fire suppressant. And the fire inspector figured something valuable had been stored at the warehouse. It doesn't take a genius to put two and two together."

"Yeah? I never heard the inspector say that."

"Maybe you're out of the loop, then." Shannon was right; not a flicker of an eyelash. This guy was cool.

"That Freon stuff's illegal," Odom added. "Who do you think would be smuggling it in?"

John shrugged, holding the man's gaze. "No idea." He wondered how far to take this, and decided the hell with it. He might as well go for broke. "I don't give a shit who's doing it. I'm just interested in getting in on the deal."

"Yeah? And what makes you think there's any money to be made?"

"You never know your luck. I've always found that information can be valuable, in the right hands."

"What information would that be?"

"I took a good look around that warehouse after the second fire, and I found evidence."

"Withholding evidence can get you in a lot of trouble. Your wisest move would be to hand it over. What did you find?"

"Straps. The kind that are used to secure cylinders of Freon."

"Straps." Odom laughed. "Straps can be used for anything."

"Not this kind. They're special."

"And where are they now?"

"Still at the warehouse. I stashed them in a safe place."

Odom chewed on that for a few moments, sucking on his cigarette. "When's your shift over?"

"Tomorrow morning."

"Meet me at the warehouse, four tomorrow afternoon. I'd like to have a look at these straps of yours. And Forester?"

"Yes, sir?"

"This conversation stays between you and me, understood?"

"Absolutely." John opened the car door and slid out. The Olds pulled away, and he took deep, hungry gulps of the fresh, moist evening air. It wasn't just cigarette smoke that polluted the car's interior. Odom was rotten through and through, well past his expiry date. And if things went the way John planned, the battalion chief would be off the shelves and in the discard bin very soon. It was a satisfying feeling.

He hurried back to the hall, and Shannon all but pounced on him the moment he slid through the door leading to Bay One.

"Do I owe you money on the bet we made?"

"You sure do."

"First time I've enjoyed losing a bet." She whipped out a twenty and handed it over. She did a quick check to see if anyone was around and then turned back to John. "So tell me what went down."

He related most of the conversation. "He swallowed the bait. I'm meeting him at the warehouse tomorrow afternoon."

"What time?"

"Four."

"I'm coming along."

"No, you absolutely are not." This was exactly what he'd been concerned about. "Joe will be there, acting as backup. If I'm right about this, Odom will set up some kind of ambush, and I don't want you anywhere near that warehouse, is that clear? You have no training in this sort of thing, and I can't go in worrying about your safety, because it'll jeopardize my own."

"I can take care of myself. There's no way you'd have to worry about me."

He was familiar with the stubborn look on her face. "You promised me, remember? No second-guessing, no rebellions. That was the deal we made. When the chips are down, my word is the only one that counts. And I'm *ordering* you to stay the hell away. Got that, O'Shea?"

Her blue eyes flashed cold fire and her chin took on a stubborn set. He stared her down, but it took a long time, and he could see that it almost killed her. Finally she nodded reluctantly.

"Okay, John. Have it your way."

YOUR WAY, BE DAMNED, Shannon seethed.

If John thought for one moment that she was going to disappear into the woodwork while he nailed Odom, he was sadly mistaken. She'd thought up the idea to trap the creep, and damned if she was going to stay away for the exciting part. All she had to do was get to the warehouse tomorrow before any of the action started.

CHAPTER NINETEEN

As SHE JOGGED UP her street the following morning after her shift, Shannon could see that there was definitely action going on at her house. She'd been immersed in plans for the warehouse gig, and at first she didn't pay attention to the hammering.

As she got closer, she saw a green pickup truck with a canopy parked in her driveway. A compact looking man wearing a baseball cap had a sawhorse set up in the front yard, and it looked as if he was reconstructing her front steps.

Cleo and Pepsi lay on the grass a respectful distance away, watching him. Cleo bounded over to greet her, but Pepsi didn't so much as glance her way.

"Hi." Shannon gave the guy a big smile. She didn't know him, but she'd welcome Jack the Ripper if it meant being able to use her front entrance instead of that ramp in the back.

"You must be Shannon." He took a halting step toward her and held out a callused hand for her to shake. She realized who he was an instant before he introduced himself. "I'm Aaron Redmond. Willow's my mom."

"Of course. Glad to meet you, Aaron. I recognize you now from the picture she showed me." And from the pronounced limp, but that was quickly forgotten when he smiled. He had the kind of open, honest face that shone with goodwill and optimism, and his green eyes had lovely laugh lines radiating from the corners.

"I drove through to check up on Mom. I got here late last night, so I slept in the truck, but she said maybe you'd let me bunk in that other upstairs bedroom for a couple days if I repaired a few things around here."

"Absolutely. Fix my damaged house and the bedroom's yours as long as you want it." She hesitated, and then added, "I'd appreciate it if you'd check with me first before you tear anything else out, though. In the house, I mean." She had learned from Willow. And he was her son.

He shook his head. "I won't be doing that. I had a look around and it'll take me all my time to fix the stuff that Mom showed me." He gave Shannon a knowing look. "I can see she's been up to her old tricks again. She means well, but she always bites off more than she can chew."

"I know she meant to get around to rebuilding these stairs and doing the other stuff," Shannon said, anxious to give Willow the benefit of the doubt. "But then she got that job at the clinic." *And got herself seduced by my notorious uncle Donald.*

"Mom's always been better at knocking things down than putting them back together."

Shannon wasn't going to argue with that. Instead, she said, "I hope Willow told you there's no bed in that upstairs room."

"No problem. I have a chunk of foam and a sleeping bag. I'll be fine. I hope you don't mind your dogs keeping me company. We sort of bonded." He bent and rubbed Pepsi's ears, and to Shannon's amazement, didn't get nipped for his trouble. In fact, Pepsi licked his hand. Shannon frowned at him. Maybe the little louse was sick?

She made her way around the back and up the ramp, and before the kitchen door closed behind her, she heard the magical sound of Aaron's hammer starting up again.

By noon, there were strong, well-built steps leading to the front door, and Aaron was already starting on the back deck. Shannon had been on the phone much of the morning—she wanted to be certain Linda was doing okay. Also, her cover shot and interview in *California Woman* were getting her a lot of unwanted attention.

At least the calls took her mind off the warehouse and the meeting scheduled for later that afternoon. As the hours passed, Shannon found herself getting more than a little nervous. John was going to be livid when he found out she'd ignored his direct orders.

For lunch she threw together egg salad sandwiches and made a pot of coffee, then stuck her head out the door.

"You want some lunch, Aaron?"

"Thanks, I sure do." He came in and took his cap off. His hair was light brown, and she was surprised to see that he already had a few gray hairs at his temples. Up close, he looked older than thirty-eight.

He asked if he could use the bathroom, and then sat across from her at the table.

"My steps look fantastic, Aaron. I can't thank you enough."

"Glad I could build them for you." He jerked a thumb toward the cupboards. "We oughta get some Arborite and fix that countertop." He took a huge bite of his sandwich, chewed and swallowed. "Mom says you work for the fire department?"

"Yeah, I do. It's a great job. I really enjoy it." *Although I've recently gone into the espionage business, just for variety.* She glanced at the clock. Another two and a half hours, and she'd head for the warehouse. She wanted to get there good and early, before anybody else could show up.

"My dad was a cop. He's retired now."

"Yeah, your mom said." And Shannon had to be careful not to let her voice reflect the negative way she felt about Steve Redmond, the wife beater. "She also said that you're a talented artist, Aaron. Do you work in oils or acrylics? Or maybe watercolors? I don't know much about artists," she confessed. "My sister-in-law, Linda, is the closest I've come to one, and she's a photographer."

"I'm no artist. I do wood carvings for fun, but Mom exaggerates about how good they are. My dad, now, he's the artist. He picks up bits of scrap, uses old pipes and things, and he makes stuff. It's called assemblage art."

"Your dad?" Willow had never mentioned this. It took Shannon a little adjusting to get her mind around the fact that Redmond the wife beater could also be an artist. But then again, why not?

"Dad had a show at one of the New York galleries a while ago. He sold quite a bit of stuff and got great reviews. Mom didn't tell you about that, huh?"

"No, she didn't." More adjustment needed. Now the wife beater was a *successful* artist.

Aaron nodded. "That's why she left this time," he said in a matter-of-fact tone.

"This time?" Shannon almost choked on her sandwich. "You mean she's left before?"

"Oh, yeah." Aaron nodded and got up to refill their coffee cups. "She takes off every now and then, but she always comes back. Mom sort of needs to be the center of attention. She's like a little kid that way."

Shannon wasn't understanding any of this. "You—you mean that Willow…that she left—because she was—*jealous?* Of your father's success?"

Maybe Aaron didn't know his father was abusive. Maybe he just didn't want to know. After all, there'd been things Shannon hadn't known about her own mother, either.

"I wouldn't say jealous, exactly. The way I see it, Mom just hasn't ever found her purpose in life. She's fooled around with all sorts of things, taken classes in everything under the sun. She doesn't ever narrow in on any one thing, though. I guess she gets frustrated, and then she quits whatever it is and starts something new."

Astrology, carpentry, electronics. Shannon remembered all too well the list of things Willow had claimed she'd studied. And she and Lisa both had firsthand evidence that Willow wasn't nearly as talented as she claimed. Everything

Aaron was saying was beginning to make sense in a bizarre sort of way.

"How...how does your father react to all that? Her taking courses, and then quitting?" Maybe she'd been right about Redmond being relieved Willow was gone.

Aaron shrugged. "Oh, I guess Dad's just used to it. It's been the same ever since I can remember." But his expression showed clearly his high regard for his father. Pride and affection glowed in his eyes. "He pretty much supports Mom at whatever it is she wants to do."

"Wasn't it hard on you? Her leaving? When you were a kid?" For some reason Shannon was thinking about John and his mother, about guys who took on the responsibility for their parents. She had the feeling this wasn't the first time Aaron had chased after Willow and repaired things she'd broken.

"When I was little, it was tough," Aaron admitted. "I always thought it was because of my leg that she left us. But my dad talked to me about it. He made me see that me being crippled had nothing to do with her going away or coming back, either. He said it was because of Mom's insecurity. It had nothing to do with me."

Lordy. And Willow had subtly used Aaron's disability for her own purposes, to gain sympathy and support. She'd also hinted that her husband was cruel. And it looked as if none of it was true.

Shannon's mind went to her uncle Donald. She knew for a fact that Willow was having sex with him. Did the woman always have affairs when she left her husband and son? It wasn't something Shannon could ask Aaron, and she felt a sudden pang of sympathy for Donald. This time, she'd bet he wouldn't be the one who did the dumping.

But Shannon wanted to be absolutely sure she wasn't making still another mistaken judgment. "You must have had a pretty turbulent time of it. I'd guess that your dad would have pretty strong reactions to your mom's behavior?"

Aaron laughed and shook his head. "Nope, Dad's not a fighter. He's not your typical cop, either. Law enforcement was tough for him. He's a gentle guy, a hippie at heart. I think he only went into law enforcement because Mom wanted him to. All her male relatives are either policemen or firemen. And of course it paid reasonable wages, although he doesn't much care about material stuff. It's Mom who likes the good things in life."

Shannon detected the slightest undertone of bitterness there.

"Well, I'll get back to work, Shannon. Thanks again for the food." Aaron picked up his plate and carefully rinsed it and his cup in the sink. Then he put his cap on and headed outside again, calling the dogs as he went out the door.

Stunned at the revelations about Willow, Shannon slumped back in her chair. Lately it seemed as if everyone around her dealt in secrets and lies.

The phone rang again. It was Mary.

"I thought you and I could go over to the hospital and visit Linda this afternoon. Sean's working, so she'll be alone, and I know how upset she must be about losing the baby. Also, I've made a few casseroles and a nice lasagna for them for freezing, and I baked one of those orange cakes Sean loves. We can drop them off at their house."

"Mom, I'm sorry, I just can't do that today." Shannon rolled her eyes in frustration, hoping Mary wouldn't ask why—but she did.

"Why ever not, dear?" She sounded both puzzled and disappointed. "Linda needs family around her."

"I—I have this appointment, and I can't get out of it." That was as near the truth as she could manage.

There was a moment of silence that spoke volumes. "All right then, Shannon. I'll go by myself. What do you want me to tell Linda?"

"Tell her—tell her I'll see her tomorrow and I'll explain everything."

Shannon hung up the phone and groaned. Damned if she hadn't just become a full-fledged member of the secrets and lies club.

BY THREE, Aaron had the supports up for the back deck and was cutting cedar for the flooring. Shannon changed into a black track suit that was far too warm for the sunny California day and loaded her lightweight backpack with the items she was taking.

She'd given a lot of thought to what she could use as a weapon if things got out of hand, and she'd decided on a small fire extinguisher. It was portable, it would blast out a stream of chemicals, and most important of all, she knew exactly how to use it. She also had her industrial flashlight and a big bottle of water—it was going to be hot in that warehouse, and she'd have a couple of hours to wait before anyone showed up.

Aaron saw her leave. He was cutting boards in the shade beside the house.

"Going for a jog?" He eyed her long-sleeved, hooded top, but he didn't comment. "I guess you'll want to take the dogs."

"No. Nope, not this time. I'm taking the car. The, uh, jogging path is quite far away. They can stay here with you."

Shannon noticed that again Pepsi wasn't paying any attention to her. Cleo came ambling over, wagging her tail, but Pepsi stayed as close as he could get to Aaron. The guy must have hypnotized the little rat.

She drove toward the warehouse, parking her car when she was blocks away and jogging the last quarter mile. As she neared the building, Shannon began to get a really bad feeling.

There was no way of telling whether or not anyone was inside. She'd have to rely on luck, because she had no plausible reason for being there if she got caught. She circled the warehouse until she found the side entrance John had used when he'd brought her and Salvage out.

It was hot inside. The exterior walls hadn't suffered much damage, and the holes the firefighters had knocked open in the roof didn't allow much daylight to penetrate. The interior stank, and it had an eerie, ominous feeling. But maybe that was just her, Shannon told herself.

She was more than a little nervous about being here. She turned her flashlight on and shivered. Piles of rubble were strewn around haphazardly, and she spent precious moments trying to figure out where John would most likely stage the meeting. After some scouting, she settled on an area close to the spot where she'd found Salvage. She'd first encountered John there, and he'd said it was exactly where he'd found the straps that had been used to secure the heavy cylinders of Freon.

If she was wrong, she'd hear their voices, figure out where they were, and do her best to move. She fervently hoped she wouldn't have to; dark as it was, she was more than liable to fall over something and be discovered.

After some scouting, she found a hiding place behind a massive steel beam and hunkered down. She took her stuff out of her backpack and made certain the extinguisher was close at hand. Her heart was hammering, and now, unfortunately, there was ample time to think about the consequences of what she was doing.

John was going to be incensed, that was a given. She was breaking her word, and that bothered her. She hated to think of losing his respect. But the promise had been made under duress, she reminded herself. He'd forced it out of her. And realistically, what could he do to her?

It wasn't as if they had anything like a future together; he'd gone out of his way to make sure she understood that. And although he'd insisted she promise, had he made *her* a single promise in return? *Not in this lifetime.*

He'd said he was crazy about her, but he hadn't come any-where near telling her he loved her. Why did that hurt so

damn much? And he hadn't said a word about any future between them, apart from hinting that he might call her from
time to time. Big deal, Forester. I should get breathless because you might phone me once or twice a year? Ha.

So what if he gave her a tongue-lashing when he found out
she hadn't obeyed his precious instructions? What did she
have to lose?

But even during her brave pep talk, she knew she didn't
relish the thought of having John really angry with her. Her
stomach gave a nervous little rumble when she remembered
the expression of cold fury on his face after Odom had done
his touchy-feely thing with her at the door of the office.

She hadn't yet seen John truly lose his temper. Sure, he'd
been steamed when he chased her up the mountain, and that
had been more than a little scary, but she'd realized afterward
that he'd actually been pretty much in control.

When and if he headed over the brink, she'd make herself
scarce, she decided. She had a feeling it wouldn't be pretty.

Lordy, it was dank and cold and miserable in this godforsaken
place. The wind or something made strange sounds, and she
squirmed around, trying to ignore them, trying to get halfway
comfortable. Maybe she shouldn't have come quite so early.

She was about to unscrew the top on her water bottle when
she heard footsteps. She peered out from behind the beam, but
it was too dark to distinguish anything other than a shape with
a flashlight, heading more or less her way.

Shannon's heart hammered until she realized it had to be
Joe. John had said Joe would be backing him up. It made sense
he'd be here early. She debated for a moment whether to let
him know she was there, but decided against it.

Joe might also be pissed off with her for horning in. Who
knew what went on in the minds of men? Better just stay
anonymous and quiet—unless, of course, he decided to hide
behind the same beam that was her cover. She grinned. That
would likely scare the hell out of her captain.

She waited, but he didn't come near. He did hunker down nearby, which reassured her about the location she'd chosen. Having Joe maybe eight feet away gave her a lot more confidence. When he doused his light, it was impossible to tell there was anyone there, but it raised Shannon's spirits and gave her a feeling of optimism, knowing John had both Joe and herself as backup. *If he needed it.*

It seemed an eternity before anything else happened. Her legs were stiff, she had to pee, and despite the heat outside, she felt thoroughly chilled before she finally heard male voices approaching.

She peered around the edge of the beam, waiting, and at first she couldn't make out what they were saying. She knew Odom's voice, and of course she knew John's, but they were much closer to her hiding place before their conversation became clear.

At last she could make out their faces in the beams from their flashlights, and she could hear what John was saying.

"Everyone with half a brain knows there's more danger to the ozone layer from car exhaust than from Freon." He was obviously trying to get Odom to open up to him.

"I couldn't care less about these tree-hugger types who go off half-cocked about the environment," he added. "If there's money to be made, I wanna be in on it. Don't lots of auto repair shops still use the stuff in the cooling system of old cars? Must be one hell of a good market out there."

But Odom was being cautious. "Just show me these straps you found, Forester."

John shook his head. "Not until I know what the deal is."

Odom's voice became sarcastic. "Far as I know, there's no deal, asshole. You're just pointing out something you stumbled over, remember?"

"Oh, yeah? Well, if that's your attitude, I can still go to Captain Ripani. He's gonna wonder why you insisted on meeting me here alone."

The battalion chief laughed. "It's your word against mine, and I've got one hell of a lot more clout around the firehouse than you have. Plus Ripani's gonna wonder why you didn't come forward sooner with this strap bullshit. So don't try any of your dumb threats on me."

John's voice went cold and Shannon shivered. "What I know, Odom, is that you set the fire here, the first one. I've got proof of that, as well as evidence that says Freon was being stored here. Put those two together, and a whole lot of people are gonna start taking a real close interest in you."

Shannon tensed. She knew John was bluffing. Would Odom know? Her palms were damp and her heart was hammering so hard, she wondered why nobody heard it except her.

And then, in the space of a heartbeat, all hell broke loose.

CHAPTER TWENTY

ODOM PULLED OUT A GUN and leveled it at John.

Before Shannon could even think of making use of her extinguisher, Joe came leaping out from behind a stack of rubble and knocked Odom to the floor. The gun went flying.

John pounced, and in an instant, he'd dragged Odom up. John held him with one arm and drew the other way back, his fist aimed at Odom's jaw. It connected with a dull crunch, and Odom went sprawling backward, squealing with pain.

John took a lunging step toward him and hauled him up again, and now Shannon saw the gun John had drawn.

"Start talking, asshole," he growled.

Joe was crouched down, searching for Odom's weapon with his flashlight beam.

Shannon stayed where she was, desperately trying to figure out what was going on, because she knew now that it hadn't been Joe who was hiding near her. He'd appeared from an entirely different direction.

Suddenly another light clicked on, and someone stepped out of the shadows. Shannon could see that it was a woman. She was wearing a helmet with a light attached to it, and she, too, had a gun. This one was larger than John's handgun, maybe some sort of semiautomatic. She held it with both hands, easily, as if she was familiar with it, and she pointed it at Joe.

"Toss your gun away," she ordered John, "or your partner's dead."

John released Odom and took a slow step back. He dropped his gun at his feet.

"Good girl, Rachel," Odom hollered, and started to walk toward her.

Shannon just had time to see the triumphant smile that gleamed in the light from the woman's helmet before the gun exploded, and Odom went flying backward, landing spread-eagled on the cement. Blood began to pool around him.

The muzzle of the gun was swinging toward John as Shannon took two long, lurching steps and brought the extinguisher down as hard as she could on the woman's back. It made a satisfying sound, a dull, heavy thwack, and Rachel went flying forward, landing on her belly. Shannon was lifting the cylinder in case she had to hit her again when something big struck her full force.

She flew several feet and then hit the floor. The air was knocked out of her lungs and her head smashed against one of the beams. Light exploded in her brain, and she couldn't breathe. She could hear the noises she made, ugly, gasping sounds, and was fighting hard to stay conscious when a powerful flashlight beam shone straight down into her face.

"Jesus, it's you."

The light began to turn in concentric circles, making her dizzy, drawing her into a vortex. The last thing she heard was John's horrified voice.

"*Shannon?* God almighty, Shannon. Don't pass out. Stay with me here—"

His panicked voice seemed to come from far away, but she knew that she was safe with him, that she could let go. She heard him cursing as the light faded and she slid down into darkness.

JOHN KNEW THAT RIPANI had Rachel Gruber. He could hear the woman cursing as Joe struggled with her. He must have subdued her somehow, because she let out a yelp and then shut up, and John heard Ripani's gasping voice calling 911 on his cell.

Odom had begun screaming intermittently, but those sounds seemed faint and faraway. All John was really conscious of was Shannon, sprawled on the cement beside him. He could see in the beam of his flashlight that the side of her face was scraped and bleeding where she'd connected with the steel post. Her skin was pasty-white, her breathing barely discernable. God, what had he done to her? How badly had he hurt her? He'd lunged at her, hitting her with the full force of his body.

"John, you okay? Who've you got over there?" Joe's voice steadied him.

John drew in a ragged breath and hollered, "It's Shannon. Get an ambulance here as fast as you can. She's unconscious."

"They're on their way. What the *hell* was O'Shea doing here, anyway? How bad's she hurt?"

She was backing me up. Doing everything she could to keep me safe.

"I dunno. I think maybe bad. I knocked her down."

John felt sick in body and soul, and he was shaking. He'd tackled her hard, probably broken some of her bones. In the confusion and the darkness, he'd had no idea who the blurred shape was that had jumped out and walloped Rachel Gruber. For all he knew, it could have been yet another accomplice of Odom's. John had simply reacted.

"I think Odom's still alive," Joe called. "Is O'Shea bleeding? Did she stop a bullet?"

Jesus. He hadn't even thought of that. He did a fast assessment. There was no major bleeding, and he couldn't determine if anything was broken. He didn't think it was.

He stripped off his jacket, tucked it around her, started to pull her into his arms and stopped abruptly. What if she had a spinal injury? He pressed his lips to the scratches on the palm of her hand and prayed harder than ever.

He could hear Joe, still scuffling with Gruber, warning her not to move.

Odom made groaning noises.

Shannon didn't budge, and John put a finger on her throat, relieved beyond measure at the strong, steady pulse beating there. After an interminable time, he finally heard sirens in the distance. They grew closer and suddenly stopped, and then there were voices shouting outside. Within moments, powerful lights were making paths through the darkened warehouse.

"Over here, hurry up," he bellowed, and when he looked down at Shannon's face again, he realized her eyelids were flickering. She groaned and struggled to sit up, but he put both hands on her shoulders and held her down.

"Let me go," she moaned, trying to break his hold with her hands.

"Lie still. You're not moving until a medic has a look at you."

"I'm fine, I must have hit my head. Geez, John, why did you tackle me like that, anyway? You really whacked me a good one." She struggled with him. "Let me go. I need to get up."

"You stay the hell where you are," he told her through gritted teeth, practically sitting on her to keep her immobile. "Medic?" he roared. "Over here. *Now.*"

A young man appeared beside them, setting down a large portable light and a first aid case. He knelt at Shannon's side. "Hey, Biceps, what'd you do to yourself? Lie still. Let's have a look—"

"I'm fine, Bernie. I just got knocked out for a minute. *Ouch*—I must have banged my shoulder, too. Let me up. There's nothing broken, honest. I'd know if there was…"

Bernie finished a careful examination. "I can't find anything broken, but if you were unconscious, you better go to the hospital and let them check you over. You could have a concussion."

"I don't need the hospital, I don't have a concussion, I'm absolutely fine." She sat up, and then, using John's arm as a fulcrum, struggled to her feet. She was unsteady at first, and

John looped an arm about her, but after a few minutes she slid away from him and looked around.

"What happened to that woman with the gun, John? And where's Joe? He's okay, right? Is Odom alive?"

All that mattered to him right now was Shannon.

"Joe's fine. I don't know about Odom, and I don't care." He'd lost interest in the bastard. He'd lost interest in everything except her. "Are you dizzy? Feel sick? Maybe you oughta sit down again."

"John, read my lips. I've got a few bruises, but that's it. Don't you have better things to do right now than fuss over me?"

For the first time since he'd knocked her down, he really looked around.

The scene was controlled chaos. Ambulance attendants, firemen and police officers were milling around, and still more were pouring into the warehouse. He needed to find the police officer in charge and brief him as to what the operation had been about.

With Shannon close beside him, he made his way over to the group surrounding Odom. Joe introduced John to the police officer in charge. Rachel Gruber was in handcuffs, alternately swearing and crying, and the medics were about to load Odom onto a stretcher.

"It was all his idea," Rachel wailed as an officer led her away. "Stupid fucking idiot. I should have known he'd mess up."

John showed his ID to the senior police officer. "I'll want to question Gruber, and Odom as well, if he's gonna live long enough."

"They figure he is," the officer said. "She's either a lousy shot or the guy's got horseshoes. She didn't hit any major organs. He's out of it right now, but we'll have him under guard at the hospital. I'll have them call you the moment he comes to."

"John, have a look at this." Joe held up a fuse and a container of liquid accelerant. "Gruber had these with her. She was planning to shoot us all. I'll bet she was gonna make it look like we'd shot one another. Then she'd use this to torch the place. There wouldn't have been much left as evidence. She'd have been long gone with all Odom's money by the time we got the fire out and anybody started to figure out what was going on." He turned his attention to Shannon. "You okay, O'Shea?"

"Fine. A few bruises, nothing to worry about."

Joe nodded. "I have no idea how you ended up here, Shannon, but John and I sure as hell owe you one for smacking Gruber with that extinguisher before she had a chance to pull the trigger again."

"My pleasure, Captain." Shannon gave John a sidewise glance. He narrowed his eyes and glared at her. He wasn't about to thank her for anything. Now that he knew he hadn't crippled her for life, he had more than a few things he planned to say to her, and thanks wasn't one of them. But this wasn't the moment.

"If you don't need me here," she said, "I think I'll head home. My car's just a couple blocks away. I'll find my backpack and—"

"You're not driving anywhere." John encircled her upper arm in a none too gentle grip. "You heard the medic. You need to go to the hospital, get x-rayed, make sure your ribs aren't cracked or something. You still could have a concussion." He started worrying all over again.

"I *don't have concussion*. And if something were broken, I'd know it. Don't treat me like a bimbo, Forester. I know when I need medical attention and when I don't."

Damn it all. With her, everything was a battle. "Okay, but you're still not driving yourself home." John turned to Joe. "I'll drop her off and then I'll head over to the police station. See you there."

"That's not necessary." Shannon was trying to unhook his fingers from her arm. "You don't have to drive me anywhere. I have my own car, and I'm perfectly capable of—"

Aware that there were lots of interested observers, John leaned over until his mouth was an inch from her ear and hissed, *"Shut up and do as you're told for once, or so help me—"*

He didn't expect threats to have any effect, but amazingly, she stopped struggling. One of the young officers handed over her backpack and John took it, still holding on to her arm with one hand. He marched her out the side door of the building, and just as he'd expected, the moment they were outside, she started in all over again.

"You're bruising my arm, John. You don't have to *drag* me, for heaven's sake. If you're so set on driving me home, fine. Let go of me and I'll come of my own free will."

Deep breaths, that was the answer. He released her arm, counted to ten several times, opened the passenger door on his car for her and managed not to slam it once she was inside.

He tossed her pack in the back and got behind the wheel, but he didn't start the car. He held on to the steering wheel in hopes it would keep him from throttling her.

"I really thought we had an agreement." He was trying hard to keep his voice under control. "You gave me your word. You promised you wouldn't come anywhere near here today." He could feel himself losing it just a little. "What the *hell* did you think you were doing, Shannon?" His voice was rising. "Do you have any idea how foolhardy that stunt was? You could have been shot. It's a bloody wonder I didn't shoot you myself, instead of knocking you down." That sent a spasm of icy fear through his gut. "Your word's not worth a tinker's damn. Why I ever thought I could trust you…" He swallowed hard. It took two stabs to get the damn keys in the ignition, and then he burned rubber for half a block. It didn't help.

She didn't say anything. He kept expecting her to—mouthing off wasn't something she had problems with—but they got all the way to her house and she still hadn't said a word. He pulled in at the curb.

There was a guy in a billed cap sawing lumber at the side

of her house, and he looked up when the Corvette stopped. The dogs were lying on the grass beside him, and neither of them budged, not even when Shannon opened the car door, almost before the car stopped moving. She got out, back and shoulders hunched. She slammed the door and went limping along the sidewalk and up the new steps at the front of her house.

It was the final straw. John rolled the window down and bellowed, "That's it, then? You're just going to walk away from me?"

She didn't answer, and the front door wasn't locked. She opened it and went inside without a single backward glance.

CHAPTER TWENTY-ONE

JOHN WATCHED THE DOOR close behind her, and his anger kicked up a notch.

Okay, if that's how she wanted to play it, then good riddance. It was better this way, easier. He had enough on his plate without fighting with Shannon O'Shea. He started the car again, reached for the gearshift, swore and turned the ignition off.

He was out the door and up the sidewalk before he could begin to think what he planned to do. He only knew that he was so furious he was on the verge of exploding. He knocked once, more of a thump, but he didn't wait for her to come to the door. Instead, he turned the knob and marched straight in.

She was sprawled on the sofa in the living room, bent double, a throw pillow on her lap, her face pressed into it. She didn't even look up when he stormed in, and he stopped short just inside the door, because she was crying, huge, choking sobs that sounded as if something was ripping open inside of her.

"Shannon?" Rage evaporated, and confusion took its place. He wasn't sure what to do. He'd dealt with female tears before. His mother cried a lot, maudlin, drunken tears that meant less than nothing. But he'd never heard a woman cry like this. He could feel it in his own chest, and it hurt him somewhere deep inside.

He moved over beside her and put a tentative hand on her soft hair.

She raised her head. Her blue eyes were bloodshot, her face

blotchy and soaking wet. Her nose was running. She was incredibly beautiful.

"Shannon, please don't cry." His throat tightened, and he had to clear it. "Don't, please." He hunkered down, one knee on the floor. "I didn't mean those things I said. I got scared, see. I thought when I hit you and you went down like that I'd maybe broken some ribs or damaged your spine—"

Before she could answer, a male voice from right behind him said, "Shannon? You want me to get this guy out of here?"

John, still down on one knee, turned toward the door. It was the carpenter he'd seen outside, and the two dogs were with him. Cleo was barking like a fool, and Pepsi started growling deep in his throat, then dashed over and bit into John's pant leg, doing his best to rip the fabric and reach flesh.

John tried to dislodge the animal without hurting him, and got nipped in the process. He swore under his breath and tried again to shove the dog away. The man was giving him a threatening look from under his billed cap.

"You gonna hit the dog, too?" he said. "He's small enough."

This was just about enough. John had to raise his voice over the noise of Cleo's barking. "Look, mister, clear out, okay? And take these damn dogs with you. We're trying to have a private conversation here."

"Yeah? And is that what you were having when you hit her?"

Speechless, John gaped at him. "It—I—hey, it wasn't like that," he managed to stammer.

The guy took several steps toward him, and John saw that he had a pronounced limp. "Oh, yeah? I just heard you admit that you'd hit her. Look at her face, all bruised up. Ask me, she oughta be calling the cops. What kind of a spineless creep hits a woman and knocks her down, anyhow?"

John backed up and raised both hands. "Look, I don't know who you are, but you've got the wrong idea here—"

"Aaron," Shannon managed to say through a stuffed nose. "It's okay, we're just—"

Before she could say anything else, the front door burst open and Patrick appeared. He ignored Aaron and John and the dogs and sat down beside his sister, throwing a protective arm around her.

"Hey, kid, I just heard. Are you okay?"

Pepsi was on the attack again, gnawing John's shoelaces, and Cleo was giving out woofs loud enough to make the windows rattle.

"Shut up, Cleo," Patrick hollered, and for a moment the dog did. Patrick turned back to Shannon. "Are you hurt? Sean called me. He said there was some kind of shoot-out over at that damn warehouse, and you were there. He said Bernie told him you were knocked out cold. What the hell happened?"

Aaron was bent over, quieting Cleo. He stood up again. "What happened," he said heatedly, "is that this dude here hit her. I heard him admit it just now. Said he knocked her down. And far as I can see, she doesn't want him around. She came running in the house and he followed her in uninvited."

"John didn't mean to hit me," Shannon said in a muffled tone, but then she started sobbing again.

Patrick got to his feet and advanced on John, fists balled. *"You punched my sister?"*

There was a coffee table between them, but John wasn't about to back up this time. He didn't want a fistfight with Patrick, but neither was he going to let Shannon's brother land one on him over a misunderstanding. He tried to move around the table and almost tripped on Pepsi, still worrying away at his shoelaces.

"Stop this. Stop it, Patrick." Shannon sprang up and put herself between Patrick and John. "Let me explain."

"Get away from me, kid," Patrick ordered, trying to push her to one side, but Shannon clung to him. "I checked on you, Forester," he said. "You're no fireman. Nobody seems to know who the hell you are—"

"Listen, Patrick, just *listen* to me here," Shannon said, trying to intervene. "I *know* who he is—"

"What the hell's going on in here?"

Along with everyone else, John turned toward the door. Shannon's father had just come in. Cleo started barking again.

"Shannon?" Caleb raised his voice over the noise of the dog. "Are you all right, honey?" He took in Shannon's swollen eyes and scraped cheek and scowled. "Look at you. Sean called me, said you'd been involved in some shoot-up over at the warehouse. He said you might have a concussion or some such thing."

"Yeah, thanks to Forester here," Patrick snarled. "He punched her out."

"He *what?*" Caleb's expression turned thunderous.

"He did no such thing." It was obvious nobody was listening to Shannon. She turned to John. "Please, please, just go now. *Leave.* I can't take any more of this. Please, John?"

The quaver in her voice and the pleading look she shot him did it.

John turned, dragging Pepsi, who was attached to his pants again, and headed for the door.

"Pepsi, enough." Aaron snapped his fingers at the animal, and miraculously, it let go and settled meekly at his feet.

John was halfway down the sidewalk when Willow and Donald parked across the street. They were in Donald's half ton. They got out, and Donald tried to take Willow's hand, but she jerked it away. They were obviously still arguing as John started the Corvette.

He was just pulling away from the curb when a red van arrived and Shannon's mother scrambled out.

When he was halfway down the block, a fire truck passed him. It didn't have its sirens on, and he could see through the rearview that it, too, pulled up in front of Shannon's house. Sean jumped down and went trotting up the sidewalk.

Family.

John had taken on a lot of powerful organizations over the years, and he'd almost always won. The O'Shea establishment was way too strong for him to challenge.

He swallowed against a tightness in his throat. At least he didn't have to worry about her being alone. He should never have gotten involved with her, he'd known that, but the attraction had been more than he could resist. Now it was time to walk away, but some weak and needy part of him wouldn't let go.

Feeling worse than he'd felt in his entire life, John headed for the peace and quiet—the familiarity—of the police station.

He had work to do. If Odom was conscious, he'd put pressure on him right away, let him know in no uncertain terms what happened to criminals who tried to murder FBI agents. He could play him and Gruber off against each other. John had a hunch they'd give up the names of the other smugglers without too much coaxing. He could probably get through all of that tonight, and then he had no reason to stay on in Courage Bay. He'd pack up his stuff at the motel, drive to L.A., return the Corvette to the rental agency and catch the first flight back to New York in the morning.

"HE CHECKED OUT?" Shannon stared at the desk clerk. She couldn't get enough air into her lungs, and her voice came out reedy and thin. "When? When did he check out?"

"It must have been sometime during the night." The clerk punched something into the computer. "Here we go, J. Forester, checkout time 2:00 a.m."

It was 9:25. He'd be on a flight to New York by now. So that was that.

Shannon turned away from the motel desk and walked out into the California sunshine. It was a glorious morning and was going to be a hot day. She didn't have to go to work. She could go to the beach; she hadn't been to the beach for weeks. The salt water and sun would help her aching muscles. Or she could drop in on Linda at the hospital. Or she could go home and help Aaron finish the back deck. Just because an affair had ended, there was no reason to curl up and die, right?

Wrong. The sun seeped into her skin and her teeth began to chatter.

She'd never felt as cold or alone in her life, and she had only herself to blame. This was what hysterical tears got you. She'd always known crying was a waste of time and effort. If she'd managed to get hold of herself yesterday, at least she and John could have had a discussion, reached a mutual truce, parted like reasonable adults.

But no, she'd started bawling and couldn't stop, and then Aaron got the wrong idea, and her entire family had converged on her, and everything went spiraling out of control. She could have handled either John or her relatives, but the combination did her in.

After he left, it had seemed to take her forever to explain what had gone on at the warehouse, because she couldn't stop crying when she got to the part about the woman pointing that gun at John. And because she hardly ever cried, Patrick and her father and Sean—and especially her mother—had all freaked. They'd decided she had a concussion, and they'd hauled her, practically kicking and screaming, off to Emergency.

There, the damn E.R. doctor had ordered X rays in case she had a hairline fracture, decided she might actually have a minor concussion, and kept her under observation for hours, with her father and Patrick standing guard as if she were some sort of prisoner.

She'd finally thought to ask if Odom had survived. When the doctor confirmed that he had, Shannon couldn't figure out whether she felt relieved or disappointed.

It was four in the morning by the time she got home, and by then she was too exhausted to do anything except crawl into bed.

This morning, Willow had awakened her at eight with coffee, a freshly baked muffin and the news that she was leaving. She'd decided to drive back to New Jersey with Aaron.

They were going as soon as the back deck was completed, probably in two days.

"I'll work at the clinic today, getting things in order, and then I'm sure Lisa can find someone else on a moment's notice. It's a really good job," Willow added, for all the world as if she was doing Lisa a favor by walking out. And maybe she was.

"I feel I should give my marriage one more chance," Willow had declared with a dramatic sigh. "For Aaron's sake as much as anything. Being around you and your family has taught me that no matter how old children are, they still need their parents."

It was tough, but Shannon held her tongue. She hadn't been able to resist one question, however. "What about Uncle Donald?"

Willow hadn't batted an eyelid. "As I told him last night, we've been such good friends. He's helped me through a very difficult time in my life. But I'm afraid the chemistry just isn't there. I'm sure there's a wonderful lady for him somewhere."

Uncle Donald had met his match, but Shannon couldn't help feeling sorry for him. She knew firsthand how much it hurt to be dumped. Maybe she should find her uncle, and the two of them could be miserable together.

But the fact was she had no energy for anything, and she needed a long rest from her relatives. She'd go home and spend the day lying on the couch watching soaps. And with effort, maybe she could keep from crying.

SHE PULLED IN BEHIND Aaron's pickup and got out, wondering if her legs would carry her into the house.

There was no sign of the dogs. Male voices sounded from the backyard. One stood out, and a shiver of recognition made the hair stand up on the back of her neck. Slowly, knowing she must be wrong but unable to stop herself from hoping, she walked around the corner.

Cleo came bounding toward her, barking a welcome. Pepsi stayed beside Aaron, who was measuring a piece of cedar while John held it. He saw Shannon and let go, and the board toppled off the sawhorse. Aaron bent to pick it up, and John started toward her.

Don't make a fool of yourself, she warned. *He probably just needs a statement from you to complete his investigation.*

"Shannon." He stopped two feet away, and she wrapped her arms around herself to keep from touching him. She centered her gaze on the half-finished deck to avoid looking at him. But she could smell him, the sun on his shirt, the scent of his aftershave.

"Hi, John." *Good. Really cool, O'Shea.* "What are you doing here? I thought you were on a plane heading for New York." *Doofus. Now he knows you checked on him. Keep talking, distract him.* "Where's your Corvette? I didn't see it out front."

"I returned it to the rental place."

"In L.A.? So how did you get back here?" *Stick to the trivial stuff.*

"Taxi. I had to come back. I forgot something."

She was right. He just needed her version of the warehouse thing.

"How'd the investigation go?"

"About like I figured it would. Odom wants clemency in exchange for giving up his buddies. He swears it was Gruber who set the warehouse fire. She's singing a different tune, insisting it was all Odom. They both coughed up the same names, and their accomplices will be in custody by tonight."

"So I guess you need me to sign a statement or swear out a deposition or something?" She was tough; she could handle this. She managed to look up at him, and the intensity in his bloodshot brown eyes made her catch her breath.

"No." He shook his head. "I came back because I didn't tell you thanks for saving my life yesterday."

"Oh. *That.* Well." It wasn't what she'd expected him to say. At least he wasn't hollering at her anymore for being there in the first place. "I probably never thanked you for saving Salvage and me, either."

"Yeah, I got to thinking about that. There's an old Chinese proverb that says if you save someone's life, that life is your responsibility forever after."

"Wow." This was one strange conversation. She was having problems keeping up. Maybe that concussion had been more serious than she realized. "I guess that puts a whole new twist on rescue work, huh?"

He nodded, but he didn't smile the way she'd thought he might. "I saved your life, and then you saved mine, which means we're responsible for one another forever, right? So I decided the only solution was for you to marry me."

"Marry you?" Shannon gaped at him. It was the last thing she'd expected him to say, and all she seemed able to do was repeat it. *"Marry you?"*

"Yeah." He looked her straight in the eye. "I know it sounds like a crazy idea. We come from different backgrounds, we live at opposite ends of the country and there's all sorts of problems. Like my mother, she's a biggie. You'd have to put up with her. And then there's your family. I'm not really good at families. And your brother Patrick isn't a big fan of mine."

She was shaking her head. "No, I mean he understands now. I explained to all of them about you, who you were, what happened yesterday." John wasn't really listening, she could tell. As usual, he had some sort of agenda, and he was doggedly making his way through it.

"And then there's the whole issue of babies. I'm not really sure whether I want babies. They're so—small."

Babies? She was starting to get annoyed here. He hadn't kissed her or anything, and now he was on to babies? "Let me get this straight, Forester. McManus. Sebastian." Lordy, she could barely get his name straight. "You're trying to talk me out of this before I even give you an answer? So why ask in the first place?"

She heard him swallow hard. He looked a little green around the edges.

"Because—because I love you."

The simplicity of his words took her breath away.

"I want to spend the rest of my life with you. I don't care where—here, New York, wherever. As long as we're together."

She was marginally aware of Pepsi sneaking up on them, growling deep in his throat, but then John reached for her and pulled her close, and everything went out of her head. His mouth felt so good, hot and arousing and familiar. She kissed him back hard, startled when he jerked away.

"*Ouch.* Damn." He hopped on one foot, trying to dislodge Pepsi, who was attached to his right ankle.

"*Pepsi.*" Shannon bent down and tugged at him, and the cursed animal nipped her hand.

From somewhere nearby, Aaron said in a quiet voice, "Pepsi. Come here."

The dog let go and scampered off.

Shannon sighed and moved in for a replay of the kiss, but John caught her shoulders and held her away.

"Are you going to give me an answer or not?" He was starting to look annoyed, and she could feel the tension in his arms. "You've never said you loved me. Although why I'd take your word for anything is beyond me."

"What were the questions again?" Damn, she was starting to enjoy herself.

He narrowed his eyes at her. "*Do you love me? Will—you—marry—me?*" When she still didn't say anything, he started to look a little uncertain. "My mother's not really that bad. When she's sober, she can be a lot of fun. And you do have Pepsi. I'd take my mother any old day over that miserable dog."

She wasn't going to have Pepsi much longer. She'd decided

a minute ago she was giving him to Aaron. They actually liked each other. But she didn't tell John that. Let him sweat a little.

"I'll take you to Tortola on our honeymoon. You'll like it there."

Bribery, no less. This was getting better and better. "Tortola? Where the heck is Tortola?"

"In the Virgin Islands." His hands tightened on her shoulders and he gave her a little shake. "Shannon, stop changing the subject. Are you going to marry me, or do I have to arm wrestle you first?"

"Nope, that's not a good way to start a relationship, because I'd win. And for the rest of our lives, you'd go around telling people I trapped you."

He thought that over for a second.

"So you do love me. And you will marry me." His voice shook with emotion. "Say it, O'Shea. I want to hear you say it."

"I do. I will. Yes."

He started to smile a little, but she saw the tears in his eyes, and she understood for the first time how terribly vulnerable he was. He needed honesty from her. It was time to stop teasing and tell him the absolute truth. It took great courage, but she did it.

"You are my knight in shining armor, John Sebastian McManus." Her own eyes were brimming, but her voice was strong. "And I will love you with all of my heart, for as long as I live, and on through eternity."

She felt the muscles in his arms relax, and then he kissed her.

And the dogs barked, and Aaron cheered.

Ordinary people. Extraordinary circumstances.
Meet a new generation of heroes—
the men and women of
Courage Bay Emergency Services.

CODE RED

A new Harlequin continuity series continues
September 2004 with

LINE OF FIRE
by Julie Elizabeth Leto
Attorney Faith Lawton steps outside the courthouse.
Shots ring out from a nearby rooftop. The concrete
around Faith explodes with expended bullets as a pair
of strong arms pull her back into the building. Faith
welcomes the strong embrace of Chief of Detectives
Adam Guthrie—for the moment.
His fast actions saved her life.
But it's nothing personal….

Here's a preview!

ONE LAST sweep through the living room, decorated in a palm-tree motif, and Adam decided no one had invaded her home.

No one but him.

"We're all clear," he reported to Faith, who waited in the foyer, a semipatient smile on her face.

"Good to know," she answered. From that tiny, somewhat predatory smile, he figured she hadn't been worried.

He took one last look out her front window, which was safely darkened by sturdy wood blinds. The street was quiet. In this tiny collection of homes on a cul-de-sac, no one parked on the street, but tucked their cars safely in their garages. Small lawns dotted with tall skinny palms didn't provide many places for anyone to hide. Adam could, for the moment, assume they were safe.

"Yeah," he agreed. "In the morning, we'll review the case and try and figure out who might want to hurt you."

"Or you."

Adam expected Faith to shy away from this discussion, but he should have known better. Neither exhaustion nor needful desire would keep her from a good argument.

"We can debate that point all night," he said.

"I can think of more interesting things to do all night." Her soft whisper crawled along his collar, teasing the sensitive skin of his neck, making him wonder if she would deepen the effect by applying her tongue to the same area.

"There's no harm in thinking," he said.

"Is there harm in doing?"

"You know there is."

Her smiled turned down on one side. "The harm is in the long run, sometime in the future, near or far, when we have to stare down each other in a courtroom. We've faced each other twice in two years, Detective. Those odds aren't too intimidating."

He agreed, but Adam wasn't the type to simply grasp at straws because they made his life easier—even his love life. Faith had presented nothing more than a circumstantial argument. Much like evidence of the same kind, relying on such flimsy statistics could lead them down a primrose path to destruction.

"Admittedly, the odd are in our favor," he answered. "But that doesn't mean we should act on our first instinct."

"I can't remember the last time I acted on my first instinct."

"Because it's not in your nature."

"Not usually."

"Then why now?"

"Maybe because I almost died today?"

She tossed the keys on the hall table and closed the distance between them. When she slid her arms around his neck, he did the same with her waist. Holding her felt so good.

"Come on, Adam. You're a cop. It's a well-documented phenomena that people who've faced their mortality often react by doing something outside the norm."

"That's true. But Faith, I'm used to looking death in the eye. Only takes once or twice in your life before you build up coping mechanisms that don't include jumping into bed with someone you shouldn't."

He knew he'd said too much when he caught the dark reflection in her eyes—a mirror of the danger and death he'd faced in his career, and his life. But if she wanted him to recount any of the shadows from his past, she didn't ask.

"So far, Detective Guthrie, you haven't said anything to dissuade me."

"I don't want to dissuade you," he said.

"Then shut up and kiss me."

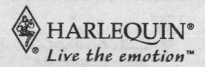

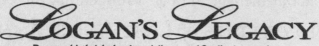

Return to Trueblood, Texas, with this brand-new novel of thrilling romantic suspense…

P.I. Dean Harding's search for the mother of an abandoned baby leads him to an Austin, Texas, hospital—and to Dr. Kate Purvis, a secretive OB who knows more than she's telling. So Dean goes undercover, hoping to get information in a more personal way.

Finders Keepers: bringing families together

Available in September 2004.

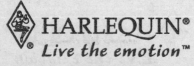

www.eHarlequin.com

CPLUC

Maybe this time they'll make it down the aisle

USA TODAY bestselling author

Anne McAllister

AND

Tori Carrington

The attraction continues to spark in these two full-length novels in which two couples are reunited after several years. The feelings haven't changed...but they have! Is a future possible?

Coming in September 2004.

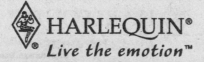

HARLEQUIN®
Live the emotion™

If you enjoyed what you just read,
then we've got an offer you can't resist!

Take 2 bestselling novels FREE!
Plus get a FREE surprise gift!

Clip this page and mail it to MIRA®

IN U.S.A.
3010 Walden Ave.
P.O. Box 1867
Buffalo, N.Y. 14240-1867

IN CANADA
P.O. Box 609
Fort Erie, Ontario
L2A 5X3

YES! Please send me 2 free MIRA® novels and my free surprise gift. After receiving them, if I don't wish to receive anymore, I can return the shipping statement marked cancel. If I don't cancel, I will receive 4 brand-new novels every month, before they're available in stores! In the U.S.A., bill me at the bargain price of $4.99 plus 25¢ shipping and handling per book and applicable sales tax, if any*. In Canada, bill me at the bargain price of $5.49 plus 25¢ shipping and handling per book and applicable taxes**. That's the complete price and a savings of over 20% off the cover prices—what a great deal! I understand that accepting the 2 free books and gift places me under no obligation ever to buy any books. I can always return a shipment and cancel at any time. Even if I never buy another The Best of the Best™ book, the 2 free books and gift are mine to keep forever.

185 MDN DZ7J
385 MDN DZ7K

Name	(PLEASE PRINT)
Address	Apt.#
City	State/Prov.	Zip/Postal Code

*Not valid to current The Best of the Best™, Mira®,
suspense and romance subscribers.*

*Want to try two free books from another series?
Call 1-800-873-8635 or visit www.morefreebooks.com.*

* Terms and prices subject to change without notice. Sales tax applicable in N.Y.
** Canadian residents will be charged applicable provincial taxes and GST.
All orders subject to approval. Offer limited to one per household.
® and ™are registered trademarks owned and used by the trademark owner and or its licensee.

BOB04R   ©2004 Harlequin Enterprises Limited